The Urbana Free Library

To renew materials call
217-367-4057

Pecos Valley Revival

PECOS VALLEY REVIVAL

ALICE DUNCAN

FIVE STAR

A part of Gale, Cengage Learning

GALE
CENGAGE Learning

Detroit • New York • San Francisco • New Haven, Conn • Waterville, Maine • London

GALE
CENGAGE Learning

LIBRARY OF CONGRESS CATALOGING-IN-PUBLICATION DATA

Duncan, Alice, 1945–
    Pecos Valley revival / Alice Duncan. — 1st ed.
      p. cm.
    ISBN-13: 978-1-59414-926-9
    ISBN-10: 1-59414-926-7
    1. New Mexico—Fiction. 2. Murder—Investigation—Fiction. I. Title.
PS3554.U463394P43 2011
813'.54—dc22   2010041576

Published in 2011 in conjunction with Tekno Books.

Printed in Mexico
3 4 5 6 7 15 14 13 12 11

This is Mimi Riser's book, for sure! If it weren't for Mimi, I'd never have written it.

CHAPTER ONE

"Herd's comin' through!"

Jack, my obnoxious twelve-year-old brother, didn't have to make that announcement twice.

"Oh, Lord."

As I hurried to close the front door of our parents' dry-goods store, leaving my best friend Myrtle Howell gaping after me, Jack raced to the windows and started slamming them closed and latching them against what we knew was sure to follow the herd of which Jack spoke. In those days Second Street wasn't paved and during October, when the fall cattle drive was going on and all the ranches within hundreds of miles drove their herds through Rosedale, New Mexico, the dust the animals kicked up on their jaunt down Second would have been unbelievable if we hadn't seen it ourselves for so many years.

Fortunately the weather was cool that fall day, or we'd have suffocated. Suffocation was what generally happened during the spring cattle drives, although the May drives had become somewhat less stifling since the advent of electricity to town. Now the big rotating electrical fan we'd ordered from Missouri kept us from dying during the two weeks of the spring drives. Anyhow, around here you could never depend on the weather. It's been known to snow in southeastern New Mexico in April, and we've had heat waves in October (although we've also had snow in October and heat waves in April). Even though the Twentieth Century had rolled in some two-dozen years earlier,

7

and we'd been a state since 1912, life was still a little on the edgy side in our neck of the woods back then.

As soon as we'd secured the store against the storm of dust to come, Jack, Myrtle and I, along with the few customers lingering in the store at the time, gathered around the windows to observe the action. Uncomfortable as the drives could be, they were also a whole lot of fun to watch. It was easy to get lost in the adventure of the action and to romanticize those men, the cowboys, who whooped and hollered through town, riding like centaurs and keeping the cattle confined to the street when the occasional cow or steer seemed inclined to stray onto the boardwalks in front of the stores and offices. Once or twice over the years a stray had lumbered through a window or a door, much to the dismay of it, the owner of the property, and the cowboys who had to get the animal out again.

I know for a fact that my idiot brother (I have another brother who isn't an idiot) had a glorified notion of what cowboys did on a daily basis, probably because he read a lot of Zane Grey novels. He'd even told me once that when he grew up, he aimed to move "west." I asked him where he thought we lived if it wasn't in the west, where the dad-gummed legend of the so-called western cowboy originated, but he only sneered at me.

For the most part, I had no sympathy for my brother. Watching the drive from behind the glass panes of the store window, though, I could understand how he'd formed his opinion of cowboys as noble—if somewhat rugged and dusty—heroes, however unrealistic the image might be.

As you observed the cowboys working, it was easy to let your mind wander to open plains and campfires and fabulous adventures featuring bad guys, red Indians, cattle rustlers, and fainting maidens. The unfortunate truth was that a cowboy's life was hard work, blazing heat (or frigid cold), danger and boredom for the most part—but that was no fun to think about, and it was definitely not romantic.

Suddenly Myrtle cried, "Oh, Annabelle! Isn't that Kenny Sawyer?"

"Where?"

She pointed. "There. Oh, my, doesn't he look handsome!"

I spotted him. "Ah," said I. "I see him now." And he did indeed look handsome, mainly because he was handsome. He also looked more at home on a horse than any other man I'd ever seen except maybe my special friend Phil Gunderson. I didn't say so, since I liked to consider myself above such adolescent fancies, even though I wasn't. Myrtle and I were only nineteen in 1923, after all. "So I guess that must be the cattle from Texico."

The Texico Ranch, owned and run by a family by the name of Baldwin, straddled the border between New Mexico and Texas on the east side of the state, near Clovis and Portales. The Baldwins had decided to honor both states when they named their ranch. Their brand was T-X-O, which I thought was kind of clever, although I'm not sure why. The Baldwins' Texico Ranch was not quite as far away from Rosedale as some of the herds, being almost a hundred and twenty-five miles away, but it was pretty darned far. Therefore, I figured, if the Texico herd had reached town, the drive must be about over, since theirs was the last herd to hit town most years. And none too soon, if you asked me, mainly because the big party and rodeo held annually to celebrate the end-of-the-year drive was scheduled to start in only a couple of days.

Everybody in town loved the rodeo because it meant several days of campfires, sing-alongs, dances, and barbecues, not to mention competition between cowboys from various ranches to see who was the best bull rider, broncobuster, calf roper and bulldogger, in the area. It was, in effect, a huge town party, and we all looked forward to it.

In 1923, rodeos weren't the huge moneymaking operations they became a few years later, with men who considered themselves professional rodeo performers. In those days they were more in the nature of big festivals, celebrations of a whole lot of hard work completed, during which real cowboys who worked on real ranches demonstrated their real skills to an admiring, if somewhat restricted, public. At the time, only about 20,000 folks lived in our fair city. Well, sort of fair.

We in Rosedale got to host the party because Rosedale was the hub of the ranching world for an area almost two hundred miles in diameter. Since Rosedale itself, as noted above, only boasted around 20,000 people, you can tell we weren't exactly the hub of western civilization. Still, we liked where we lived. Once in the spring and once in the fall, ranchers drove their cattle through Rosedale to the big pens a little bit east of town, where the beasts were rounded up and guided onto railroad cars and chugged on to Kansas City. There the poor animals would be slaughtered and distributed—I guess to the entire nation. Which made us pretty darned important, even though I'm sure few people outside of the town itself had ever heard of Rosedale, New Mexico, much less thought about Rosedale as they ate their pot roasts, T-bone steaks or beef stews.

That particular October was an unusually interesting one for us, because not only did we have the cattle drive going on, which was a big deal in itself, but a tent revivalist had also come to our town, thereby giving the citizens of Rosedale two forms of entertainment. I don't think I'm supposed to look upon tent revivals as entertainment, but I do. Those revivalist preachers can get folks more stirred up than anything else I know of, barring a big bank robbery or the smashing of a bootlegger's still.

Not that I'm a heathen or anything. In fact, I'm a good, churchgoing, Christian girl, and I sing an almost-on-key alto in the choir at the Methodist-Episcopal Church (North) in town.

But, darn it, I don't like people telling me I'm going to hell if I don't believe exactly as they do. From everything I've read in the Bible, Jesus Himself didn't consign people to hell as often as did most of the revivalist preachers who've come through town.

Unfortunately Myrtle, who, as I already mentioned, is my best friend, and my other best friend, Phil Gunderson, had both gone to some of the revival meetings and been "saved." Ever since then they'd been begging me to go to a meeting or three. They weren't the only ones, either. Worse even than Myrtle or Phil, my mother thought it would be a good idea for my obnoxious brother Jack and me both to go. I guess she thought we were sliding into sin or something, unless she just wanted to get rid of us for a couple of hours in the evening. I guess I couldn't blame her for that, but I still didn't want to go.

This was especially true since the preacher, Reverend Milo Strickland, had the world's most beautiful sister. This sister was a young woman named Esther, about whom both Myrtle and Phil had been waxing ecstatic for several days. Myrtle's infatuation with the Stricklands I could stand, if barely. However, I found Phil's rhapsodizing very trying, since for years he'd been sweet on my own personal self. Mind you, I didn't want to wed him anytime soon, desiring to experience an adventure or two before I got married and faded into obscurity. My personal ambitions aside, I sure as heck didn't want to lose Phil to some female revivalist. Or any other kind of female, either, for that matter.

It's not that I'm ugly or anything. I'm actually kind of pretty. But my plain brown hair and blue eyes are no match for Esther Strickland's beautiful blonde hair and ethereally lovely azure eyes. And I was a normal-sized person, being approximately five feet, four inches tall. Esther was tiny and fairy-like. Shoot, I didn't even know the woman, and I hated her. Which maybe indicates that I *should* go to the next tent revival that hits town. But I didn't want to go to the one conducted by Reverend Strickland and his teensy, gorgeous, angel-like darned sister.

"The rodeo begins the day after tomorrow, Annabelle," Myrtle said, excitement shimmering in her voice. "What are you going to wear to it?"

I looked at her slanty-eyed. "Wear? What do you mean?" I glanced down at my plain old white shirtwaist and blue skirt, covered by a big, more-or-less white apron. This constituted my usual costume when I was minding the store. "I guess I'll wear trousers and a shirt. And I'll take a sweater in case it gets cold."

"You're going to wear *trousers?*" she all but shrieked.

"Well . . . yeah. Why not? I always wear trousers to the rodeo. You do, too."

She tilted her head to one side and pursed her lips. "I used to."

"Used to?" I didn't like the sound of that.

Myrtle lowered her eyelashes and fluttered them slightly. I considered this an alarming sign and, putting two and two together, anticipated what was coming next. Lousy revivalists. "But Reverend Strickland believes women should be feminine at all times. It's what the Bible wants us to be, he says."

"He would," I muttered, wishing Reverend Strickland and his beautiful blasted sister to the devil. Evil of me, I know.

Myrtle turned on me with a frown. "You know it's true, Annabelle. The Bible says that men should act like men, and women should act like women."

"Yeah? Where?"

Myrtle smirked at me, and I instantly knew it had been a mistake to ask. Darn it, she'd been listening to the stupid preacher too closely if she had a reference handy. "Titus. Chapter Two. Read it, if you don't believe me." She sniffed. "It might do you some good."

"Nuts. Anyhow, back then everybody wore skirts," I reminded her. "Including the men. Wouldn't you just love to see Kenny Sawyer in a dress?"

She huffed. "You're avoiding the issue. Wearing trousers is dressing like a man. And trousers show off your shape. According to that chapter in Titus, women are supposed to be discreet and chaste and not . . . not. . . ." She struggled to find the right word. I waited, irked. "Not seductive."

My irritation suffered a keen and blood-boiling spike. "*Seductive?* What's seductive about wearing a ratty old pair of blue jeans while you're sitting on a fence watching a rodeo? I should think having your skirts blow up around your neck would be more *seductive* than that, Myrtle Howell!"

"You're being deliberately obtuse, Annabelle. You know what I mean."

This conversation was really beginning to aggravate me. "Darn it, Myrtle, you've always worn trousers at the rodeo. We both have. Wearing a skirt to a rodeo is stupid unless you're old and can't climb fences."

She lifted her chin. "Nevertheless, I believe Reverend Strickland is right. And his sister *never* wears anything but modest, feminine clothing. She's a shining example of what a woman ought to dress like."

"I just bet she is." How else could she make all the men in her brother's congregation drool over her? I didn't say that last part out loud, since it sounded spiteful—probably because it was.

"Well, I'm going to wear a skirt and shirtwaist," Myrtle said firmly, her chin tilting obstinately upward. "It's modest and . . . and feminine and polite."

"What's so polite about wearing a skirt and a blouse?"

"It shows a proper respect," Myrtle said. If her chin tilted any higher, she'd be staring at the ceiling.

"Towards whom, exactly? The cowboys who will be rolling in the dirt when they fall off their horses and bulls? Or maybe it's the horses you want to respect? I know! You want to impress the bulls!"

"Annabelle Blue, you ought to be ashamed of yourself," said Myrtle, as annoyed as I'd ever seen her (Myrtle being a very even-tempered girl, unlike yours truly, who can be a trifle touchy at times). "It wouldn't do you any harm to go to one of Reverend Strickland's meetings, you know. Listening to the word of God might put a civil tongue in your head."

"Oh, pooh. I don't believe God cares what kinds of clothes young women wear to rodeos and barbecues," I said back at her. "In fact, anybody who'd turn water into wine so that the wedding guests could keep on slurping it up doesn't sound anywhere near as stuffy as your precious reverend and his silly sister."

"That's blasphemous, Annabelle Blue!"

"No, it's not. It's the truth. You can read about it yourself in John, Chapter Two!" I was really proud that I'd remembered which chapter this bit of biographical (and miraculous) information came from. My brain isn't always that quick.

The herd had passed the store by that time, although there was still a pall of dust hovering in the air outdoors. Therefore, I didn't open the windows or the door before I stamped back to the counter and ducked under it. I rose on the other side just in time to see the front door open and Phil Gunderson stroll in. I was about to greet him with enthusiasm when I saw him step aside and hold the door open for someone else to enter.

When I saw who the someone else was, I felt as if God had decided to punish me for my ugly words to Myrtle and for using His word to establish my own petty argument. Esther Strickland, looking as delicate and waiflike and beautiful as Sleeping Beauty and Cinderella and the Princess with the stupid Pea all rolled into one divine human package, wafted into the store. She smiled at Phil as if he held the key to all her happiness. I wanted to drown her. Unfortunately, I lived on a desert.

For all the tea in China, I wouldn't allow Phil to know I was jealous of the woman. Rather, I smiled brightly at the couple— the *couple*, for Pete's sake! I could hardly stand it—and spoke in a friendly manner. "Hello, Miss Strickland. Hey, Phil. Hope you guys didn't get all dusty out there." I noticed that Phil was carrying the princess's sweater. Nuts. He never carried *my* sweaters. Not that I wanted or needed him to, since I was an able-bodied, independent young woman.

"We watched the herd go by from Mrs. Pruitt's store," said Phil, taking Esther's arm and guiding her as if she might fall down or bump into something if he didn't, her being so fragile and feminine and all. To give Phil credit, she did walk as if she existed in some sort of unearthly haze. Cynical creature that I am, I wondered how she did that. I was pretty sure I knew *why* she did it.

"Is Reverend Strickland with you?" Myrtle's voice sounded rather wistful, as if she were hoping the answer would be in the affirmative.

"No, he's working on tonight's sermon, Miss Howell." Esther Strickland gave Myrtle a sickly-sweet smile. Oh, very well. It wasn't sickly-sweet. It was just a lovely smile, and I had the dreadful suspicion that Miss Strickland was a genuinely nice person, which meant that Phil's interest in her was probably justified, confound it. "But thank you for asking. I'll be certain to tell him you asked after him. We've found the citizens of Rosedale to be truly filled with the spirit of the Lord, Miss Howell. You're all so kind to us traveling servants of God."

I suppressed my incredulous snort.

"I'm sure the sermon will be wonderful," murmured Myrtle. "I'm looking forward to going to the meeting tonight." She added fervently, "Mr. Strickland preaches the most wonderful sermons!"

"It's very kind of you to say so, Miss Howell." Esther's fabulous blue eyes scanned the store. She wore a pretty brown-checked dress with three-quarter sleeves, a white lacy collar and a dropped waist that tied behind with a big puffy bow, and she was wearing a pretty brown hat with a bow that matched the one on her dress. You'd have thought she was going to a tea party.

For some reason, just her being in Blue's Dry Goods and Mercantile made the place look dumpy. I'd never thought of the family business as lacking in any way before the advent of this woman, probably because she looked as if she ought to be perched on a throne somewhere. Heaven would be nice—and it would get her out of my hair and away from my special gentle-man friend.

"What a wonderful store," she purred. Her speaking voice was as lovely as her person, blast it. There wasn't a nasal twang or a lisp or anything else in it that a person might find objection-able. Smiling at me—and, although I hate to admit it, her smile seemed to hold nothing but honest admiration—she said, "It's so . . . so precious."

Precious? My parents' store was precious? The store my Grandpa Blue had established in 1892 was *precious?* For some reason I resented that, perhaps because the word made it sound as if she considered us quaint and old fashioned. And heck, maybe we were—but I preferred to think of us as up to date and modern. We weren't back-country hicks, after all, even though we did sort of live at the edge of the universe.

"Really?" I said, in a fairly icy tone of voice. "I've never thought of it as particularly *precious.*"

"Oh, I meant no disparagement," Esther hurried to say, her voice conveying honest worry lest I take offense. "Your store is utterly charming. It preserves the atmosphere of the Old West to perfection, don't you think so?" She didn't wait for me to answer what had probably been meant as a rhetorical question, but turned to Phil. "Did you say there were some fabrics here somewhere, Mr. Gunderson?"

Oh, brother. Why didn't she just ask me, who worked there? But, then, I knew why. Boy, did I ever.

Phil gulped. He would. "Yeah, sure. Over here." And, with Esther holding onto him with both hands—you'd have thought she needed to be anchored to this earth in order not to float up into the ether (I pictured her there, her head bumping against the ceiling, but I was probably only bitter)—he moved over to where Ma kept the fabrics and sewing notions. Esther wafted along beside him as if she were treading on clouds. Myrtle and I exchanged a glance. I hated seeing the sympathy in Myrtle's eyes.

That being the case, and because I absolutely detested having people feel sorry for me, I spoke brightly to Myrtle. "Well, whatever we both wear, I'm really looking forward to the rodeo. I can't wait to see the bulldogging."

"Me, too," said Myrtle, giving herself a little shake, I presume to help her stop staring at Miss Strickland and refocus her attention on our conversation. I could tell she wanted to be Esther Strickland. I considered it a great pity that I could hardly blame her. I mean, how often does one run across perfection, you know?

"And Ma said I can drive the car to the Gundersons' ranch every day, so I don't have to stay with my aunt Minnie." Minnie's place is close to the Gundersons, and I *hate* staying there.

There weren't a whole lot of automobiles in Rosedale, since the roads were rough and most of the folks in and surrounding the town still carried out their business on horseback or via horse and buggy (or, more commonly, mule and wagon). Most of the cars that did tootle around in the area were Model T Fords. My family had a Model T that we'd acquired a couple of years earlier. I thought it was the height of wonderfulness, although I'm sure Miss Strickland would disagree. After all, I lived in the Old West, and she was only visiting. Grumble.

"Thank God for that," Myrtle said piously.

Internally, I echoed the sentiment, although I didn't say so aloud since I didn't want Myrtle to think I was as lost in religion as she. However, I'd spent several perfectly awful days at Minnie's house during the summer that had just passed, and I never wanted to stay with Aunt Minnie again. I loved her a lot, but not only did Minnie believe in ghosts and spirits, with whom she liked to communicate—she'd forced me to participate in her little sessions, too, and even though I don't believe in ghosts, I got the jitters—but her cook and best friend, Libby Powell, is probably one of the meanest people in the entire world. Libby didn't like me one little bit, and I returned the sentiment with interest.

Besides, Minnie lived even more in the middle of absolutely nowhere than I did. I was a town girl. Maybe Rosedale wasn't a big metropolis, but I was used to being able to see my friends and go to the library or visit the Pecos Theater to see a flicker when I wanted to. I didn't like being so isolated and out of the way. I don't know how Minnie stood it. I'm sure all that vast expanse of nothingness contributed to her many oddities. Add to that her only close neighbor, a strange little old man named Olin Burgess, who was a nice fellow but who'd been horribly mutilated in the Civil War about a billion years previously and gave everyone who looked at him the creeps, and you can probably understand my feelings on the matter of staying with Aunt Minnie. Never again. Well, unless my mother made me.

"Ma's making a couple of apple pies, and I'm bringing some

yeast rolls to the barbecue Friday," Myrtle said. "What about you?"

"We're making up a big batch of beans with ham hocks and onions and chilies." My mouth watered, even thinking about all the wonderful food we'd have at the feast. We Old Westerners loved our barbecues.

"Oh, yum. I suppose the Gundersons will be contributing a steer."

"I expect." It was a tradition in Rosedale for the ranch family that hosted the rodeo to dig a big pit and roast a steer in it. Generally they added a goat or two, also, for those of us who liked the meat therefrom. The other attendees brought covered dishes, salads, desserts, pickles, etc. "I hope Libby makes a batch of her potato salad and brings that. I'm sure she'll bring pickles."

She'd darned well better bring pickles. I'd almost killed myself during the summer helping her with those stupid pickles. I didn't like Libby any more than she liked me, but she was one of the best cooks in the area. Maybe even the world. It was great to eat her cooking when she wasn't around while you were eating it. I mean, who cares how food tastes if the person who cooked it hangs around while you're eating it, carping and criticizing and giving you a stomachache?

I'd been trying very hard not to watch Miss Priss and Phil as Myrtle and I chatted about the rodeo. After all, I didn't want Phil to think I gave a rap if he wanted to transfer his affections from me to her (even though I did give a rap—several, even), so I was kind of surprised when Miss Strickland wafted back into view after only a couple of minutes. She smiled at me. "What a sweet store you have, Miss Blue."

First it was precious, and now it was sweet. I'd have to tell my mother. She might be amused. I wasn't. "Thank you. Did you see anything you liked?"

"Well . . . yes, indeed. You have a fine selection of fabrics. And I'm sure the materials in stock are most suitable for the rugged life you live here in Rosedale." She gave me a smile that would have looked right at home on one of the archangels. Except that the archangels are men, aren't they? I'm not sure about that.

I think my mouth fell open, which was a big mistake because words spewed forth. Which, of course, meant that she'd won this round. I was as certain as I was of anything that she was hoping to rile me by her supposedly kind comments that were, in reality, thinly veiled barbs. "Rugged? I'll have you know my mother orders fabrics from the best warehouses in the country!"

Her azure eyes opened wide, and her dark eyelashes—I'd bet money she used mascara, which I'm sure her brother would condemn as ungodly—fluttered. "Oh, of course. I'm sure that's so." She looked so innocent, I didn't believe her. "You have a perfectly wonderful selection of merchandise."

"We stock the *best* merchandise," I averred mulishly.

"Of course you do, dear."

Dear? I must have looked as if I aimed to throw something at her, because Phil said hastily, "You coming to the opening of the rodeo tomorrow night, Annabelle?"

"Of course, I am." I glared at him. "Don't I always?"

"Um . . . yeah." Phil shuffled his feet. He looked mighty uncomfortable, which was only fair under the circumstances. "Well, good, then. Reckon I'll see you there."

"I reckon." My voice was hard as flint (if that's the stuff that's hard. Maybe it's steel). But I was angry, darn it, mainly because I'd reacted to Miss Holier-Than-Thou Strickland's attempt to make me feel like a backwater bumpkin instead of bearing up under her attack and remaining aloof, thereby proving to her that I was not merely immune to her snide innuendoes, but better than she.

Or maybe she wasn't trying to make me look bad. It was really hard to tell, because she appeared so utterly earnest. Her very sincerity was suspicious—to me, anyway. It didn't seem to me as if anybody else suspected her of being anything but a lovely, morally upright woman. Which made her even harder for me to take. And *that,* no doubt, bespeaks my own lack of charitable personality characteristics.

Phooey.

"I'm *so* looking forward to seeing a real rodeo," Esther said, clutching Phil's arm once more. I noticed her fingernails were extremely well manicured. I hid my hands in a fold of my skirt and silently cursed myself for not filing and buffing them the evening before. Darn it, by her mere existence, Esther Strickland could make me feel like two cents. Didn't seem fair somehow. "Phil says he's going to be riding bucking broncos."

Phil shuffled some more and his tanned cheeks turned a ruddy color. The fool was *blushing,* for heaven's sake!

I said, "Yes, he's a very good bronc rider." It was the truth, and I felt as if the comment made up for some of my mental meanness about Miss Strickland.

Phil flashed me a shy smile, as if to thank me for making him look good in front of his new ladylove. I felt as if I'd just handed him over to the enemy, and that, of course, made me feel like a martyr on a cross.

That being the case, I heaped ashes upon my head and added, "He's a good bulldogger, too, and he can rope better than anyone else in Rosedale."

"I was sure of it." She all but glowed at Phil, whose face was now redder than any brick I'd seen in Rosedale, primarily because any brick in Rosedale was covered in dust by that time.

The front door opened before I could say anything else, which was probably a good thing, because I didn't have anything nice to say. Two men walked in and immediately approached Miss

Strickland. One of them was about as tall as Phil and had a long face that reminded me of pictures of a basset hound I'd seen in a magazine. The other one was shorter and balding and looked rather like Mrs. Sepulveda's overweight Chihuahua. They were both clad in sober dark suits and reminded me of undertakers.

"Miss Strickland," said the tall undertaker.

Esther turned, and her perfect features were marred by a frown when she spotted them. "Charles and Edward, what are you two doing here?" Although she wasn't rude to either of the men, she was clearly not pleased to see them.

The Chihuahua said, "Reverend Strickland asked us to find you, Miss Strickland. He hadn't expected you to . . . er . . . visit town without saying anything to him."

The revival tent had been set up a couple of hundred yards west of the town limits. It wasn't that far away, and I wondered why Reverend Strickland would send out a search party for his sister. Unless he didn't trust the people in town, which made me see red for an instant before it occurred to me that he actually might not trust *her* for some reason or other.

Hmm. That was an interesting notion. I allowed myself to speculate for a couple of seconds about why Esther Strickland needed to be followed around, but didn't come to any conclusion other than that Milo Strickland was a loving brother who didn't want his sister getting into trouble in a strange—and some (Esther Strickland, for instance) might say rough and ready—frontier outpost. Not that we were, of course, but I understood that's what people back east thought about us out here in the west. That being the case, I reluctantly acquitted Milo and Esther Strickland of a mean-spirited attempt to make me feel like a country yokel. Almost.

The celestial blue eyes rolled. "Oh, heavenly days. Milo does worry about me, doesn't he?"

"Yes, ma'am," said the shorter of the two men, sounding emphatic.

"I'm sure I'm quite safe with Mr. Gunderson," said Esther, endowing Phil with a look that made my stomach give a hard spasm. Then she turned toward Myrtle and me and said, "Miss Blue and Miss Howell, please allow me to introduce you to two of my brother's most valued and trusted associates, Charles Peabody and Edward Grant."

Was there malice in her eyes? Probably not. By that time, I'd decided I hated her guts, and I was sure I was only projecting my own distaste (my high school psychology teacher taught us all about projection). I smiled at the two men, who nodded, sober as a couple of judges. I decided then and there that I didn't want any part of a religion that turned people into sticks of wood. "Happy to meet you, gentlemen," I said.

"Likewise," said Myrtle, who sounded a trifle flustered.

"Miss Blue. Miss Howell," said the tall undertaker, bowing slightly.

"Pleased to meet you, Miss Blue and Miss Howell," said the pudgy Chihuahua, and he bowed too.

I still didn't know which one of them was Charles and which one was Edward. Stupid people.

"Well, since Milo sent you after me, I suppose I'd best be getting back to him." And then Esther Strickland, hanging onto Phil and gazing up at him with adoring eyes, and Phil Gunderson, his face flaming with embarrassment, left Blue's Dry Goods and Mercantile Emporium with Charles and Edward trailing in their wake. Myrtle and I gazed after them.

I said, "I hate that woman."

Myrtle gasped, shocked.

Jack, the fiend, who'd been hiding behind a stack of Franco-American Spaghetti cans, snickered.

CHAPTER TWO

Two days later, on Thursday, the rodeo was set to begin. The morning dawned clear and perfect, with big fluffy clouds cluttering up the sky and with almost no wind, which was something of a miracle. We could get hideous winds in Rosedale. The winds primarily tortured us in the springtime, although no season was immune. But there wasn't a breeze to be felt that day and the temperature was probably around seventy degrees, which was great weather for a rodeo, by gum.

I could hardly wait for the store to close so my family could all pile into our Model T and head out to the Gundersons' ranch for opening day of the big rodeo and party. As I'd mentioned to Myrtle a couple of days before, Ma and Pa were going to let me drive, since I was nineteen and knew how because my older brother had taught me. Jack, as might be expected, objected to this arrangement.

"I don't know why I can't drive," he said, sulking. He sulked a lot. I think it's required of twelve-year-old boys that they irritate their families in every way possible, and sulking is one of the best.

"You can't drive because you're twelve," I told him, making no bones about it. Sometimes I amused myself by thinking of ways to get back at my brother for being such a drip. My favorite so far was burying him in the desert near a red-ant hole, pouring molasses on him, and having the ants bite him until he shrieked for mercy. Sometimes I'm not very nice. But, darn it,

24

Jack was not nice *all* the time.

"Huh. Davy gets to drive his father's truck." Davy was Phil Gunderson's younger brother. According to Phil, Davy was every bit as obnoxious as Jack, but he wasn't around me all the time like Jack was, so I liked him better than I liked Jack.

I pointed out the obvious. "Davy has to help on the ranch. Lots of farm and ranch kids drive early."

"And we have to own a stupid store in town," Jack grumbled, clearly believing that Grandpa Blue had opened the store in the full knowledge that one day his having done so would irk my brother. Boys are *really* difficult to take sometimes.

"That's enough, both of you," said Ma.

I thought she was being unfair since I wasn't the one doing the grousing, but I was used to it. The only children of William and Susanna Blue, my parents, who didn't get ragged on were my older brother and two older sisters. George, the older brother, was a member of the U.S. Army Air Service and a war hero, so he'd have been above being scolded even if he was home, which he wasn't. Hannah and Zilpha, my sisters, were married and out of the running. So that left Jack and me. Sometimes I wondered if marrying Phil might not be such a bad idea after all. Not that it was an option any longer, I guess, thanks to Miss Esther Strickland. The notion made my heart twang, and I told it to stop.

However, there wasn't anything I could do about Ma's impartial disciplinary measures. This was mainly because if I objected, Pa would smack me and make me stay home, and I *really* wanted to go to the rodeo. Therefore, I shut up and drove.

As I've mentioned already, the roads weren't very good in Rosedale, and the Gunderson ranch is a good twelve miles to the west of town. Still, it didn't take too very long to get there. This was in spite of there being more traffic than usual because the entire citizenship was going in the same direction for the same purpose. Mrs. Gunderson, who is a lovely person in spite of having to live at the back of beyond and having had to raise five sons with no daughters to help her or add brightness and joy to her life, greeted us shortly after we all tumbled out of the Model T.

"It's so good to see you, Susanna!" she cried, throwing her arms around my mother. I imagine she got lonely, stuck out there on the ranch all the time, with no other women to talk to. When she let Ma go, she took my hand in both of hers and beamed at me. "And Annabelle, just look at you! You're growing prettier by the day!"

I was? Boy, I didn't know that, but it was nice to hear, even if it was from Mrs. Gunderson and not a young man. And this was in spite of my trousers and shirt. Take *that*, Myrtle Howell. "Thank you," I said politely, wishing there were a mirror nearby so I could check this evidence of attractiveness for myself.

"She cleans up pretty good," my father said with a chuckle. I grinned at him. Pa's really got a good sense of humor.

"Humph," came a voice from behind him. We all turned to see Aunt Minnie and Libby Powell. "You sure couldn't tell it by *that* outfit." Naturally, this disparaging comment had come from Libby. Have I mentioned that she didn't like me? Well, she didn't. I didn't take it too personally since Libby pretty much didn't like anybody, but I still thought she was poisonous as a rattler.

Naturally, Minnie and Libby were clad in dresses. Both of them looked as if they'd stepped right out of 1880 and ended up in 1923 by accident, with their long skirts and corsets and bonnets and stuff. Of course, that mode of costume wasn't unique to them. Lots of older women in Rosedale still dressed the way they had when they were younger. For a second, I wondered if old ladies in New York or San Francisco did that, too, or if they were more modern in big cities and followed the latest fashions even though they were older. With my luck, I'd never get to find out.

"Good evening to you, too, Miss Libby," I said with as much sarcasm as I dared, with my parents being there and all. "Hi, Aunt Minnie." As I've mentioned, I loved my aunt in spite of her eccentricities. She was never deliberately cruel, like Libby. "Is that a bag of cookies I see there?"

"It is," she said, beaming. "They're Libby's famous chocolate-drop cookies."

"I'm sure they'll be good anyway," I muttered.

My mother said, "Annabelle," right before she stooped to kiss Minnie on the cheek. "It's good to see you, Minnie." Minnie is as short and round as a pumpkin. Libby is big as a house and also round, although I don't think any of her largeness is due to fat. She's just big.

"We always enjoy watching the men ride those bulls and things," said Minnie. "My Joe does so love the rodeos." Uncle Joe Blue, my father's older brother, passed away several years earlier, but Minnie claims to keep up with him through her Ouija board. I guess he still watches the rodeo from the Other Side, whatever that is. Minnie explained it to me once, but I wasn't paying attention.

"It looks as if there's quite a crowd here already," said Pa, surveying the milling throng.

He was right. We'd had to wait until the store closed at five o'clock before heading out, but other people, especially the cowboys from outlying ranches who'd been camping out in the desert around Rosedale for a few days, had arrived several hours earlier than we. I was eager to find my friends and get a good seat on the fence surrounding the pasture where most of the activity would take place.

"I'm going to find Myrtle," I said.

Before I could get away, Ma said, "Take a sandwich with you,

Annabelle. You haven't eaten dinner yet." We'd brought a picnic to the rodeo so we wouldn't have to waste time eating a real dinner at home.

"There's Davy!" Jack cried suddenly. Before he could take off, Ma caught him by his shirttail, which was always coming out of his trousers.

"You take a sandwich, too, Jack Blue."

"Aw, Ma."

But he took the sandwich. So did I. Ma very rarely raised her voice. She didn't need to. So Jack and I both obediently thanked her for our sandwiches, and Jack took off like a spooked jackrabbit in the direction of Davy Gunderson.

I took my time, munching and watching, and wondering if Mrs. Gunderson had been right about me. Was I really getting prettier every day? It was a comforting thought, I guess, especially since I seemed to have lost my one true beau to a usurping blonde revivalist.

Myrtle came running up to me after I'd taken my second bite of sandwich. The sandwich was good, by the way, being made of leftover roast beef and slapped between two pieces of Ma's homemade bread. With mustard. "Annabelle!"

"Myrtle!" I noticed that she wore a pretty white shirtwaist and a striped skirt. The skirt was surely going to get in her way when she tried to climb the fence to watch the calf-roping competition that was supposed to be the first activity on the rodeo menu that evening. She carried a blue sweater, in case it got cold.

Until electricity had come to our vicinity, a body pretty much had to stay home at night unless the moon was full, in which case you could almost see your hands if you held them in front of your face. This was especially true if it had been snowing, which it didn't do very often. But when there was a coating of white on the ground, night was almost as bright as day. If it weren't for Mr. Edison and his light bulb, however, Rosedale never would have planned an outdoor event on a Thursday night because the horses and cows would be running into the fences and killing their riders in the dark. And spectators would have been flat out of luck as they tried to see the death and destruction, too.

For the past two years, though, Rosedale's fledgling electric company had strung temporary lighting around the pasture of the ranch family hosting the rodeo. The excitement of actually being able to see past six o'clock was still a novelty that year, so everybody's spirits were high. Including mine, which is why I didn't point out to Myrtle the impracticality of her skirt, given the event about to transpire. I doubt that Myrtle would have thanked me for my self-control, as she was still convinced she was doing what God—or at least Reverend Strickland—wanted.

Since I believed that God saved His rules for important things like war and peace and famine and earthquakes and floods and fires and famines and stuff like that, and that the requirement that women wear dresses under all circumstances had been ordained by a much lower power than He, I hurried over to the fence to get a good spot on which to sit. Perhaps I hurried a little more than usual—I was also wearing sensible shoes, as opposed to Myrtle's pretty black-strapped pumps that were already gray with dust—because she hollered at me to slow down. And maybe I smirked ever so slightly as I turned around and waited for a puffing Myrtle to catch up with me, but I figured I'd earned it.

Then, as I clambered up the slats and perched myself on the top of the fence and leaned my back against a conveniently situated cottonwood tree, she looked at the fence in dismay. I smiled beneficently down upon her. "Why, whatever is the matter, Myrtle?"

"I can't climb the fence," she said, sounding bleak. "It's

unladylike."

Unladylike? Nuts. "I suppose you can fold your arms on the top rung and lean against it from behind," I suggested helpfully. "Although that might get your pretty blouse dirty." I regret to say I sniffed. "Personally, I'm glad I'm not ladylike."

"You would be," she muttered. Then, to my great appreciation, she hiked up her skirt and climbed the fence in spite of God, Reverend Milo Strickland and his seductress of a sister.

I didn't mean that. Miss Strickland had thus far—in my vicinity at least—displayed nothing but a modest friendliness to my own personal beau.

Of course, I don't know what she did behind my back.

Oh, never mind. I was just feeling a little put-upon that evening, is all.

However, I was darned proud of Myrtle.

"This is going to ruin my stockings," she muttered.

Not to mention her skirt. Nevertheless, I only smiled. Not once during the entire evening did I tell her she'd been stupid to wear a skirt and shirtwaist instead of trousers and a shirt. I believe my restraint should be commended. It took a few minutes, but Myrtle finally found a position that wasn't horribly uncomfortable. I shared my cottonwood backrest with her.

Mr. Gunderson had just stepped up onto a platform Phil and he had erected at the far end of the pasture. He was greeting one and all, to thunderous applause, when I heard my name spoken by a voice I recognized.

"Annabelle, move over."

Turning, I saw my sister Zilpha, accompanied by my other sister Hannah, hurrying up to the fence. Zilpha and Hannah are the sisters Ma no longer scolds because they're married and living in their own houses in town. Zilpha's husband Mayberry is a really nice fellow whom I like a lot, but his last name is Zink. Maybe it's petty of me, but I wouldn't want to be named Zilpha

Zink. I've never shared my opinion with Zilpha, who wouldn't have appreciated it.

Hannah is married to Richard MacDougall, who works at the Rosedale Farmer's and Rancher's Bank. I guess Richard is an all right sort of person, as bankers go, but he's kind of stuffy for my taste, and he likes to show off his money, which he has a lot of. But Hannah seems happy, so I don't suppose it's any of my business. Anyhow, no matter what Reverend Strickland would surely have said on the matter, I've always thought that there's nothing wrong with having plenty of money. I should think it would beat the alternative hollow.

At any rate, I moved over, happy to see that my sisters displayed the family's commonsensical trait and were wearing trousers. "Hey. How are you guys doing? Where are Mayberry and Richard?"

"Mayberry's over there." Zilpha pointed to the other side of the pasture, where I discerned her husband in a deep conversation with Phil. They were probably talking about saddles, Mayberry being a saddler and all, and Phil being a cowboy when he wasn't working in his brother's hardware store in town.

"I don't know where Richard is," said Hannah. "Probably trying to drum up business."

She didn't seem to think there was anything unusual about a man trying to drum up business at a community social event, so I guess there wasn't, although it seemed kind of sad to me that Richard was all business all the time. On the other hand, maybe that made him happy. It had definitely made him well off, which was nice for him and for Hannah. I only said, "Ah."

Myrtle and Zilpha and Hannah greeted each other. I noticed that Zilpha's eyebrows arched a little when she saw that Myrtle was wearing a skirt, but she didn't say anything. Zilpha's very nice. So is Hannah, but I think Zilpha is more filled with the milk of human kindness than is my other sister. They're both older than I am, and they were both very good to me when we were growing up, so I'm not complaining or anything. I've got friends who can't say as much about their older sisters and brothers, so I felt fortunate in my family. Well, except for Jack, but he's another matter altogether.

Mr. Gunderson lifted his megaphone, looking not one little bit like the picture of Rudy Vallee I'd seen in a recent movie magazine, and tried to get the crowd's attention. Everyone was so excited, it took him a few minutes, but eventually something resembling quiet prevailed.

"Good evening, ladies and gents!"

Everyone shouted "Good evening!" back at him. We're friendly folks in Rosedale.

He went on to greet everyone and thank all the hard-working cowboys for bringing the herds to town without any notable catastrophes breaking out. One year a frightened steer ran right through Joyce Pruitt's front door and proceeded to kick out two windows and flatten two shelves of patent medicine. Maybe that was the animal we later ate at the barbecue that year; I never asked. And then Mr. Gunderson did something I could have lived without.

"And now, to get the festivities off to a good start, we have two special guests. Miss Esther Strickland is going to start us off with a song, and then her brother, Reverend Milo Strickland, will say a prayer that all these gallant lads will survive their competition in one piece!"

That got a laugh from most of the crowd, with the possible exception of my own personal self, who could have lived forever without hearing Esther sing or Milo pray. Oh, well. Nobody asked me.

And then, with help from Phil—naturally—Esther took the stage. Or the platform. With her on it, it looked like a stage. Mr. Gunderson handed her the megaphone, and she smiled sweetly at the crowd, which was stomping, clapping, and hollering by that time.

The whole thing made me sick, although I'm willing to chalk up some of my attitude to jealousy. Oh, very well, it was probably mostly jealousy. But, darn it, I'd never had any serious competition for Phil's affections before, and I didn't like it one little bit. I also felt a little guilty knowing Phil might well have turned to another woman in order to get the appreciation he didn't get from me.

You see, I think Phil is a swell fellow. But he and I have known each other all our lives. And I was only nineteen years old. Can't a girl have an adventure or two before she shackles herself to a husband and gives up living? All I'd done my whole life was live in Rosedale, New Mexico, and read about adventures in books. I wanted one or two adventures of my own before I got married, for Pete's sake. I wanted to take an African safari. See the pyramids of Egypt. Visit the Taj Mahal. At least go to New York City and maybe Boston or Salem, Massachusetts, where the witch trials were held. And I wouldn't have minded if one or two really exciting and adventurous men exhibited some interest in me along the way. I wouldn't do anything untoward with any of them. Honest, I wouldn't. I'm not that sort of girl. Is that kind of ambition so hard to understand?

But back to the rodeo. . . .

"Thank you so much," Esther said in her sugary voice. "You have all been so kind to Milo and me. May God bless you and keep you all safe in His arms."

Then Esther started to sing "We Gather Together," a song we folks in Rosedale usually sang around Thanksgiving time, although I suppose it's logical to sing it during cattle-harvesting season, since we were definitely gathered together that night. Whatever its appropriateness, the song held the attention of everyone in the audience, and I made up my mind then and there to run away and see the world all by myself, and to heck with Phil Gunderson. Let him have the preacher's sister if he wanted her. Insipid, sneaking creature.

She sure had a voice in her, though. Sweet and pure, it carried clear out to where the cows used to be on the open plains surrounding the Gunderson ranch. I'd never minded having to sing alto in the Methodist choir before that evening. On that particular Thursday night, listening to that gorgeous woman sing in her magnificent, vibrant soprano voice, I couldn't help but wonder why God had made me the way He had. I mean, if I couldn't be fabulously beautiful or rich or live in an interesting or charming place, couldn't I at least have been blessed with a voice like Esther Strickland's?

I was so annoyed, I stopped looking at her, with one hand clasped to her bosom, the other holding the megaphone, and her ethereal face practically proclaiming her to be one of God's holy angels. Rather, I scanned the crowd. There were Charles and Edward—or Edward and Charles (I still don't know which was which)—sitting next to Reverend Strickland and watching Miss Strickland, which was appropriate. As you might expect, most everyone's attention was riveted upon the stunning Miss Strickland. They were lapping her up like a kitten laps cream. It was as if she was a witch and she'd enchanted the entire town.

There were two exceptions to this rapturous attention—well, besides me, I mean. What's more, one of those exceptions was none other than Richard MacDougall, my own sister's husband.

Unsure of what I was seeing, I squinted harder. Yup. It was Richard, all right, and he seemed to be getting awfully cozy with—good heavens, was it really . . . ? Yes, by gum, it was: Josephine Contreras. Josephine, who was married to none other than Armando Contreras. Hmm. What was this meeting all about? I sure didn't want to think that Richard and Josephine had designs on each other. They were both married to other people, for one thing, and for another thing, one of the other people was my sister Hannah, whom I didn't want to see hurt.

But there they were. And they were definitely together and being secretive. Well . . . they were being as secretive as they could be, given the occasion and the fact that the entire town was there with them, if not exactly *with* them, if you know what I mean. I told myself I was only suffering residual upset over the Phil–Esther affair—if that was the right word for it, and I hoped it wasn't—and was reading into Richard and Josephine's tête-à-tête things that weren't there. I still didn't like it, though. I sneaked a quick glance at Hannah, but she was listening raptly to Miss Strickland.

However, at that moment, the song ended (to more thunderous applause, of course), Esther Strickland threw a kiss to her audience, which seemed to thrill everyone, Phil helped her down from the platform (again of course), and her brother took to the platform, sans megaphone. I guess he figured God would amplify his voice and he wouldn't need further help.

He was right. Boy, like his sister, that man had a voice! It wasn't anything you'd expect if you just looked at him and waited to listen to him speak. Milo Strickland was really kind of thin and reedy, with scant, floppy, sand-colored hair, narrow shoulders, and a pointy chin that made him look kind of like a weasel. He sure didn't look like his sister, except that they were both smallish and blondish.

But when he let loose, look out! He prayed for the cowboys and for the city of Rosedale. He prayed for the city fathers. He prayed for the sailors at sea and all the soldiers, wherever they were. He prayed for the herds. He prayed for the ranchers. He prayed for the sinners in Africa and India. He prayed for the consecrated and the unconsecrated. He prayed for the President and for Congress, both of which needed all the prayers they could get. He prayed for the Supreme Court and the people involved with the Scopes trial, which had concluded not too many months prior. I'm sure he was on the anti-evolutionist side of the issue, although I still can't figure out how those anti-evolution people can argue with science. He prayed for the churches in town and out of town, and for the people who didn't attend any of them, that they'd find their ways to the Lord. He prayed for the king of England and for all the starving Russians in Russia, and he prayed that they'd be guided back to the Lord (evidently, after the revolution there, the people in charge had axed religion). He even prayed for the pope, for Pete's sake, even though he wasn't a Catholic. Reverend Strickland, I mean, not the pope.

He prayed so long and so hard, I was thoroughly sick of him before he finally intoned the last sonorous "Amen" that I'd started praying for myself. I probably sound like a thoroughly sinful young woman, but I'm not, really. I go to church. I believe in God. I try to love my neighbor as I do myself, even though I find that somewhat difficult, as you can probably tell. I sing in the choir, for pity's sake. Anyhow, a swelling chorus of "Amens" from the spectators followed the rev's amen. It's my theory that people were so glad he'd shut up, they said the word out of a sense of relief.

Whatever the emotions of the crowd, Mr. Gunderson took to the platform again and announced the first event, which, as I mentioned before, was calf roping.

Most of the guys who were performing that evening had been born nearby and had known each other for a number of years and were friendly with each other. The only one of the gang who didn't quite fit in was Kenny Sawyer, the cowboy Myrtle and I had watched from the store window of Blue's Dry Goods. Kenny had been born in Rosedale, too, and his mother and sister still lived in town, but from there on, he differed from his fellow cowboys. For one thing, he was a little over six feet tall and handsome as sin. He knew it, too; and whereas most of the cowboys I knew were humble fellows, Kenny was quite full of himself.

He was darned good, though, at everything he did. He was a great roper, a wonderful rider, and he could stick to the meanest bull God ever invented. If he was inclined to take himself seriously, and if he swaggered a little too much, and if he wasn't precisely a man's man, it didn't seem to bother any of the women in town. He collected females the way spilled honey collected ants, and this in spite of the fact that he and Sarah Molina were supposed to be engaged to be married. He was kind of a wanderer, if you know what I mean.

Kenny and Phil were generally the best of the cowboys in most of the events held in our annual rodeo. Kenny had beat Phil in overall points for the past two years, but Phil was older and bigger now than he'd been then. Phil had just turned twenty-one, and he'd completely lost any babyishness he'd once had. He was good-looking too, but he wasn't spectacular like Kenny was. Kenny could have been a movie star; he was that handsome. And he wasn't at all shy, as Phil could sometimes be. He even flirted with me sometimes, even though he knew Phil was sweet on me—had once been sweet on me, anyhow. Or maybe he flirted with me *because* he thought Phil was sweet on me. That possibility wouldn't have surprised me. I didn't like Kenny a whole lot.

However, he sure could rope a calf, which didn't merely entail work on the cowboy's part. The cowboy had to have a horse that he'd trained especially for the purpose. Both Kenny and Phil were wonderful with horses, and both had trained their mounts themselves. It was exciting to watch Phil work with his horse and his cattle, even when he was only doing his regular job on his father's ranch. I'm sure the same could be said of

Kenny, but I only saw him a few times a year, when he came to town.

A lot of work had gone into fixing the Gundersons' pasture so that the rodeo could take place. Chutes had been built to hold the broncos before they were let loose to rattle the cowboys' bones, and runs were made to be used by the calves, bulls and steers as they were shooed into the pasture. The calves and the cowboys entered the pasture through the run, the cowboys chasing the calves—one at a time, naturally, so the different events could be timed by Mr. Gunderson and a couple of the other ranch owners, using big stopwatches. Sometimes they had to confer with each other. I guess they added all the times up and divided by three in order to come up with the cowboy's official time. As I said, rodeo wasn't very formal in those days.

And I sure don't know all the rules of the various events, but I do know that in calf roping, a calf would be set to run into the pasture, and a couple of seconds later a cowboy would chase after it on his horse. He'd have to rope the calf, then leap off his horse, run to the calf, catch it and flank it, and then tie at least three of its legs together with what Phil told me was a "pigging string," which was another name for a small rope, and which he carried in his teeth. I guess every profession has its own argot. Anyhow, when the cowboy was through tying up the calf's legs, he'd throw his hands in air as a signal to the judges that he'd finished the job. Then he'd remount his horse and let the rope go slack. If the calf kicked free of the rope in a certain number of seconds, the tie was considered invalid. It was a lot of work to do in a short space of time, and it took a lot of strength, skill, and a great horse. The horse was very important, because it not only had to respond to every tiny cue the cowboy gave it, both with his knees and his hands, but after the calf had been roped the horse had to stand there, perfectly still while the cowboy worked with the calf. If the horse wasn't perfectly trained, all of the cowboy's careful efforts would be ruined.

Phil and Kenny both had all of the attributes necessary to perform the task, but that evening Kenny beat Phil by something like a tenth of a second. I'd have felt sorrier for Phil if I hadn't been mad at him. Still, he was a gentleman about it and shook Kenny's hand. Kenny, smirking, slapped Phil on the back and said something I could tell Phil didn't like much. But Phil really *is* a gentleman, and he didn't react by more than a tightening of his lips.

Then something happened that made me smirk inside, even though I knew it was mean of me. Esther Strickland, the woman who had been treating Phil as if he were her own personal box of candy, started fawning over Kenny Sawyer.

Oh, all right, she didn't actually *fawn* over him. But she came over and shook his hand, tilting her head back shyly and smiling up at him as if she thought he was the most thrilling thing to come along in a month of Sundays. She looked gorgeous and appealing and sweet and charming. Kind of like Mary Pickford, actually. She had that same air of innocent beauty about her.

Have I mentioned recently that I hated her?

Phil, looking a little lonely, wandered off. Kenny, with Esther hanging on him instead of Phil for a change, got ready for the steer wrestling, which was next. Phil wasn't entered in that event, and I wondered if he'd bother to look up little old me, or if he was going to lick his wounds somewhere else.

Sometimes I worry about perhaps being a trifle too catty. But not often.

Anyway, I'd wronged poor Phil. Right after the steer wrestling began, darned if he didn't show up at my section of the fence.

"Hey, Annabelle."

I turned, and he was standing right there behind me, smiling his self-deprecating smile, and holding a glass of lemonade (rodeoing is thirsty work). "Hey, Phil. Wanna sit here?" I scooted over closer to Myrtle and patted the fence beside me. "Good event for you."

He shrugged. "I lost anyway."

"Pooh. You came in second by a hair. Anyhow, it's supposed to be all in fun."

He climbed up, slung his long legs over the top rung of the fence, and settled in, leaning against my cottonwood (it was a big tree). "Tell that to Kenny Sawyer," he muttered darkly.

"Don't pay any attention to him. He's a swell-headed dummy."

Phil said, "Hmm," and resumed slurping his lemonade.

"Hey, Phil," said Myrtle, leaning over and looking around me so she could smile at Phil. "You did a great job with the calf. Your horse was perfect, and you almost won."

"Hey, Myrtle. Thanks." He squinted at her skirt but didn't say anything. Then he greeted my sisters, both of whom liked Phil and expected me to marry him someday. *Everybody* expected me to marry him someday. Even me, until recently.

"Good meeting last night at the revival tent, wasn't it?" Myrtle asked him.

Phil nodded. "Reverend Strickland is a great speaker." He nudged me with his elbow. "You ought to come to a meeting with us, Annabelle. You'd be impressed. I don't think they'll be in town much longer."

Thank God for that, said I to myself. To Phil, I said, "Hmm."

And then I heard my name again. It sounded kind of snuffly this time. "Annabelle?"

I turned once more, and spotted Sarah Molina, the woman who was, ostensibly, Kenny Sawyer's ladylove, although you wouldn't necessarily know it from the way Kenny behaved around other women. "Hey, Sarah." Although the lighting wasn't the best, I saw that she'd been crying. "What's the matter?"

She sniffled again. "Oh . . . nothing."

That was clearly a lie, as Sarah was obviously in distress. Because I like Sarah and am a nice person in spite of my occasional lapses, I gestured for Phil to move over a little and let me get down. Playing the gent again—as I said before, he really *is* a gentleman (I don't think he can help it)—Phil slid down from the fence and helped me lower myself to the ground, even though I didn't really need his help. Nevertheless, because I'd learned my lesson in coquetry from a mistress of the art, I smiled and said, "Thanks, Phil."

"Sure."

I took Sarah's arm and led her a foot or two away from the fence. "Now, Sarah, I can tell something's wrong. Please tell me what it is. You've been crying. Whatever's wrong, I'm sorry you feel bad."

She made a gesture of helplessness. "Oh, it's . . . it's nothing. Really." She was lying through her teeth. If ever there was a miserable person in the world, that person was Sarah Molina.

"Nuts."

She heaved a huge sigh. As I said before, I like Sarah. However, the girl lived life as if it were a drama being staged for general humanity's benefit, and she was kind of extreme in her emotions. If she was happy, the whole world knew it, and if she was sad, she was sure to make as many people be sad with her as she could. Since I had a hunch she was unhappy this time because of a certain blonde evangelist, however, I had more sympathy for her than was usually the case when Sarah believed that she'd been wronged by another person.

"Come on, Sarah, tell me. I hate to see you like this."

She sniffled some more and then came out with it. "Oh, Annabelle! It's that *girl!* That preacher's sister! She's trying to steal Kenny from me!" And she burst into tears.

I put my arms around her and glanced over her shaking

shoulders to Phil, who stood there looking uncomfortable and clearly not knowing what to do. Men. They're totally useless most of the time. I mean, Phil was always opening doors for girls when they could open them for themselves and helping them down from fences when they didn't need help, but when he saw a girl in true distress, all he could do was stand there and look uncomfortable.

Turning my attention back to my sobbing companion, I said soothingly, "I'm sure it's nothing, Sarah. But I do know what you mean." I didn't look at Phil that time. I took a deep breath, said a silent prayer that God would forgive me for my next words, and went on, "Although I must say that, from what I've seen and for such a religious person, Esther Strickland shows every symptom of being a hussy."

That made Sarah cry harder, but I think she sobbed, "Yes!" It was sort of hard to tell since her tears were getting in the way of her speech.

Phil stiffened a trifle. "Miss Strickland is a good Christian lady, Miss Molina. I'm sure she doesn't have designs on Kenny."

I said, "Hmm."

Sarah continued to cry. I was getting a little tired of the waterworks by that time, but I was irked at Phil because he was so darned naïve, so I tried not to show my impatience. I only patted Sarah's back and muttered comforting sounds.

After watching us for a minute or two, Phil shuffled, shrugged again, and said, "I'd better get back to the chutes. Gotta help put the steers in the pens."

"Very well," I said in a voice that meant a lot more than that, if Phil could read the undertones—which he probably couldn't, being a man and all. What those undertones meant was that, for all her supposedly chaste ways, I thought Miss Esther Strickland was a conniving harpy who stole other girls' male friends for fun, and that sort of behavior didn't seem very godly to me.

Mind you, I had no proof of this bad behavior on Miss Strickland's part. And I had to admit that if she *was* a conniving harpy, she put on a magnificent show of innocence. However, I was hurting internally, and I didn't allow common sense or charity to cloud—or clear—my vision.

It probably didn't matter anyway, since I'm sure Phil didn't understand the full significance of my underlying meaning. He strode off, drooping a little. I guess he was smarting some over losing to Kenny, although I don't think he had anything to feel bad about. He'd done a great job and was better than all the other entrants except Kenny. I guess that salve to the pride only works when you're the one who didn't lose.

Anyhow, what he *should* have been drooping about was his habit of hanging out with Miss Esther—the man-stealer—Strickland and making me, Annabelle Blue—his intended bride, even if he hadn't asked and I hadn't answered—feel bad.

CHAPTER THREE

Eventually Sarah stopped crying, thank heaven, and wandered off to make somebody else miserable. I got back on the fence in time to see the steer wrestlers at work.

The event was pretty exciting, although I'm not sure why anybody would want to do it competitively. I mean, when you're a cowboy, you occasionally have to wrestle a steer to the ground in order to brand it or medicate it or whatever else people need to do to steers. But steers are big and they have horns and, while horns make okay handles if you absolutely have to handle them, they scare me. Maybe my attitude reflects the fact that I grew up in a dry-goods store and not on a ranch, although I don't think so. Why would anyone want to wrestle a steer unless he or she had to?

Right before Kenny Sawyer was supposed to show us how well equipped he was to wrestle his steer, I heard my name spoken yet *again*. I guess when you live in a small community, you pretty much know everybody, but I wasn't at all sure why everyone in town seemed to want to talk to me that particular evening. Not only that, but I wish they'd stop doing so. Even though I don't much like steers, I wanted to see the competition. Nevertheless, I turned with a cheery smile to see who sought my attention this time.

My cheer suffered a slight dent when I saw Hazel Fish standing there beside the fence, grinning up at me. Hazel Fish was the nosiest person I knew and the worst gossip in town. Her grin conveyed titillation, too, which probably meant that she'd seen Phil with Esther and wanted to needle me about losing my man to a conniving revivalist. Only, naturally, she wouldn't come right out and *say* that's what she was doing. She'd coat her barbs in sugar, rather like Esther Strickland had done hers. Only Hazel was much more obvious than Esther Strickland. I don't know which one of the women I detested more at that moment in time.

Just what I needed.

"H'lo, Hazel," I said unenthusiastically.

Hazel didn't wait to be invited, but climbed up to sit next to me on the fence where Phil had been. Naturally, she wore trousers. Any female with a brain in her head was wearing trousers that evening, except Myrtle. And Esther Strickland. But Esther Strickland didn't have to climb any fences since a row of folding chairs had been set up near the platform for the preacher and his entourage. As if they were royalty or something. I did not approve.

"Hey, Annabelle. Is Phil in the steer wrestling?"

"No. He didn't enter this event."

"Where is he, then? He's usually with you, isn't he?"

See what I mean? Hazel Fish was a little cat. "He has to work on the chutes whether he's competing or not, Hazel. It takes a lot of men to get the animals in and out of the pens, you know, and his family is hosting the whole rodeo."

"Of course. I just wondered. You see, I think I just saw him and Miss Strickland together a minute ago. She's so pretty." Hazel sighed meaningfully. "I'm sure all the men want to be around her."

What *I* wanted was to push her off the fence. Instead, I said, "Hmm."

Leaning over, Hazel glanced at my sisters, who were chatting together on the other side of Myrtle. Lowering her voice, she said, "Did you see Mr. MacDougall and that Contreras woman? They looked mighty cozy together. I wonder what's going on *there*."

Even though I'd noticed and wondered the exact same things not an hour earlier, it irked me that Hazel was talking like a gossipy old hen about a member of my family. I could just imagine her brewing up rumors to spread—and she would spread them, too. Hazel had no discretion when it came to perceived scandals. Therefore, since I didn't want my family's name dragged through the mud by this vicious scandalmonger, I turned and frowned at her, deciding not to let her get away with spreading any tittle-tattle this time. "And exactly what do you mean by that, Hazel Fish? Are you implying that there's something—"

Hazel wasn't accustomed to people boldly questioning her gossipy spitefulness. She backed down instantly. "Heavens, no! Why, I never thought anything about it, Annabelle. I mean, they were only . . . talking."

"Exactly."

"I didn't mean anything."

"Like heck you didn't," I snapped, wanting her to perceive that I wasn't going to allow her to get away with any of her darned implications and innuendoes.

"No, really," she said. It sounded as if she were pleading with me. Hazel loved to spread idle rumors, but she'd never admit it.

I stared at her hard for almost a minute. She seemed to wither at my scorn. "It's a darned good thing, Hazel Fish."

Lifting her chin in a feeble effort at defiance, Hazel said, "You're awfully touchy tonight, Annabelle Blue. I wonder why that is."

"I don't like gossips," I snarled. Even I, who am not particularly noted for my tact, don't generally call a spade a spade in so direct a manner. But I was angry, darn it. And

Hazel Fish was a pain in the neck.

"*Well!*"

I sniffed, turned back to watch the show, and Hazel descended from the fence. I guess she'd decided to peddle her malice elsewhere. Good thing, too. If she'd started in on me about Phil and the preacher's sister again with me feeling the way I did then, I really might have shoved her off the fence. Preferably in the path of an unwrestled steer.

Kenny put on quite a performance with his steer, eventually winning that part of the competition, too. I hate to admit it, but I was glad, because it meant that Esther Strickland might continue gushing over him and not return her attention to Phil. Or she might not. I wasn't used to *femmes fatales,* so I wasn't sure what to expect from that quarter, although I was sure that, whatever it was, it would be nothing good.

After the steer wrestling, the competition was over for the evening. The rodeo's competitive events were scheduled to start again on Friday a little after noon, including a demonstration by some of the ranch women, who would compete in something they called "barrel racing." I wasn't sure what that was, because I generally didn't pay much attention when the ladies competed. I think that's because I felt left out, since I could no more race a barrel than I could wrestle a steer.

However, even though the competition was over, there was more fun ahead for us that evening. Every day of the rodeo, after the events ended, we all gathered around a huge campfire and sang songs and ate cookies and toasted marshmallows. I guess that sounds kind of tame, but that's only because you didn't live in Rosedale, New Mexico, in 1923. For us, it was the epitome of entertainment.

So I helped Myrtle down from the fence (she snagged a good pair of cotton stockings, by the way, on a rough board, which points out another argument in favor of girls wearing trousers if they're going to be climbing wooden fences), and we made our way to the campfire circle, along with most everybody else in town. Hannah and Zilpha walked a few feet behind us, still chatting.

As we moseyed along, I espied Josephine Contreras again. This time she was with Kenny Sawyer, who seemed to be paying her a good deal of attention. And *that* meant Phil was probably in the clutches of Esther Strickland. Rats! Looking around, I spotted them, together as I'd feared. Esther was clutching Phil's arm as if she was afraid he'd get away if she let him go. She wasn't looking at Phil, however, but at Josephine and Kenny. Her beautiful face seemed totally blank, as if any expression had been erased. I thought that was kind of strange.

Stranger still was the fact that the determined duo, Charles and Edward, walked up at that moment and said something to Phil and Esther. Esther said something back, and then she walked off with the two men whom I'd begun to think of as her keepers. What was that all about, anyhow? Did Reverend Strickland have a couple of goons specifically assigned to keep his sister out of mischief? Now *that* would be *really* strange. Especially since, although I hated to admit it, Esther seemed quite pleasant. And it didn't look to me as if she were suffering from some malady. I mean, she didn't look as if she was going to faint or anything. Or run away. Or have a tantrum. Since I couldn't figure out Esther and her keepers, I turned back to Josephine and Kenny.

As I observed the pair, Josephine's husband Armando arrived upon the scene. Armando was known all over town as a rather jealous sort, and he didn't appear pleased when he took Josephine's arm and led her away from Kenny. Really, it was more of a yank than a lead. And then Sarah Molina showed up, and Kenny put his arm around her shoulder.

Curious to see what Esther Strickland might make of the

Kenny-and-Sarah team, I glanced at Esther and her two bodyguards, trying not to be obvious. The holy strumpet's expression was easier to read this time. She was annoyed. And it wasn't with her brother, was my guess. Was she angry because Kenny was showing affection to the woman with whom he was supposed to be in love and not to the gorgeous Esther? Hmm.

Well, well, well. What did it all mean? I hadn't a clue, although I was glad that Kenny had finally decided to pay some attention to his purported fiancée.

Would that I could have said the same thing about my own personal special gentleman friend who, the next time I sneaked a peak, seemed to have vanished along with Miss Strickland, Charles and Edward. I imagined her slipping away from Charles and Edward—sort of like in a fairy tale when the oppressed princess finally escapes from her imprisoning tower—and seeking out Phil, the handsome knight whom she hopes will rescue her from her travail. Then I imagined her and Phil in all sorts of compromising situations. I told myself that I was overreacting a trifle. Myself didn't believe it.

And myself turned out to be right, too, although I don't suppose the situation in which I discovered the two of them was exactly compromising. Myrtle and I had just followed the fence around the corner of the pasture and were headed out to where the fire pit had been laid with lots of logs and rocks surrounding it for seats, when I saw Phil. He was taller than most folks, so his head stuck up out of a crowd. And he was with Esther, who evidently had escaped from her keepers. I felt as if somebody had socked me in the solar plexus.

They weren't alone, though. As I watched, while pretending not to, I saw Kenny and Sarah walk up to the two of them. And then Esther said something to Sarah with one of her ingenuous smiles. Sarah looked shocked for a moment. Then Kenny said something to Phil, Phil said something back to him, Sarah looked more shocked, and then Phil and Kenny exchanged a few more heated words, and Sarah turned tail and ran off.

With one parting word—probably a nasty one—for Phil, Kenny turned and went after her.

Hmm, thought I to myself. *Esther Strickland might possibly be as poisonous as Libby. But she's more dangerous, because she's subtle. Also, she only seems to instigate stuff. She doesn't just come out and batter you with mean words like Libby does, but she digs and jibes and pokes and prods, all the while looking and sounding blameless and naïve and absolutely innocent, and she makes other people do her dirty work for her.*

I'd have loved to say this aloud to someone, preferably Myrtle, since she's my best friend, but because it concerned a woman of whom I was frightfully jealous, I didn't dare. I already had people sympathizing with me—or needling me—about losing Phil to the evangelist's sister. If I said anything negative about her, they'd surely think my words were motivated by sour grapes. But I didn't think they were. Maybe a fraction of my opinion was born of sour grapes. Maybe twenty-five percent.

Oh, very well. It was probably more like seventy-five percent. Still, just because I was jealous and hurt didn't mean I was wrong in my opinion, did it? No, it did not.

I did have to admit, only to myself (again), that I was perhaps being too hard on Esther Strickland. After all, I didn't know what she'd just said to Sarah Molina that had sent her—or seemed to send her—running off. And she hadn't actually said anything *bad* about Blue's Dry Goods. She'd called the store *precious* and implied we Blues were old-fashioned bumpkins, but I couldn't pinpoint anything truly negative that she'd said.

Pooh. I was confusing myself.

Deciding not to think any more about Esther Strickland or Phil Gunderson or anything else of a disturbing nature, I found a seat on a log next to Myrtle and prepared to enjoy the rest of the evening.

And I did enjoy myself. The campfire and sing-along were fun. And Phil came and sat beside me for most of it, so maybe all wasn't lost yet. We'd see, I reckon.

There was a slight disruption in the jollity, after about a half hour. As we were singing "She'll Be Coming Around the Mountain," I heard a scuffling sound behind me. When I turned my head, I saw that Kenny Sawyer and Armando Contreras were having some kind of altercation. They were a few yards off, and I couldn't hear what either of them said, but I did see Kenny push Armando pretty hard, making him stumble backwards and almost lose his balance. When Armando regained his balance, he tried to lunge at Kenny, who was ready for him with his fists up, but another man (I think it was one of Armando's brothers) caught Armando by the arm and hauled him off, struggling.

Boy, that Kenny could make more people angry in one evening than anybody else I'd ever met.

Well, except for Esther Strickland.

The next day, Friday, we were going to close the store at noon so that the whole family could enjoy the second day of the rodeo. I had to work in the morning, though, and it seemed to me as if everybody in the entire town of Rosedale visited Blue's. Some folks came to stock up on goods, but most wanted to chatter excitedly about the rodeo. We all loved the rodeo, although I must admit that I'd loved it a lot more in prior years, but my lack of enthusiasm had nothing to do with the competition. At least not the competition going on in the pasture.

"It looks as if that Sawyer feller's gonna take it all again this year," said Mr. John O'Dell, the closest thing Rosedale had to a rich man. He dealt in real estate, primarily farming and ranching land. I'd suspected him of dire dealings a couple of months earlier, but he'd been proved innocent. Or, if not entirely innocent, at least not guilty of the particular crime of which I'd suspected him. Since I'd misjudged him once, however, I made it a point to be extra nice to him every time I saw him.

"He sure did a good job last night," I said, thinking of Phil. Phil had also done a good job, but I didn't dare say so.

What a stupid situation to be in! And what was worse was that I couldn't figure out if it was all in my head or if I really had something to worry about. But there I was, supposedly almost betrothed to Phil Gunderson, and afraid to talk to anyone about him for fear people would look at each other and shake their heads, as if to say "poor Annabelle." And this befuddlement on my part was all because a snake had slithered into Eden. Okay, so Rosedale, New Mexico, wasn't exactly Eden, being more in the nature of an Arabian desert than a lush garden. Still. . . .

"He's an alley cat, though," said Mr. O'Dell, shaking his head. "He don't know how to treat his woman."

"Oh, boy, isn't that the truth? I don't think he's very nice to Sarah, and they're supposed to be engaged. And I guess he and Mr. Contreras had a scuffle, too."

"I seen 'em." Mr. O'Dell put a can of pomade on the counter and started digging in his trouser pockets for money. "Fool thing to do, getting into a fistfight at the rodeo."

"Well, somebody—I think it was one of Mr. Contreras's brothers—separated them before it could come to that."

"I reckon." Mr. O'Dell counted out sixty-three cents and shoved it at me. I took it and shoved the pomade at him. "And that young feller of yours showed himself right proud, too," went on Mr. O'Dell. Neither his tone of voice nor his words implied anything other than what he'd said, and I appreciated him for it. Of course, since he was a man and therefore blind to everything that went on around him unless it directly affected him or created a fistfight, he probably hadn't noticed my "young feller" and Esther Strickland being cozy together.

Nevertheless, I smiled and said, "He did a darned good job." I rang up Mr. O'Dell's sale on our lovely old Nelson cash register. I liked the way it chinked.

"He's getting better every year. I expect he'll be winnin' it all come next May."

"I'm sure we all hope so." After all, Phil was a local boy. Well, Kenny was a local boy, in that he'd been born in Rosedale, but he didn't live here any longer. My comment couldn't be taken as anything but a general wish for success in the community and certainly not in any way a lament for a lost love, no matter who was listening.

See what I mean about Esther Strickland having complicated my life? Darn her!

Mr. O'Dell left, and I went over to a pyramid of Franco-American Spaghetti that looked a little shaky. My obnoxious brother Jack is supposed to see to it that the displays are maintained in good order, but he usually doesn't.

I'd just straightened the display and wondered if I should pep it up with a couple of cans of Campbell's Tomato Soup (I don't know why I remembered this, but the Joseph Campbell Company had acquired the Franco-American Company a few years earlier, and I thought that was interesting enough to be noted in our displays) when Myrtle and Sarah came in. Myrtle must have been on a break from her job at Pruitt's drugstore. I'm not sure what Sarah was doing in town.

Myrtle rushed over to me. "I've decided you're right, Annabelle. I'm going to wear my old blue jeans to the rodeo today. I don't want to go against God, or anything, but I don't want to ruin another pair of stockings, either."

"Good idea. I'm positive that God doesn't care what you wear to the rodeo, Myrtle. Maybe you could get Reverend

Strickland to pray over the pair of stockings that got snagged last night and get God to heal them." I was only joking, but Myrtle didn't like my comment anyway.

"Annabelle, it's just wrong to say things like that!"

With a sigh, I said, "I didn't mean anything by it. I was just teasing."

"You should watch your tongue, though, because other people might take the things you say wrong."

She was right, so I didn't argue. Sarah appeared to be a little blue and droopy that morning. Fearing the answer but figuring it would be friendly to ask, I said, "Hey, Sarah. How are you today? Kenny did swell yesterday. He pretty much won everything."

I didn't know whether to roll my eyes in annoyance or rush to hug her when tears started rolling down her face. "I hate that Esther Strickland," Sarah said, her words shaking with emotion. "She's a hussy and a man-stealer!"

Myrtle gasped. "Oh, Sarah, no!"

Huh. If Myrtle had a gentleman friend to steal, she might not be so shocked by Sarah's words. I'm sure she'd be ever so shocked by Esther Strickland, though. I entirely agreed with Sarah. However, since I didn't want anybody—especially not Myrtle or my family—to know how much Phil's maybe-defection was hurting me, I patted Sarah on the back and spoke soothingly at her. "I'm sure that's not so, Sarah. Miss Strickland is . . . um . . . very friendly." That was one word for it. "She seems quite nice. Sweet, really."

"Friendly? Sweet? *Nice?*" Sarah, trembling with hurt and indignation, fumbled in her handbag for a handkerchief. She wiped her face and blew her nose, then said, "It's not being friendly or nice or *sweet* to try to steal another woman's man."

Boy, wasn't *that* the truth! Nevertheless, I said in a consoling tone, "She won't be here long, Sarah, and then you won't have anything to worry about." Except Kenny, who was, as Mr. O'Dell had pointed out, kind of an alley cat, but she didn't need to hear that assessment of her beloved at the moment. I wondered if Sarah had noticed the altercation between Kenny and Armando Contreras the evening before, but didn't ask. I can be discreet sometimes, when my brain works faster than my mouth. Some people would say that's not very often. Heck, even *I* admit that's not very often. "And she actually does seem quite . . . charming." It almost killed me to say that, but when I mentally looked over my interactions with Miss Strickland, I had to admit it was true. "She can't help being pretty and . . . um . . . appealing." And blonde and tiny and gorgeous and all that other stuff that made me want to choke her.

"Huh," said Sarah, which pretty much summed up my own thinking on the matter of Esther Strickland.

"I'm sure you're wrong about Miss Strickland, Sarah," Myrtle said, taking over for me. This was a good thing, since she meant what she said in favor of Miss Demon Strickland, and I wasn't altogether sure I did. In fact, I knew I didn't. "She's awfully pretty, and she told me the rodeo is all new to her, so naturally she's curious. She told me she's never been to a rodeo before and she finds it all fascinating. Really, Sarah, she's a good Christian woman who helps her brother with his mission. She's only interested in the rodeo, is all."

"She's only interested in the *men*," Sarah said stubbornly. "Including Phil."

For once when I didn't know what to say, I kept my stupid mouth shut.

"Oh, Sarah, no!" Myrtle looked at me. I looked back at her, endeavoring to keep my expression neutral. After all, it had been Myrtle who'd been offering me sympathy yesterday because Phil had showed up with Esther. I wondered how she was going to work her way out of this paradox. If Esther Strickland wasn't a man-stealer, what was she doing with so many other women's men? Answer *that*, Myrtle Howell! She didn't. Instead, she said, "Why, that's not so. Phil sat with Annabelle at the sing-along last night. And didn't Kenny sit with you?"

Still faintly sniffling, Sarah said, "Yes, but he kept looking at *her*."

"Where was she?" I said, genuinely interested since I hadn't bothered to locate her in the crowd around the campfire. I must admit, however, that I'd been pleased to see her drive off with her brother and her keepers before my family and I left to go home. I didn't want to think of her loose on the Gunderson ranch without Charles and Edward or the citizens of Rosedale there to monitor her behavior. Overnight. With Phil around.

"She sat with Reverend Strickland and some of his group," said Myrtle. "Across the fire from where we were sitting."

"Ah." *So,* I wondered, *had Phil been looking at her, too?* I hadn't noticed in particular, but I'd been having fun singing the old camp songs and hadn't paid a whole lot of attention. Maybe I'd better start keeping a better eye on Phil.

No! I'd be darned if I was going to play the fool for a man. Any man. Including Phil Gunderson, the philandering so-and-so!

I didn't mean that.

Or maybe I did.

I was obviously still confused.

And then, as if he'd been waiting until that particular moment to make his entrance, Phil walked into the store. The three of us girls must have stared or jumped or something, because he halted, looked nervous, and said, "Oh. Hey, Annabelle. Hey, Sarah and Myrtle."

"Hey, Phil," we chorused.

After a second or two of silence, Myrtle asked brightly, "Are you going to be in the bronc riding and the bull riding today, Phil?"

He came out of his embarrassment-induced stupor and walked toward us, removing his Stetson as he did so. He's *such* a gentleman. His boots made a clomp-clomp sound on the scarred wooden floor of our store, but so did everybody else's. We live in a cow town, for Pete's sake. Clomping boots go with the territory. "Yeah. Both of those. Mr. Baldwin and Mr. Hanks and Mr. Molina are bringing bulls, so there should be some lively competition."

"I hope you win," said Sarah unexpectedly, since one would anticipate her to root for her boyfriend. Unless you were me. Heck, I'd been hoping Kenny would win yesterday, because I was mad at Phil. So I understood, although Phil clearly didn't.

"Yeah? Well. . . ." He shuffled, looked unsure of himself, and twiddled with the hat in his hands. "Well . . . thanks, Sarah."

She sniffed, but I think that had more to do with her recent bout of tears than any indignation regarding Phil or Kenny.

"Good luck tonight, Phil," said Myrtle, who was a very nice person.

"Thanks, Myrtle." He gave her one of his lovely smiles. He really did have a winning smile. It had melted my own innards a time or two. Today, it was with a stony heart that I watched his teeth flash, thinking how treacherous good looks could be. "Say, Annabelle, do you stock any kind of candy here? You know, like those boxes you see at Christmas time? The ones that are shaped like a heart and have that stuff that looks like a footstool on the boxes?"

Candy? He was asking about candy? I squinted at him. I wanted to ask exactly whom he aimed to give a Whitman's Sampler to, but I didn't want him to perceive how jealous I was. "You mean like Whitman's Samplers?" That was the only kind of boxed candy our store carried.

"Is that the one that comes in the box that looks like a chair cushion?" he asked.

"If you mean is it the one that comes in a box that looks like an old-fashioned needlework sampler, yes, it is."

"Oh. Good. Can I have one of those?"

"Sure. Be right back." I had to go into the back of the store—into the yard at the back of our house, which was behind the store, in actual fact—because we only put out the Whitman's Samplers on special occasions. We generally didn't keep a big supply of them around, since people only bought them at Christmas and Valentine's Day. Sometimes, though, like today, somebody would want to give a Sampler to a person for a special occasion. I swore to myself I wouldn't ask Phil to whom he aimed to give this one. Ma kept the candy, which was chocolate and could melt, in the stone cooler out in our backyard, so I got one and carried it back to the store.

"Here's one. Who's it for?"

Darn! So much for fervent resolutions.

"Esther Strickland. She's feeling a little puny today."

I swear to heaven, he didn't stutter, he didn't stammer, he didn't stumble over the words, he didn't blush, he didn't hesitate. He didn't indicate in any way whatsoever that what he'd just told me was tantamount to a declaration of his independence from yours truly. Inside, I was reeling. Outside, I was as calm and collected as a nun. I'm assuming nuns are calm. I don't know this from actual fact.

That being the case, and because both Myrtle and Sarah had gasped and were now staring at the two of us as if they were watching a murder being committed, I said casually, "Oh? I'm sorry to hear that. What's the matter with her?"

He shrugged. "I don't know."

"Oh. Well, here you go." And I handed him the box. He

handed me some money. I rang up the sale and made change. Phil left.

As soon as the door closed behind him, Myrtle said, *"Annabelle!"* in a tragic whisper.

Sarah said, *"Annabelle!"* in a sympathetic whisper.

I said, "Nuts."

Fortunately for me, I got a break at about eleven o'clock that morning, because I really needed to escape from the store. So many people were coming in, and I kept imagining them all looking at me with the same sympathetic curiosity I'd seen in the eyes of Myrtle and Sarah. I didn't want to be reminded of my blighted love life, and when I asked if I could run to the library before it closed for the weekend, Ma made my bratty brother watch the store for a while in spite of his many and vocal protests.

"For heaven's sake, Jack Blue, stop your whining right this minute and mind the store." Ma spoke more sternly than was usual for her.

Jack said, "Aw . . . shucks." I got the feeling he wanted to say something else, but didn't quite dare. Our mother and father didn't believe in sparing the rod when it came to misbehavior, or bad words, from their offspring.

The library isn't far from Blue's Dry Goods and Mercantile Emporium. Several years before, it had been funded by the Carnegie Foundation, which had provided a whole lot of small towns with libraries, a charity with which I am in full sympathy. For most of us who lived in out-of-the-way places like Rosedale, the only adventures we ever experienced were through books. Well, books and the occasional flicker that came to the Pecos Theater on Main Street a year or so after the rest of the country saw it.

So I hung up my apron, put on my sweater because the

weather was a little blustery, and headed to the library. I'd been on a Mary Roberts Rinehart kick lately. I was taking back *The Man in Lower Ten* and *The Window at the White Cat,* and I aimed to pick up another couple of her books if I could find them. *The Circular Staircase* had been checked out last week, so I was hoping it would be back in circulation that day. Bless Mrs. Rinehart, she was a prolific writer, so if *Staircase* wasn't in, I was sure I could find something else of hers to keep me company. Now that my man had deserted me.

Oh, very well, I was feeling a little low, if you want to know the truth.

When I pushed open the door, I took a deep whiff. I guess I'll always associate that smell with books and libraries: it's a combination of old paper, leather, floor wax, and I don't know what else, but every time I catch a sniff of it, I think of reading, which is probably one of the things I like to do best in the world. And books never disappoint, either, unlike people. Sure, I've picked up a couple of books that I didn't care for, but I never felt betrayed by a book, if you know what I mean.

Since most folks were already headed to the Gundersons' place, the library was deserted except for the librarian, Miss Whitesmith. She was a nice, elderly lady, who fully approved of my reading tastes—unlike my mother, who thought mystery stories were too sensational for her daughter. But I figured that if I stuck to writers like Mary Roberts Rinehart and Agatha Christie, Ma really couldn't complain too much. Both of those authors were ladies, and they were also both considerably better off financially than any Blue I knew about; therefore, when Ma scolded me for reading "trash," I only had to point out those salient facts to shut her up.

I'd turned in my books, smiled at Miss Whitesmith, and was wandering through the "R" stack. I'd just picked up a book when I saw a sight that made my breath catch. Head down, pretending to be engrossed in thumbing through *The Case of Jennie Brice,* I edged toward the table isolated at the end of the stacks, between the R's and S's.

"Do you really think it will work?" whispered Josephine Contreras.

When I lifted my head slightly, I saw her hunched over, almost nose to nose with my brother-in-law Richard MacDougall. Armando Contreras's wife. With Hannah's husband. My heart sank into my sensible shoes. Darn it, I didn't want to see those two together!

"I'm sure it will. Monday night. Don't let me down," said Richard, his voice soft. "What about Armando?"

"You let me worry about Armando. I'll take care of him."

"And I'll take care of Hannah."

Good heavens! What were these two fiends plotting? It was bad enough to think they were having an illicit affair without worrying that they were out to do something dreadful to their respective spouses.

I reminded myself that I had a sometimes-too-vivid imagination, and that Josephine and Richard were probably only planning . . . something else. Something benign. Or even something festive. A party, perhaps, for Hannah's birthday, which was coming up soon.

Surely Richard would have invited Hannah's family to any party he was contemplating. And why would he be planning a party for Hannah with Josephine Contreras? Why not with one of Hannah's sisters? I hadn't figured out that last question before my attention was caught by something else.

Was that Sarah Molina who'd just risen from the table in the corner? Squinting down the stacks at the swinging doors, I saw a figure leave the library. I was pretty sure it was Sarah, and I contemplated following her and saying howdy. Then I decided not to. I'd already seen Sarah plenty that day, and I didn't feel like being cried at anymore until I couldn't avoid it any longer.

Besides, what did I care about her unhappy affair with Kenny Sawyer when it looked as if there was another affair going on that hit much closer to my own personal home?

That being the case, and because I really wanted Richard to think better of what he was doing—provided he was doing something despicable—I decided that Richard and Josephine weren't going to get away with their devious plans scot-free. I was going to make my presence known. Perhaps if he realized that a member of his wife's family knew what was going on, Richard would be jolted back to his senses, dump Josephine and head back home to his lovely wife Hannah. Heck, stranger things have happened. At least I think they have.

So I walked right up to the couple, hugging *Jennie Brice* to my bosom. In a perky whisper, I said, "Richard! Josephine! What are you guys doing here?"

My ploy partially worked. Both of them started as if I'd stuck them with pins. Richard leaped to his feet. If the chairs in the library weren't so heavy, his would probably have toppled over backwards. As it was, it was Richard who had to fight for his balance and not his chair. "Annabelle! You scared the dickens out of us!"

He's spoken kind of loudly, and the three of us heard a "Shh!" from the front of the library. As I mentioned, I liked Miss White-smith, but see was kind of a stickler about library etiquette. There really wasn't any reason for her to shush Richard, since we were the only people in the library at the time. However, I digress.

"Mercy sakes, Annabelle, I didn't think there was anybody else in here," said Josephine, pressing a hand to her heart.

Yeah. I'd already figured that out. I only smiled. "I wanted to stock up on books because I've read all the ones I picked up last week."

Richard sat again with a grunt. "Shoot, I don't know when you're planning to read that." He gestured at the book I held. "The entire weekend is going to be given over to the rodeo."

"Maybe, but I don't like to be without something to read." And he hadn't answered my question about what he and Josephine were doing there, so snuggly close and all, talking about taking care of Josephine's husband and Richard's wife.

He stood again, this time pushing his chair back first. "Well, you two, I have to get back to the bank. See you this afternoon at the Gundersons'?"

"We'll be there," said Josephine brightly. She, too, stood.

"You know we'll be there," I told him. My voice was kind of cold.

"Well, then. . . ." He stood there looking nervous for a couple of seconds, then said, "Well, then, I'll see you both later." And he walked toward the library door.

Josephine tugged her skirt into alignment. "I guess I'd better be going, too. Armando's probably in a dither to get to the Gundersons'."

"Ah."

She frowned slightly. "I hope to heaven he doesn't have another fight with Kenny Sawyer. What's the matter with him, anyhow?"

I didn't know whether she referred to her husband or Kenny, so I said, "I don't know," because the answer applied equally to both men.

"I don't, either. Men! See you, Annabelle." And with a jaunty wave, Josephine, too, left.

So I ambled back to the "R" stack, my mind troubled, and grabbed a couple more Rinehart books. Then I hit the "C" stack, picked out *The Murder on the Links,* which was a brand-new book by Agatha Christie that I was the first person to check out—it pays to go to the library when everybody else is at a party—and moseyed back to the front desk. I had to pass the table where I thought I'd seen Sarah, and I glanced at the book she'd left on it—if it actually had been Sarah. *The Book of Poisons* sat there, squat and fat and out of place, and opened to a page titled "Arsenic and Its Uses."

Merciful heavens, what had the girl been reading about poisons for? I considered whether I ought to warn Kenny to watch what he ate for the next couple of days.

At the time, I thought I was being funny.

CHAPTER FOUR

If you think that I felt pretty lousy for the rest of the morning, what with Phil having jilted me for Esther Strickland, Sarah Molina trying to figure out a way to poison Kenny Sawyer (or perhaps Esther Strickland), and my sister's husband showing every indication of carrying on a secret affair with Josephine Contreras, you're absolutely right.

In fact, the last notion was almost as appalling as the first two. Maybe it was more appalling, actually. I mean, Phil and I weren't married or anything. We weren't even officially engaged, as were Sarah and Kenny. Just because everybody in town, including me, assumed Phil was sweet on me, he hadn't really *said* anything about it. At least not to me. Therefore, no matter how crummy I felt, there was no way I could say Phil had treated me badly. Well, I *could*, but I'd be stretching the truth.

Actually, I'd been the one who didn't want things to get hot and heavy between us, because of my desire to have adventures before I got married and became mired in the matrimonial and maternal muck for all eternity. That's what it looked like from my perspective anyway. Maybe my perspective had been skewed by reading too many novels. They used to claim novels weakened women's brains. I think that's bunkum, but perhaps it isn't. Perhaps I was the end result of a novel-weakened brain.

No. That's just nuts. Probably men made up that claim in order to keep women from gaining the equality they deserved. Not only that, but . . . oh, never mind. I sometimes get carried away when I think about how women are oppressed by their male counterparts.

Getting back to the issues at hand, I wondered if I should tell Ma my worries about Richard and Josephine. It would make me feel better to share my suspicions, even though I'm sure sharing them would make Ma miserable. But then I decided I'd better keep the matter to myself. After all, I might be wrong.

Fat chance, men being the fickle fiends they were.

Still, you never knew.

I didn't let on that I was down in the dumps, however. I went back to the store and took over clerking duties from my idiot brother, who didn't even thank me, which was typical. I *could* have left him there for the rest of the morning, after all, but I didn't, good sister that I am. He doesn't deserve me. Neither does Phil. That notion made me feel better for approximately ten seconds, and then gloom descended upon me again.

Nevertheless, I was as cheerful as cheerful could be, talking to friends and customers. Anybody watching me would have had no idea that my heart had been broken in twain and then stomped flat. And I wouldn't listen to any fussing by Myrtle or Sarah, who came back to the store around noonish. If Sarah wanted to parade her wounds around town for everyone to see, that was her lookout. That sort of overt wallowing wasn't for me.

It crossed my mind to ask Sarah why she'd been reading about poisons in the library. I mean, it seemed unlikely that she was *really* planning on poisoning Kenny or Esther. At least I think it was. But I didn't really feel like having a conversation with her. Or with anybody else, for that matter.

I mainly just wanted to be left alone. Since there was no way of that ever happening, the second-best option—and the only one available to me—was to pretend that everything in my life was fine and dandy. I guess it was a matter of pride and self-respect. Maybe dignity. I just *hated* the notion of people gossiping about how Phil had forsaken me for another woman, and I'd be darned if I'd let anyone see my inner hurt.

Anyhow, as I said before, it wasn't that I was madly in love with Phil or anything. Sure, I liked him better than most people. And it was also true that I'd always sort of figured I'd marry him someday. But I can't honestly say that we shared a deathless passion like Romeo and Juliet—who were a couple of ridiculous adolescents, if you ask me. Not that anybody ever did. Still and all, it was really humiliating to think that a guy who'd shown every indication of being sweet on me for years and who had made his attentions plain, had taken one look at a bit of goods like Esther Strickland and abandoned me without a backward glance. That's what it felt like, at any rate.

Since I'd rather be burned at the stake than admit how hurt I was, I kept up my jaunty demeanor when I drove the family Model T out to the Gundersons' ranch. We had the backseat packed solid, what with Jack and Pa crammed in there along with the pot of beans and the applesauce and two pans of chocolate brownies (made with pecans, and very yummy) Ma had made to bring to the barbecue. And really, except for the aforementioned broken heart, I was eagerly anticipating the events of the day to come. The rodeo was about the most exciting thing that ever happened in Rosedale, barring natural disasters like windstorms, floods, and the occasional tornado, and at least the rodeo was fun.

As soon as I pulled the Ford to a stop underneath a big old elm tree, and before the family even got out of it, I saw Phil and Esther together. Oh, boy, what a thrill. I also noticed that Miss Esther Strickland didn't look the least little bit under the weather to me. So what was all that nonsense Phil had flung at me about the box of candy? Hmm. This looked very unpromising, and I wondered why God was punishing me. Was I *that* bad a person?

I put a stop to that line of thinking instantly. If God didn't care if women wore trousers to rodeos, I'm sure He had better things to do than taunt me with glimpses of my lost . . . well, whatever Phil was. I was going to say "lost love," but I'd already decided that's not what Phil was to me. Still, I'd sure be glad to see the dust from Milo and Esther Strickland's caravan as they headed out of town forever, and no mistake. Where the heck were Charles and Edward when I needed them?

"Ooh, ooh, Annabelle, looks like you lost your beau," Jack said in that high-pitched, taunting voice he used when being horrid, which meant most of the time. Perhaps, like the devil, God used earthly beings to carry out His plans.

But, no. While I could feature Jack being in league with the devil, I couldn't feature a benevolent God having anything at all to do with the little monster.

"Shut up, Jack," I muttered, peeved.

"That's enough, you two," said my mother mildly, again including both of her children in her admonition, even though only one of them (Jack) was being beastly. I got really tired of her evenhandedness sometimes.

I rolled my eyes and wondered why life wasn't fair. Which was a stupid thing to wonder, I guess. Life was just life. Always had been. Always would be. Life had nothing against me, in particular. It got everyone pretty much equally. "I'll take a pan of brownies," I said, changing the subject and hoping it would stay changed.

"I'll carry one, as well," said Ma. She looked sternly at Jack. "Before you run off and play, young man, you take that pot of beans to the tables, and mind you be careful with it. None of your horsing around yet." At least she acknowledged that Jack was a lazy, sloppy, clumsy good-for-nothing. Sort of.

"I'll get the applesauce," said Pa, and did.

Then, armed with our foodstuffs, the Blue family walked over to the tables where several of the women from town, along with Mrs. Gunderson, were already setting up for the big barbecue that was going to be held after the first two events of the day. A barbecue pit had been dug days earlier, a steer lowered into it, and the aroma from the beef and mutton being smoked made my mouth water—and I'd just eaten lunch! There's just nothing in the world like a barbeque, though. I wished we could barbeque a steer in our backyard from time to time. Heck, the whole town could partake of it. I'm generous. I doubt that Ma would appreciate having her vegetable garden dug up for the event, however, and that's about the only place we could have dug a pit. That's probably why they hold these things on ranches.

Davy Gunderson ran up to us as soon as he spotted Jack. He was a cute kid, with light-brown hair and freckles splashed across his nose and cheeks. I remembered Phil looking like that a few years earlier and heaved a sigh.

Some people thought Jack was a cute kid, too, but I didn't, undoubtedly because I couldn't see past his obnoxious personality. He probably was good-looking, though, because everyone else in the family was—including me, darn it. I might not have blonde hair and heavenly blue eyes, and I know I wasn't as delicate as a blasted fairy princess, but I was sure no hound dog.

"Jack! Come on and play baseball with us! Did you remember your bat?"

"Yeah, I remembered it. I'll be there in a minute, Davy. Gotta get them beans on the table." He nodded at the pot he carried.

"These," said I, unable to help myself. "Not them."

Jack stuck his tongue out at me. Figures.

Myrtle was already at the picnic tables, wearing her sensible trousers and adjusting the pies she and her mother had baked. I joined her at the desserts table, glad to leave my horrible brother. "Hey, Myrtle."

"Hey, Annabelle." She spied the pan I carried. "Oh, those look delicious!"

"They are. Ma's specialty. Or," I amended, "one of her specialties." My mother was a good cook. "I love them. Chocolate brownies. She puts pecans in them."

Looking around to see if anyone was watching, Myrtle murmured, "I wonder if anybody would notice if I took one."

"Oh, pooh, why worry about it? Here." I dug out a brownie and handed it over. "I've already eaten two of them. If I eat any more, I'm afraid I'll be sick before the rodeo begins."

Myrtle chuckled and took the brownie. "Let's go find a place on the fence."

"Good idea."

So, with Myrtle munching and me trying to look eager and not miserable, we began to make our way to the pasture. We hadn't got far when Phil and Esther strolled into my line of vision again. Oh, goody. "Are you going to help serve up the barbecue?" I asked Myrtle in an effort to pretend the sight of Phil with another woman wasn't excruciating.

"Sure. Might as well."

I think she was going to say something more, but at that moment Jack and Davy showed up, grinning like fiends. Which they were. I guess Jack had gone back to the car to get his baseball bat, because he was swinging it as if he were Babe Ruth. Huh.

"Annabelle's boyfriend's got a new girlfriend!" Jack taunted.

"*Poor* Annabelle!" said Davy.

At that moment, I wished all little boys to Hades.

"Annabelle's lost her beau!" screeched Jack.

I'd had it. "Jack Blue, shut your mouth!" And I swatted him

a good one with the back of my hand. He tried to avoid it, but I connected with the side of his head and sent him staggering. It hurt. That is to say, it hurt me. I hope it hurt Jack, too, but he took off running and didn't say so. He was the type of beast who'd withhold that sort of information in order to provide the maximum amount of torture to his victim.

"Stupid brother," I growled, rubbing the back of my hand and glowering after Jack and Davy, who were headed straight for Phil and Esther. The despicable brutes!

"Woo, hoo, Phil! Looks like you have a new girlfriend!" Davy shouted, sticking his tongue out at his big brother.

"Annabelle's *so* sad!" hollered Jack, looking over his shoulder at me and sticking out *his* tongue. Fiend. The boy was a fiend.

I could tell that Phil was mightily irritated. He frowned at his brother and mine, and said, "Get lost, and quit being stupid!"

The two junior demons laughed uproariously and took off running toward a field where, I supposed, they aimed to play baseball in spite of the rodeo going on, since Jack was still swinging his bat. Now why would a couple of red-blooded American boys play baseball when they could watch a rodeo? Heck, they could play baseball any day of the week. An answer eluded me, but I wished I could have used the bat on both of them.

"I hate my brother sometimes." I actually hated him most of the time, but didn't think it would be prudent to say so, Myrtle being a little on the zealously religious side lately.

Myrtle swallowed the last bite of her brownie. "I don't blame you. I'm glad I don't have one."

I heaved a huge sigh. "You don't know how lucky you are, Myrtle."

By that time we were at the fence, so we climbed up, Myrtle having a much easier time of it today than she'd had the prior evening, since she was clad in a pair of old blue jeans and a plaid shirt. Similarly attired, I hopped up, too. We found the same places we'd had before, with that convenient cottonwood tree to use as a backrest.

To open the rodeo that day, Esther Strickland sang *God Bless America,* which was kind of nice. I believe I've already mentioned that she had a beautiful voice to go along with her beautiful looks. Some people get everything. After the song, Reverend Milo Strickland gave us another prayer, this one not quite as long as his prior one. Then Mr. Gunderson announced the first event of the day, which was bronc riding.

Before the first bronco left the chute, Hazel Fish, not, as I believe I've already mentioned, my favorite person, joined us.

"Hey, Hazel," said I, resigned to hearing the latest slander whether I wanted to or not.

"Hey, Annabelle. Did you bring anything for the barbecue?"

Everyone brought something to the barbecue. To do otherwise would be to let down the entire town. I didn't say so. What I said was, "Brownies, beans, and applesauce."

"We brought a big mess of acorn squash."

"Sounds good to me. I like squash." I pretended to be fascinated by the ongoing preparations for the rodeo, in hope that my lack of interest in her would keep Hazel from slinging dirt. I should have known better.

"Did you hear that Kenny Sawyer and one of the cowboys from the Ruidoso Ranch got into a fistfight this morning?" I could hear the glee in her voice.

"No, I hadn't heard about it. We just got here," I pointed out. Shoot, Kenny was really outdoing himself. Last night it was Armando Contreras, and this morning it was a cowboy from another ranch.

"Well, they did. I don't know why, but I guess Mr. Gunderson had to separate them. Kenny gave the other guy a bloody nose, and I think he got a big bruise on his cheek."

"That's a shame." Not that I much cared, except that I

deplored fighting. Men. They were so silly. When they weren't being treacherous.

"It was because of a girl, too. Kenny was flirting with the other cowboy's girl. He does that all the time. I don't know how Sarah stands it."

I didn't either, and I also thought I detected a sly note to Hazel's voice, indicating she didn't know how I stood Phil's straying. Hazel was such a busybody. I didn't say so. "Hmm," was what I said, in an effort to discourage her. Again, I should have known better.

"Kenny's not the only one, though," she said in crafty tones.

"Hmm." If she was going to start in about Phil, I aimed to push her off the fence. I could later say it was an accident.

"And it's not always men who do it, either."

"It, what?" Myrtle said. Maybe I'd push her off the fence, too.

"Stray from the straight and narrow," Hazel said. "It's not only men who do it. I've seen some things today that you wouldn't believe."

Oh, brother. I remained silent and pretended to be looking for someone in the crowd.

"I know you don't want to think about it, Annabelle," Hazel said in her low, confidential voice—the voice that always presaged messages of a scurrilous nature. "But I just saw your brother-in-law and Josephine Contreras together again, and they were looking might friendly with each other."

Drat. I didn't want to think about Richard and Josephine having some sort of illicit alliance. And if they *were* having one, I sure as heck didn't want to know about it—and I didn't want Hannah to know about it, either. And I definitely didn't want Hazel Fish to start a rumor. Rumors spread like wildfire in a small town like Rosedale.

"And that was after I saw Kenny and Josephine together,"

Hazel said. "I don't know what Kenny's up to. I saw him with Miss Strickland, too."

"That Kenny," I said. "He does get around, doesn't he?"

"I'll say he does." Hazel nudged me. "But what about Josephine and your brother-in-law, Annabelle. What do you think is going on there? I sure hope they aren't . . . well, you know."

I certainly did know. And I also knew that Hazel had just lied to me. She'd absolutely *love* it if she found out Richard and Josephine were cheating on their respective spouses. Even if she didn't find out anything that firmly pointed to the two having an affair, she might start gossip about an assumed affair, which would be embarrassing for the entire family and ruinous to various reputations.

That being the case, and because I couldn't think of any other way to shut Hazel up, I lied like a rug. "I'm sure Josephine and Richard were just talking about the birthday party we're having for Hannah the day after tomorrow. She probably wants to know what to bring." Hannah's birthday really *was* the day after tomorrow, so that fib was the first thing that popped into my mind on the spur of the moment—but, because of the rodeo, we *weren't* having a party or anything. I hoped God wouldn't fling Phil and Esther in my line of vision as my punishment for lying. "So if you think you're going to spread a lot of gossip about them, you'd better think again."

Hazel said, "Oh. I didn't realize that." She sounded disappointed. I wished she'd take up reading as a hobby and give gossip the go-by, but I doubted that would happen anytime soon.

I was right. "I saw Miss Strickland and Phil a few minutes ago," she said next, having given up Josephine and Richard as meager pickings, I guess.

"Huh."

"She sure is pretty. And she's real nice, too. A fine Christian woman. I've gone to all the revival meetings. They're very uplifting. You should go to one, Annabelle."

"Yeah. Maybe I will."

After a moment of silence—relatively speaking (there was quite a bit of noise surrounding us)—Hazel said, "I must say you're taking it really well, Annabelle."

I eyed her with disfavor. "Taking what well, Hazel?"

With wide-eyed innocence on her face and evil in her heart, she said, "Why, the way Phil's fallen in love with Esther Strickland, of course! I wonder if he'll follow her when she and her brother leave Rosedale to preach in another town."

Boy, there's something I'd never thought about before. The notion appalled me. "I'm sure I wouldn't know."

Myrtle, who'd heard everything and probably thought she was rescuing me—which she was—said, "Oh, look, the first rider's in the chute. Look, Annabelle, the horse looks like it's trying to squash his leg." She grimaced horribly.

Silently blessing Myrtle, I squinted at the action. It wasn't often you actually *got* action before the horse left the chute, but Myrtle was right about that horse. He evidently didn't want to be there one little bit and was showing his disfavor the only way he knew how. I grimaced along with Myrtle, and hoped the cowboy's leg wouldn't be broken. "Ow. I hope he's not hurt. Who is that, do you know?"

"I think it's Dan Ingram." The horse slammed Dan's leg against the chute again. "Oh, dear, did you see that?"

"I sure did. They'd better open the chute quick. Poor Dan." Horses are ever so much bigger and heavier than human beings. Even if the horse didn't succeed in crushing Dan's leg like an egg, it could sure make it a mess of bruises, bumping it against the side of the chute the way it was doing.

The attendants opened the chute at last, and that horse shot out of it like a bullet from a gun, stopped dead, jumped straight

75

up into the air, came down almost to its knees, leaped in the air again, and poor Dan went flying.

I said, "Ow."

Myrtle said, "Ew," and clapped her hands to her cheeks.

Hazel clutched my arm. "Is he all right?"

Seizing the opportunity, I said, "I hope so. Why don't you go look, Hazel? You can find out what happened and come back and tell us if Dan's okay."

"Good idea," said she, and jumped down from the fence and went scurrying off to get the scoop from the horse's mouth—so to speak.

Myrtle nudged me. "That was brilliant, Annabelle."

"Thanks." I thought so, too.

"Oh, my!" Myrtle's voice sounded strangely excited—and a little bit worried.

"What's the matter?"

"I don't know, but it looks as if Phil and Kenny are having words."

My heart hurting, I glanced at the chutes and saw that Myrtle was correct. "Oh, dear. I hope they don't get carried away." I knew they didn't like each other much, and I also knew that Kenny was a blowhard and a braggart, two behaviors that were totally foreign to Phil's nature and that probably annoyed him a lot. It didn't surprise me one iota to see Esther Strickland standing with the two men, holding her folded hands to her bosom and gazing upon them seraphically. I figured she'd probably egged them on somehow.

Oh, don't listen to me. I'm only being catty. However, I anticipated hearing a full report on the dispute from Hazel when she returned to us. Now I almost regretted sending her to the chutes. Oh, well. As I watched, Phil turned around and stomped away from Kenny, who glowered after him. Esther stood there, her beatific smile still in place, looking like an angel in a Renaissance painting. I've seen pictures in books, so I know what Renaissance angels look like.

The woman was strange. I don't care what anybody says.

Arguments aside, the competition continued. Phil and Kenny Sawyer were the two best riders in the bronc-riding event that day, only this time Phil took top honors. Although I was finding it difficult not to root for Kenny under the circumstances, I was still happy for Phil.

As the rodeo continued (bull riding was up next), Hazel rejoined us on the fence. I can't say that I was pleased to see her. In actual fact, I was sorry she hadn't attached herself to somebody else. "Dan's okay. His leg is bruised from where the horse bashed him against the chute, but he didn't get hurt when he got bucked off."

Now I ask you: how can a full-grown man get his leg smashed against a wooden chute several times, ride a horse that's acting like a demented cyclone, be hurled therefrom, land hard in the dirt on his back, and not be hurt? By my reckoning, such a thing is impossible. However, I knew as well as Hazel that cowboys who performed in rodeo events would sooner die than admit to being injured. One more example of the foolishness of men, I guess. What I said was, "Glad to hear it."

"And did you see Phil and Kenny fighting?" Hazel asked with unalloyed glee. "I think it had something to do with Miss Strickland. Sarah Molina was there, too, and she was crying."

I hadn't seen Sarah with the others, but it didn't surprise me any to hear that she'd been crying, since she cried a lot. I probably would, too, if I depended on Kenny for anything as important as my emotional security. I was having a hard enough time trying not to cry over Phil, although I didn't want Hazel or anyone else to know that.

However, that was another matter, and we were sitting on that fence in order to see cowboys ride bulls. I said, "Hmm," and eyed the chutes. Bull riding was another event that was exciting to watch, but sort of pointless. On your average ranch, people don't ride bulls very often, and if they do, it's generally by accident.

Those things—bulls, I mean—are wily and unpredictable, and they can weigh a couple of thousand pounds. They can be mean, too, and try to stomp or gore you once they've bucked you off their backs. Mind you, I wouldn't take it kindly if somebody locked me in a chute, dropped a body on top of me, kicked me in the ribs, and then rode me out into a pasture in front of a bunch of screaming people, either, but that's part of a bull's lot in life. The rest of the time he spends romancing the ladies—if he didn't still have his romancing equipment, he'd be a steer—so I guess it all evens out. Nevertheless, you couldn't get me to go near one of the things—bulls, I mean—much less try to ride it.

Both Kenny and Phil stayed on their bulls for the entire however-many-seconds they were supposed to stay on, but Phil's bull was meaner and less predictable than Kenny's, so Phil won that competition, too. I noticed that Kenny didn't appear to be very happy about it, and that he and Phil exchanged another few words that didn't seem awfully friendly. Then, as Esther Strickland clung to Kenny's arm (and Sarah presumably went off somewhere and cried), Phil walked away from them. I could tell by the set of his shoulders that he was peeved, and I decided to go talk to him. Maybe if he comprehended that I was proud of him and cared about him, he'd realize he'd wronged me and would return to my side.

Or something. I guess it boiled down to me not wanting to give him up without a fight, although the notion that I *had* to fight for him was really galling.

I found him looking grumpy, wandering among the tables that were laden with food. Every now and then he'd pick up and nibble something. He didn't see me, so I said, "Hey, Phil."

He looked up and frowned at me. Now, I ask you, was that any way to treat the woman to whom you'd been devoted for several years? I think not. But I pretended I didn't notice the frown. "Great job with the horses and bulls, Phil. You looked really good out there."

"Hmm. Thanks."

Gee, if he were any more happy and grateful to me for voicing my praise, he might just fall asleep. I was not amused. "Well, I just wanted to tell you I thought you did a great job."

"Hmm."

Hmm. Okay, then. I felt like telling him to take his horse and his bull and go to Hades, but I was trying my very best to pretend that nothing Phil did could affect me in any way at all, so I just said brightly, "See ya!" and turned around and headed back toward the fence. If my chest ached and my eyes burned and I wanted to scream and shout and throw things and then go to bed and cry for a year or two, I wouldn't let on.

Because I felt so rotten, I decided to take a little walk around the place before heading back to my friends and being forced to make a peppy conversation with Myrtle—or, God forbid, Hazel. I made off in an easterly direction, away from where the rodeo was going on.

In a field some yards off, I could see my brother and Davy Gunderson and a couple of the Wilson boys playing ball. I still wondered why a person with a single grain of sense would play baseball when there was a rodeo going on. On the other hand, these were boys, and boys have never been noted for their common sense. In fact, I'll never understand boys as long as I live. And then they grew up to be men, and everyone knows there's no understanding men.

I veered right, away from the baseball game, hoping Jack wouldn't see me and resume his taunts. As I neared a stand of shinnery oaks, I heard voices. Angry voices. Well, shoot. I didn't want to have anything to do with an argument; I already felt bad enough.

I took a quick turn to my left, but I wasn't quick enough to avoid seeing Kenny Sawyer stomp out of the oaks, his face red and his eyes blazing. Behind him stomped Armando Contreras, his hand clamped on Josephine's arm, hauling on her as if he was furious with her and Kenny both.

"But I swear, Mando, we weren't doing anything!" Josephine cried.

It looked to me as if Armando had her arm in a really painful grip, but I wasn't about to interfere.

"You know how people around here talk, damn it!" Armando said. "And that Kenny Sawyer is a damned snake! If anybody else had seen you, you'd never live it down, and neither would I!"

Kenny whirled around. "Who you callin' names?"

"*You,* you damned snake!"

"Why, you son of a. . . ." Kenny started back toward Armando.

I stood there, scared, wishing I could think of something to do that might defuse the situation. I didn't think fast enough to do anything useful.

In the end it was Josephine who saved the day—or maybe she only saved her husband from having his nose busted. She yanked hard on Armando's arm, he stumbled slightly, and she jumped in front of him, facing Kenny. "Just go back to the rodeo, Kenny. Please. Armando didn't mean it."

"The hell I—"

"I tell you," she cried, drowning out Armando's voice, "he doesn't understand what was going on! Just go back, Kenny. Please!"

Deciding that, while I might be generally useless, I might be able to help a tiny bit in this case, I hurried into the fray. "Kenny! Hey, Kenny, I'll go back with you."

None of them had realized they had an audience, I guess, because they all three jerked and turned toward me. Josephine whispered, "Oh, Annabelle, thank you."

Kenny said, "Well. . . ."

Armando tried to tug himself out of his wife's grip, but Josephine hung on tight, digging in her heels and making furrows in the earth.

"Come on, Kenny. There's nothing to be gained by making a fuss. This is supposed to be a party, after all. You don't want to spoil it."

"I don't let anybody call me names," Kenny said stubbornly.

Then you ought to stop flirting with other men's wives, was what I wanted to say, but I managed to restrain myself. God alone knows how. "I understand," I said instead, "but Armando's famous for his hot temper. He never means what he says when he's mad." I sent Armando a happy smile to let him know I was only teasing, but I was really glad Josephine was holding on to him when I saw the look on his face.

Being more audacious than was generally the case, I stepped boldly forward and took Kenny by the arm. Since he was a cowboy, and cowboys prided themselves on their chivalry— when other people were watching them, anyhow—he pretty much had to do as I'd suggested and walk back to the rodeo with me. My heart was hammering like a kettledrum the whole way.

"You did a great job on the bulls, Kenny," I said, trying to make polite conversation.

My attempt came to naught. "I lost."

"Well, maybe, but you still did a good job. You came in second. That's not bad at all."

"Huh."

Okay, so much for playing on his ego.

My luck was holding true to form. As we passed the barbecue tables, Phil glanced over. He'd been kind of stooping gloomily over the array of desserts, but when Kenny and I strolled into view, he straightened as if somebody'd goosed him. Wonderful. Now Phil would probably think I was two-timing him with Kenny, when all I'd done was try to stop a fight before it got started.

Then again, I thought, maybe seeing Kenny and me together had made Phil's heart lurch a little bit. That might not be such a bad thing. My own personal heart had been flipping around like an acrobat at the circus in recent days, thanks to Phil's infatuation with Esther Strickland.

What a stupid world.

But at least Kenny and Armando hadn't come to blows. I wondered what Kenny and Josephine had been doing amongst the oaks. Maybe Josephine's parents ought to have named her Jezebel. First it had been Richard, and now it was Kenny. I'd always believed Josephine and Armando to be a happy couple, but maybe I was wrong. God knows, I seemed to have been wrong a lot lately. Anyway, when we got near the chutes, I said, "I'm going to go join my friends now, Kenny."

"All right." He looked sulky. Sounded sulky, too.

Because I thought he needed at least a small scolding, I said, "Try to stay out of trouble, okay? And that means not messing with the wives of other men."

He shot me a hideous glower that looked out of place on his handsome face. He snapped, "You don't know anything about it!" and stomped off.

I sighed, internally acknowledged that I didn't know anything about a whole bunch of stuff, and turned to walk the other way.

When I got back to the fence, Hazel and Myrtle were talking. Actually, Hazel was doing all the talking. Myrtle was looking rather as if she'd like to throw Hazel in front of a rampaging bull, an emotion I understood quite well.

Glancing around with what appeared like something akin to panic, Myrtle saw me and said brightly, "Oh, Hazel, I'm so sorry, but Annabelle and I have to help with the barbecue preparations." And she shinnied down that fence faster than you could spit (that's a cowboy expression. It seemed to fit here, given the rodeo and all. If I ever said it out loud at home, my mother would skin me).

Looking back over her shoulder as we walked off, Myrtle said, "I didn't think that girl would ever shut up. Annabelle, I swear, she *lives* for gossip, and the nastier it is, the better she likes it."

"I know. It might get her in trouble someday, too."

"How?"

Excellent question, and one to which I didn't have a ready answer. That being the case, I said, "I don't know, but I'll bet somebody will really get mad at her one of these days, and then she'll be sorry."

Myrtle looked doubtful—and for good reason, I suppose, since I hadn't noticed a whole lot of divine retribution going on around me recently. "I'm glad you told her we were going to help out at the barbecue. I don't want to watch the stupid rodeo anymore."

"How come?"

"Oh, I don't know. I guess Hazel was getting to me. And Kenny and Armando just about got into a fight a few minutes ago."

Myrtle brightened up a bit. "Did they really?"

"Yes. Kenny was with Josephine. I swear, I don't know what's the matter with people."

"I don't, either, Annabelle. I never thought Josephine would two-time Armando."

"Me, neither. I sure wouldn't if I were married to him. He's got a mean temper."

"He sure does. I don't think he'd hit Josephine, though. Do you?"

I thought about it for a second. "I doubt it, but he might try to fight some man and get himself killed for his effort."

Myrtle shuddered.

"It's not just her, either," I said. "Kenny's been cozying up to all sorts of females lately."

Myrtle sighed.

I grumped along in silence for a minute, then burst out, "And there's Esther Strickland, too."

"Esther?" Myrtle sounded awfully darned surprised, which she shouldn't have been if she'd been paying attention.

"Darn it, Myrtle, that Miss Esther Strickland is a cat! Did you see her hanging all over Kenny?" I didn't mention Phil, although she'd been hanging all over him, too. "Poor Sarah." And poor me.

Myrtle put on her self-righteous expression. "She wasn't *hanging* all over anybody, Annabelle. She's only interested in what cowboys do in the rodeo, and she's friendly. She's really a lovely person. She's totally devoted to her brother." Almost as an afterthought, she added piously, "And the Lord."

"Hmm," I murmured, wishing I'd not said anything at all about the Strickland witch.

"You'd find that out for yourself if you'd come to one of the meetings with me."

"I don't want to go to one of their stupid meetings."

"They're not stupid. That's your sinful heart talking, Annabelle Blue, and you know it."

Phooey.

But, I reminded myself, as somebody—probably God—once

said, *this, too, will pass.* It couldn't pass soon enough to suit me.

Myrtle and I had a good time dishing out food at the barbecue, though. I manned the beans and helped serve up big slabs of barbecued beef, and serving duty turned out to be fun. When Josephine Contreras held out her plate for me to plop some beans onto, I wanted very much to ask her why she'd been so cozy with my brother-in-law that day and the day before, and then with Kenny, but I didn't. Which proves yet again that every now and then I can hold my tongue. Anyhow, she was with her husband, who seemed to have calmed down, and I took that as a good omen.

"Looks good enough to eat," said Armando, grinning at me, from which I presumed that all was forgiven.

Just before she moved along to the salads, Josephine leaned over and murmured, "Thanks again, Annabelle. I was afraid they were going to fight."

"Sure," I said, happy to be appreciated by someone, even if it wasn't Phil.

Zilpha and Mayberry seemed very happy when they held out their plates. "Heap 'em high, Annabelle. I'm a hungry man." Mayberry winked. He's a really nice guy.

He was also getting to be a slightly pudgy one, but I didn't point that out to him. "Sure thing, Mayberry. Here you go."

"Isn't this a wonderful party, Annabelle?" Zilpha asked. She was bright and cheery. She was pretty much always bright and cheery. She's a much nicer person than I am.

"It sure is," I said, wishing it were so.

Richard and Hannah were next in line, and they were holding hands. Was Richard holding her hand because he was genuinely devoted to her, or was he holding her hand because he didn't want Hannah or anyone else to know he was cheating on her with Josephine Contreras? I hoped like fire it was the former, although it had always seemed to me that Richard loved money above all things. Except maybe Hannah. Truth to tell, he seemed devoted to her most of the time—which made his tête-à-têtes with Josephine terribly difficult to understand.

It was driving me nuts that I couldn't think of a likely reason for Richard to have been so darned friendly with Josephine—several times within my own line of vision, and who knows how many other times out of it—other than an affair. Maybe that meant I had a low mind. I don't know. Still, I couldn't quite feature Josephine needing to chat with Richard about a business deal, which was the only reason I could imagine for Josephine and a banker to be chummy. Especially outside of the darned bank. Nuts.

I was glad to see that Kenny Sawyer and Sarah Molina had evidently made up their quarrel, if they'd had one. It seemed to me that Kenny was oblivious and Sarah was the one who was unhappy most of the time. However, now they were in line together, and he had his arm around her waist. That looked like a good sign to me. I smiled at Sarah. "Hey, Sarah."

"Hey, Annabelle, those beans look good."

"They are. Made by my own personal mother. With chilies and ham hocks. I can vouch for them."

She laughed. It was definitely an improvement over crying. Looking at her critically, I decided she was every bit as pretty as Esther Strickland—not that looks are supposed to count, but they do anyhow. Sarah was taller and quite a bit darker than Esther, and had glossy black hair that she'd left long—lots of girls in those days were getting their hair shingled at the barbershop—and big brown eyes. I thought she was lovely, and she was also very nice if somewhat weepy. I also thought that Kenny was an idiot if he didn't treat her well, which he didn't.

Kenny himself was tiny bit taller than Phil, being a shade over six feet, I guess. He had curly brown hair and greenish eyes, and most folks, including me, considered him at least as handsome as most of the cowboys in the flickers. I wouldn't have been surprised if Kenny had decided to head out to New York or Los Angeles and try to get himself a job in the motion pictures, actually. He was the type who'd like to strut and posture in front of a bunch of people. Have I mentioned before that I didn't like him much?

"I know I already told you this, Kenny, but I really meant it when I said I thought you did a good job today on the broncs and bulls," I said as I scooped beans.

"Thanks."

Sarah smiled happily and squeezed his arm. I wonder what it is about some women that they can be happy with men who treat them like dirt. It's another one of life's puzzles, I reckon. There are sure a lot of them.

Ma and Pa were next. Ma asked nervously under her breath, "How do people like the beans, Annabelle?"

"They love 'em, Ma."

"Nobody's complaining because they're too spicy, are they?"

"Everybody around here loves spicy stuff, Ma. You know that."

"I don't know." Ma always worried about her cooking, but she needn't have because she was a very good cook. "Maybe I should have left out that last chili pepper."

"Naw," I said, spooning beans onto her plate. "They're perfect."

"That's what I've been telling her," said Pa, holding out his own plate.

Then Phil showed up, looking long and lanky and ever so handsome. I smiled at him, in spite of the mean way he'd treated me not an hour earlier. He was with a couple of the other cowboys in the competition, but he said, "Hey, Annabelle, I'm sorry I was grouchy earlier."

"Oh," I said, surprised by his acknowledgement of his former crankiness. "Were you?"

"Yeah, I was. But I'm not mad at you or anything. I was thinking about something else."

Why in the world would he be mad at me? "Oh," I said, "okay," and wondered what the "something else" was. Esther Strickland, perhaps?

There I went again, making myself miserable for no good reason.

"Hey, when you're through dishing up grub, come over and sit with me, okay?"

Boy, you just never can tell, can you? One minute the wind blows one way, and the next minute it blows the other, keeping you constantly off guard. I renewed my vow to run off and have adventures on my own, since men were so unreliable.

"Sure, Phil. I'll be happy to join you."

And then, a few people down the line later, the good reverend and his not-so-good sister appeared in front of me. Although I wasn't happy to see either one of them, I smiled sweetly. "How-do, Miss Strickland, Reverend Strickland. Have you been enjoying the rodeo?"

"Oh, my, yes," Esther said in her innocent, little-girl voice. She was hugging her plate to her chest. I hoped there was no food on it yet. Or maybe I didn't. "The cowboys are ever so handsome and robust, aren't they? I've never seen so many fine-looking gentlemen. And so athletic! My goodness, I don't know how they do what they do."

"Er . . . yes. They're a bunch of great guys, all right."

Holding his plate out to me, her brother looked pained for a second but recovered at once. "Yes, indeed. They're a fine group of fellows. And good Christians, too, according to Mr. Gunderson."

"Right," I said, spooning beans onto his plate.

"None for me, thank you, dear," said Esther in her sugary voice. "You rugged westerners enjoy food much spicier than I'm used to."

Rugged westerners, were we? I wondered where she'd come from. From her accent, somewhere south, I supposed. Way, way, way south. I only smiled sweetly some more. "Sure thing, Miss Strickland." She didn't deserve any of my mother's beans anyway.

When the line thinned out and most of the rodeo attendees and participants had been fed, Myrtle and I filled our plates and wandered over to where people were scattered around on blankets spread out on the ground. Phil and his cowboy friends had been sitting on an old plaid blanket under a pecan tree, but when he saw me with my plate, he scrambled up and rushed over to me. His chivalry made me feel kind of good, so I welcomed him with a smile.

Taking my plate, Phil said, "Come on over here, Annabelle and Myrtle. You can meet Bill Carson and Sonny Clyde from the Handlebar, over near Tatum."

I nudged Myrtle and said under my breath, "Here's your chance to snare a handsome cowboy, Myrtle."

She blushed, but I know she was glad to be invited to sit with the guys. Myrtle is a pretty girl, but she's kind of shy, and I know she wishes she had a special gentleman friend in her life. After all, we were both almost twenty years old. In a year or two, people would begin to wonder—probably out loud—why we weren't married yet, and I don't think Myrtle's excuse was the same as mine. At least she'd never voiced a desire to run off and see the world before she settled down. She's around my height, which is five feet, four inches tall, and she has brown hair that's a little darker than mine, and brown eyes. She's a little skinny, but that's not a bad thing, especially since all the magazines say a "thin, boyish figure" is all the rage. People like me, who have curves, are out of fashion, but Phil never seemed to mind. Until recently.

We had a good time eating together. Sonny Clyde was very funny, telling joke after joke, and making us all laugh until our stomachs ached. He also seemed quite taken with Myrtle. It looked that way to me, anyhow, because he was eyeing her the whole time—and Tatum isn't very far away from Rosedale. My heart, which had been behaving erratically of late, alternately glowed and ached, happy for Myrtle, and confused about me.

Stupid heart. I just hate when it does stuff like that.

CHAPTER FIVE

After the barbecue, we all gathered around the campfire again. Well, all except some of the women, who had to clean up after us. I swear, not only did the women have to cook the food and serve it, but then they had to do mop-up duties. Sometimes— often, in fact—I don't think the world is a fair place. I ventured to say so to my mother once. She only laughed and recited that old saw: "Men's work ends at the setting sun, but a woman's work is never done." Which only proves my point.

The choir director from the Bethel Baptist Church and the choir director from our church (First Methodist-Episcopal Church, North) were going to lead us all in another sing-along. They didn't just have us sing religious songs, either, in spite of the Stricklands being among the sing-along participants. I thought that showed a good deal of common sense. I mean, no matter how religious a person is, he or she still likes a bit of fun every now and then. At least I do. Maybe that proves I'm a sinner. I'd ask Myrtle, but she'd probably only confirm my suspicion.

And Phil sat next to me! I was happy about that. I was less happy to see Josephine Contreras and my brother-in-law sneaking off behind one of the barns. I found Hannah in the crowd, sitting next to Zilpha and not watching what her husband was doing. I was pleased that she didn't see her husband behaving in a suspicious manner, but darn it, what was going on between Josephine and Richard, if anything?

However, other things were good. Kenny Sawyer was lavishing attention upon Sarah for a change, and Myrtle was sitting next to Sonny Clyde on the other side of Phil and me. They seemed to be getting along quite well, and I was pleased for Myrtle. Even if she had been kind of annoying in recent days, she still deserved a good man in her life.

Hmm. I wonder if that's true. It seems to me that little girls are always told they need good little boys in their lives, but why? Why can't little girls grow up to be happy women complete unto themselves? Most of the marriages I've seen haven't been all that great, my parents' happy marriage excepted. And really, I didn't know what went on between them when I wasn't around. Maybe they secretly hated each other, although it didn't seem likely and I didn't like to think about that possibility.

Oh, there I go again. Pay no attention. Back to the sing-along.

Because I was curious—and perhaps because I'm mean at heart—I scanned the crowd for the Stricklands to see how Miss Esther was enjoying the fact that both of her prey were sitting with other women. When I located the Stricklands, I regret to say—because it speaks of a petty and childish nature—that I was not pleased. Esther Strickland seemed to have her full attention focused on her brother, at whom she was smiling her appealing, innocent smile. She looked almost as if she were what she claimed to be: a nice Christian woman who believed in what she was doing with this revivalist stuff. And who, coincidentally, was the most ravishingly lovely creature on earth. When she noticed me watching her, she smiled such a sweet smile, you'd have thought she were made of spun sugar.

I didn't believe it. Nobody could be that sweet and innocent and above petty jealousies and stuff like that. Or maybe I was projecting again. Perhaps she *was* above such nonsense. All I know for sure was that I'm not, and that I didn't like her—

which proves my point, I reckon.

Naturally, the party wasn't altogether rosy. For one thing, I still harbored a lingering worry about my sister Hannah's husband. Then there was Hazel Fish, who managed to squeeze herself in between Myrtle and me and, naturally, fling some dirt in my ear.

"It looks to me," she whispered, all titillation and excitement, "that Miss Strickland has lost both of her beaux."

I turned deliberately and frowned at her. "I don't feel like listening to gossip, Hazel Fish."

She looked at me as if my words had offended her. Can you imagine that? "I'm not gossiping! I just take note of what's going on around me. Besides, it's the truth. Just look at Sarah and Kenny. And did you see the expression on Miss Strickland's face? She isn't thrilled to see you and Phil sitting together, either."

"She looks exactly the same to me." I glanced again at Miss Strickland, hoping to find some of the jealousy Hazel pretended she'd seen. Nope. Wasn't there. Darn it.

"Humph. I know what I'm talking about. She's jealous, Annabelle, and you know it as well as I do."

"I know nothing of the kind."

"You would if you were honest with yourself. And not only that, but I saw something that would surprise everybody if I wanted to tell it, but I'm not going to, because it's nobody's business. So I'm not gossiping!"

Tired of her, I said, "Here, Hazel, have a s'more." And I shoved my just-put-together campfire treat at her. Maybe if she had something sweet in her mouth, she'd stop being so sour.

"Thanks, Annabelle."

So she ate my s'more and I had to make another one. I didn't mind too much. I'd much rather listen to Hazel chew than listen to her talk.

As the evening progressed and we sang and laughed and had fun together, I stopped watching out for my sister and her husband and Josephine Contreras and Sarah and Kenny and the Stricklands. What's more, I stopped listening to Hazel Fish, who got tired of being ignored and wandered off. Therefore, I enjoyed myself. I know that people were getting up here and there and moving around, and that different people were getting refills of cocoa from the big pot by the fire and roasting marshmallows at different times and so forth. Therefore, I didn't take any special notice of Kenny Sawyer.

Until he suddenly jumped to his feet, holding his stomach, and cried out in a hoarse voice, "Holy God!"

That brought things to a standstill for a heartbeat. Then Sarah scrambled up, too, and grabbed him by the arm. "Kenny! What's wrong?"

He doubled over for a second or two, then stood upright, looking abashed. He grinned slightly and said, "Sorry for disrupting the fun, folks. Cramp. I think I'd better take a little walk." And he climbed over a few people and faded into the night. Sarah, clearly worried, went with him, still holding onto his arm.

After the shock had worn off, we all got back to singing, laughing, drinking cocoa, roasting marshmallows, squashing same between graham crackers with bars of chocolate, and having a grand old time. The incident had reminded me of Esther Strickland, though, and I sought her out in the crowd. She still sat with her brother, and she had a slightly worried expression on her face. Maybe she wanted to rush after Kenny and comfort him but didn't dare, what with Sarah having reestablished a proprietary interest in him and all. I'd sure be glad when those revival-tent people left town.

All went well for about a half hour, I suppose, and I for one had forgotten all about Kenny, when we heard a shriek from the dark, outside the circle of our big campfire. Several people leaped to their feet. Then Sarah Molina appeared, looking pretty much like I've always pictured the mad Mrs. Rochester during the fire at Thornfield Hall. Pulling at her hair and streaming tears, she rushed into the circle and shrieked, "He's *dying!* Kenny's *dying!* Where's a doctor?"

Oddly enough, Rosedale, New Mexico, boasted a whole bunch of doctors at the time. This was because it was discovered that Rosedale was a good place to live if you had consumption. And there were, unfortunately, a whole swarm of sufferers of the white plague in the United States. In actual fact, according to a magazine article I read once, we had more doctors per capita than any other city in the country! Therefore, three men immediately stood up and moved forward. Sarah grabbed Dr. Hanks and started tugging him, I presume, to Kenny. Dr. Richardson and Dr. Hilliard followed. Dr. Hilliard paused long enough to say to the assembly, "Don't worry, folks. We'll have him right as rain in a few minutes."

He waved, smiled, and left, and we who were left all sat there, stunned. That state of affairs lasted for about a minute and a half. Then Pastor Stone, from the Bethel Baptist Church, rose to his feet and said, "Well, let's sing! How about 'Onward, Christian Soldiers'? We can dedicate the rousing hymn to our very own Kenny Sawyer, who seems to be in some distress."

So we sang, getting off to a wobbly start. I know I was worried, and I'm sure everyone else was, too, because the party never did regain its full vigor. My heart lurched erratically, but I don't think any of us were surprised when Dr. Hanks, trying to be invisible (and failing at it), came up to Mr. Gunderson, knelt down beside him, and whispered something in his ear. Mr. Gunderson appeared slightly shocked, rose, and followed the doctor away from the circle. Oh, dear. This didn't bode well for poor Kenny.

A few moments later, when I felt a tap on my shoulder, I nearly jumped out of my skin. Turning, I saw Mr. Gunderson. Very softly, he said, "Will you and Phil come with me, please, Miss Annabelle?"

"Sure, Mr. Gunderson." And, making as little fuss as we could, although I could feel the eyes of the entire campfire crowd upon us, Phil and I left the circle and followed Mr. Gunderson and Dr. Hanks to the Gundersons' house, where Kenny was. Nobody said anything until we got indoors.

Then Dr. Hanks spoke to Phil and me seriously, "I want the two of you to try to keep everybody calm out there. Can you do that? This is a serious business."

"What's the matter with Kenny?" I asked, wanting some information before I promised anyone anything.

"He's very, very ill. He seems to be suffering from some sort of gastric distress. I'm not sure what the problem is, but he's in extremely bad shape."

"Gosh, I'm really sorry to hear that," I said, meaning it. I didn't much like Kenny, but I didn't want anything awful to happen to him. The doctor sounded so grave, my unreliable heart gave a sickening lurch.

Mrs. Gunderson, carrying a basin, rushed past us, realized who we were, stopped, and rushed back again. She took my arm. "Annabelle and Phil, if you've ever prayed in your life, please pray now, for Kenny." And with that, she scooted off again, turning into the parlor where I assumed they'd taken Kenny. That didn't sound good to me, but I vowed that I'd do as she'd asked. A prayer from yours truly might not mean much to God, but it sure couldn't hurt. As we went back toward the fire circle, I prayed silently, *Please, God, help Kenny get through this, whatever it is. And I promise I'll try to be more charitable from now on.*

I can just imagine what God thought of *that* prayer. I could almost hear him declare, "Don't give me any of that nonsense about *trying*, Annabelle Blue. Either do it or don't do it, but don't quibble." He said it in my father's voice, probably because that's exactly what Pa always told any of us when we told him we'd try to improve our behavior. My father was a great guy, but a tough disciplinarian. I guess that's a good thing.

Phil and I weren't moving awfully fast when we returned to the circle. In my case, my slowness was because I wasn't sure what to do or say to keep people calm. I presume the same was true for Phil, although I didn't ask. Anyhow, when we resumed our seats next to Myrtle, the singing faltered, then stopped. The entire throng stared at us, as if asking for enlightenment. And we'd just been charged with making sure nobody panicked. Oh, boy.

However, in an attempt to live up to my promise and my prayer, I smiled a small smile and said, "The doctors are with Kenny now. I'm sure everything will be fine."

"Yeah," said Phil, bless him. "A little stomach trouble is all."

I don't think anybody believed us. I know no one felt like singing anymore. We all just sat there, wondering what had gone wrong, some of us whispering. At last Reverend Stone, after conferring with Reverend Farley, our (Methodist) minister, held up his arms and said, "How about we have a prayer for our friend, Kenny Sawyer, folks. Looks like he might need one."

We all murmured our agreement, and Reverend Stone launched into a prayer that rivaled the one Reverend Strickland had said the day before. When he finally said, "Amen," and we lifted our heads (which, naturally, we'd bowed in proper, respectful style), Mr. Gunderson stood beside the two ministers. He seemed mighty grim.

He held up a hand, tried to smile, failed, and said, "I guess the party's over for this evening, folks. Y'all come back again tomorrow for some more exciting events and another campfire and sing-along. Thanks for comin'!"

So, with much whispering and shuffling, everybody got up and started to move toward the field where all the cars and wagons were parked. I don't think anyone wanted to speak too loudly for some reason. We felt solemn, almost as if we were in church or something.

Myrtle, Sonny Clyde, Phil and I made our way to the field together. Taking my arm, Myrtle said in a hushed voice, "What's going on, Annabelle?"

"I'm not sure. Dr. Hanks said Kenny is suffering from some sort of gastric upset, and that it's pretty bad."

"Phil?" Myrtle said, giving up on me as a lost cause, I guess, "do you know any more about what's wrong?"

"Sure don't," said Phil. He appeared mighty serious. "Only what Annabelle said. Doc Hanks said it was stomach trouble, and it was bad. Hope Kenny's okay. I don't like him much, but I don't want anything bad to happen to him." That seemed to be the universal sentiment regarding Kenny.

Phil was such a nice guy. Here he and Kenny had exchanged heated words, and they'd been rivals in rodeo events for eons, yet he was wishing Kenny well. Even though Kenny was a strutting-peacock sort of fellow. "Me, too," I said, feeling guilty about disliking so many people. Heck, if Phil could be generous about Kenny, I guess I shouldn't be such a meanie about Esther Strickland. Unless, of course, she continued to try to steal Phil from me. And, now that Kenny was apparently out of the running for her affections, at least for the moment, she might just concentrate her wiles in Phil's direction. Not that she seemed wily exactly.

Oh, heck, I was just a jealous cat. She was beautiful, sweet, charming, she had a great voice, and I envied her. And I didn't like the notion of Phil falling in love with another woman, darn it.

"Wonder why it happened so suddenly," said Sonny.

We all wondered the same thing. "I guess we could look for one of the doctors and ask if they know anything more by now. Or Sarah." As soon as I mentioned Sarah, I wished I hadn't. I liked Sarah, but if anything was really wrong with Kenny, I didn't want to be anywhere near her. I wasn't keen on histrionics, unless I was watching them onstage or at the flickers.

"Let's not bother Sarah or the doctors," said Phil. "They've probably got their hands full."

I considered that a good call. My parents and Jack were waiting for me beside the Model T, so Myrtle, Phil, Sonny and I parted from each other in the parking field. I'd kind of hoped I might have a second or two alone with Phil, just to see if he'd say anything to me, or maybe kiss me or something, but I didn't get it.

The only one who wanted to talk on the way home was Jack, so he did until Pa told him to shut his yapper. Before that happened, Jack had propounded his theory that one of the other cowboys in the competition had poisoned Kenny, that Kenny had ingested some sort of evil drug, that he'd drunk too much illegal booze, or that Kenny'd had a heart attack or some other kind of fit. None of those theories sounded likely to me, but I knew better than to say so. An argument with Jack was sure to end badly, especially with our parents around to hear it.

The next day was Saturday. Blue's Dry Goods and Mercantile Emporium was scheduled to close at noon so that the whole family could attend the rodeo. We were all there, Ma, Pa, Jack and me, shuffling around, restocking merchandise, straightening displays and dusting shelves. I don't know about the others, but I was just wondering how Kenny was doing when in came Hazel Fish, big with news. It was the first and only time I'd been glad to see her, because if anybody knew what had gone wrong with

Kenny and what the prognosis was, she would.

She did. And she told us. Running up to me, she took my hand, cast a tragic glance at the rest of my family and cried, "Kenny's dead!"

I'd almost expected it, but I was shocked anyway. So shocked, in fact, that I darned near staggered backward. I gasped, "Dead?" My heart gave a gigantic plunge, and I instantly said another silent prayer for Kenny's soul. I don't think Methodists are supposed to do stuff like that, but I did it anyway.

Pa said, "Dear God."

Ma said, "Dead! Sweet Lord have mercy!"

Hazel nodded solemnly. "They say he died yesterday evening, a little before midnight."

"Good heavens." Ma, a very nice person, was truly upset. "Does anybody know what happened to the poor boy?"

Hazel was in her glory now. She took a deep breath and elaborated in a dramatic whisper. "They say he was *poisoned!*"

"Ha! I knew it!" This, naturally, came from my obnoxious brother Jack.

We all ignored him, although Hazel's announcement had caught our attention with a vengeance. Ma gaped at Hazel.

I said, "Poisoned? Are you sure? Who said so?" People died of all sorts of things in Rosedale, as they do everywhere, even ptomaine poisoning, but I sensed this wasn't that kind of poisoning but more on the order of strychnine or arsenic or rat poison or something like that. If so, it was the very first time in my whole life that anyone with whom I was personally acquainted had been deliberately and maliciously poisoned. Well, anyone I knew about, anyhow.

Nodding solemnly, Hazel said, "I heard Dr. Hanks telling my father about it. At first they thought Kenny'd had a severe gastric attack or maybe ptomaine from something he ate at the picnic, but Dr. Hanks said they think it was some kind of poison. They're going to go through . . . well, they're going to check his stomach contents and make a firm determination."

I recollected the basin Mrs. Gunderson had been carrying to Kenny's sick room and grimaced. If what Hazel said was true, someone was going to analyze Kenny's throw-up. Ew.

Hazel continued her recital, thrilled to be imparting such exciting news. "Dr. Hanks thinks it might have been arsenic." She shot a glance around at my family. "He said Kenny's lips were *blue.*"

"Good heavens," I muttered, aghast. Then, of course, because I can't seem to help myself, I tried to remember novels I'd read in which people had been poisoned with arsenic. Had their lips turned blue? I didn't think so, but I wasn't sure. Still, I figured Hazel had made up that part.

"Wow," said Jack. "I gotta find Davy! I was right!" And off he ran, in spite of it being Saturday and having work to do, before Ma or Pa could stop him.

"I'm so sorry to hear about Kenny," said Ma, and we resumed our duties.

"I'm going to go next door and see if Myrtle's there," said Hazel, and she vanished as quickly as she'd appeared, eager to spread the ghastly news. For some reason, that morning she made me think of a malaria-carrying mosquito, darting all over town to spread her sickness. I guess I was still shocked.

That day at the rodeo was a demonstration day, when some of the girls who'd grown up on ranches in the area showed everyone how well they could run the barrel race and do other stuff like that. It was kind of fun, although the mood of the spectators seemed to have been negatively affected by the events of the prior evening and the news of this morning. Most of the town was still buzzing about Kenny Sawyer.

"They're having the funeral tomorrow, even though it's not

summertime and the body might keep for a little longer," Hazel told me almost as soon as I sat myself on the fence. Myrtle was with me, and we exchanged a look of irritation. Hazel was a really uncomfortable person to be around, darn it. "He's going to be buried here, in Rosedale."

That news surprised me. "Why isn't he being buried in Texico?" I could have smacked myself for asking Hazel anything at all, because once she got started, she tended never to shut up. Still, I was curious.

"Well, he was born here and his mother still lives here in Rosedale, you know. And so does Sarah. Now they're back to saying he might have died of ptomaine poisoning." She sounded disappointed. I guess she'd have preferred arsenic.

"Hmm. Wonder how he got it. The food was all either cold or hot. Heck, it's autumn, not the summertime." In the summertime, you had to watch out for ptomaine, because it got really hot in our neck of the woods and food spoiled quickly, especially stuff like eggs and things with mayonnaise in them. That was one of the main reasons folks in Rosedale were so happy to have electricity—refrigerators kept food ever so much fresher than ice boxes. Some of my friends who didn't have refrigerators seemed to be ill with stomach problems all the time, and I suspected the problem was due to lack of refrigeration.

Hazel shrugged. "Ptomaine is funny like that."

I didn't think there was a single solitary thing funny about Kenny's death.

A pall seemed to hang over the events of that day. Charles and Edward didn't allow Esther Strickland out of their sight, so she couldn't have flirted with Phil if she'd had a mind to. I was grateful for that, although Phil was too busy setting up for the rodeo to pay much attention to me, presuming he'd had any intention of doing so.

Applause during the events seemed halfhearted, and I felt bad for Gloria Detrick, who won the barrel race, because what should have been the highlight of her year had a great, big fat cloud hanging over it.

A couple of the men in town, who acted as rodeo clowns—fellows who distracted the bulls after they'd dumped their riders so the bulls wouldn't gore or stomp the downed cowboys—demonstrated the tricks of their trade. They did a good job, but even their exhibition fell kind of flat. It was difficult to cheer and laugh when someone who'd been the star of the show only the day before was dead of some kind of poisoning. Could it have been ptomaine?

Ptomaine didn't seem likely to me since nobody else seemed to be sick, although I certainly didn't know a whole lot about poisons. I also know I wasn't the only one pondering the matter. The whole town was on edge all that Saturday. Even the campfire and sing-along fizzled, and we all went home early, Mr. Gunderson's request that we all "Say a prayer in church tomorrow for Kenny Sawyer's grieving loved ones," lingering in our minds and hearts.

I thought about how I'd feel if it had been Phil who'd been struck down, and decided I was being morbid. Still, my sympathy for Sarah Molina edged up a notch. And what about Kenny's mother and sister? It's got to be the worst thing in the world to lose a child. Heck, it's hard enough to lose a friend, but a child? I decided it would be better to stop thinking at all, since my thoughts were so gloomy.

The next day was Sunday. Blue's Dry Goods—along with every other business in town—was closed, and there were no rodeo events scheduled. I was glad of it. The atmosphere that had tainted Saturday lingered, and I didn't want to pretend to be having a jolly old time when I was, in reality, worried and scared.

It was kind of odd, too, that the atmosphere should be so solemn. Kenny wasn't the first person in the world to get sick and die, after all. Maybe it affected us so greatly because he was stricken so suddenly. And via poison. The thought made me shudder.

Another idea crossed my mind, but it wasn't very nice. But it occurred to me that since the revivalists had come in among us the atmosphere in town had changed somehow, and everyone was already on edge. You didn't necessarily notice it at first, but there was just a hint of something weird going on. And it hadn't been there before the arrival of the Stricklands and their entourage.

Or maybe I was just crazy. That's probably it.

Naturally, the whole church was abuzz with gossip and speculation about Kenny's death. I didn't get three steps inside the sanctuary before Myrtle and her parents joined us. Myrtle whispered, "Oh, Annabelle, I just can't believe he's dead."

"I can't, either." I frowned. "And of ptomaine, of all things."

"It wasn't ptomaine," whispered a voice behind me. I turned to discover—who else?—Hazel Fish. She looked positively avid. "It was *arsenic*."

"Arsenic?" Myrtle and I chorused together in mutual shock. "How did they find out for certain?"

"Dr. Hanks told my father that after they did a thorough analysis of Kenny's stomach contents, they discovered it was arsenic." Hazel scurried off in her mosquito-like fashion, eager to stab somebody else with her terrible news, and I again shuddered at how analysis must have been undertaken.

Good heavens. That meant Kenny had died of deliberate, cold-blooded poisoning. Had *probably* died that way. I mean, I suppose it's possible that someone could ingest arsenic by accident, although it seemed unlikely. Heck, if some salad or something on one of the potluck dinner tables had contained arsenic, wouldn't we all have suffered? But still . . . deliberate murder? It was difficult to imagine such a thing.

And then, because it can't seem to help itself, my mind went back to the library and that book of poisons lying open on the table. And to Sarah Molina, leaving the library after looking through the book. If it had been Sarah in the library, and I'm pretty sure it had been, although she didn't turn around so I could see her face. I didn't mention it to anyone.

"Who'd do such a despicable thing?" Myrtle asked of no one in particular.

"I don't know." What a melancholy morning this was turning out to be. And the funeral was yet to come. I sighed deeply.

Myrtle and I took off toward the choir room since we both sang in the alto section, and the rest of the family, except Jack, moved forward to sit in the pew they generally occupied, about halfway up the aisle. It defeats me to understand why nobody in church ever sits in the front rows of the sanctuary, but nobody ever does.

Taking my arm, Myrtle whispered, "Do you suppose the poisoning might have been an accident?"

"An accident?" I'd already thought a good deal about this question, and still hadn't reached a conclusion. "I don't know. How do people generally eat arsenic? Can you do it by accident?"

Myrtle looked at me blankly. "How should I know?"

I was feeling pretty blank myself, actually, never having considered any of this stuff before except when I was reading mystery novels. I read stories all the time in which people in pretty little English villages poisoned each other, but—at a rodeo? I don't know. The whole poison thing didn't make any sense to me.

"If it wasn't an accident, then somebody must have wanted to kill him," Myrtle pointed out. "I can't imagine anybody we know doing something so wicked."

"Actually. . . ." I paused and thought some more. Did I really want to say what I'd been going to say?

"Actually what?" said Myrtle.

"Um . . . nothing."

What I'd been going to say was that I'd always heard that poison was a woman's weapon of choice, probably because they found it difficult to get their hands on their male kinfolks' guns. Could Sarah have poisoned Kenny because he'd been paying attention to Esther Strickland? I'd pondered that possibility before, and didn't like it. Could *Esther* have poisoned Kenny because she was angry with him for showing attention to Sarah? I liked that possibility a tiny bit better, although not by much. Both scenarios were possible, if unlikely, but I decided it would be unwise to say so since people might chalk up the Esther idea to jealousy on my part. And they might be right.

And then I remembered the altercation the day before between Kenny and Armando Contreras. Good heavens, could Armando have poisoned Kenny? He'd been going to try to beat him to a bloody pulp. Although I'd never say so to Armando, he'd probably have had better luck with poison than his fists, since Kenny was a good deal bigger and younger than Armando and no doubt in better shape. I didn't like that idea, either, mainly because I liked Armando, even though he was known to have a feisty temper. Given his temper, it seemed unlikely that he'd have used poison. If he got mad enough, he might shoot someone dead or try to pummel him to death, but poison? Unlikely.

Or—egad! Could it have been Josephine who'd done Kenny to death? She'd not only been flirting with Kenny, but with my brother-in-law Richard, too. Maybe, what with one thing and another, she'd slipped a cog and gone nuts. Those things happened sometimes. At least I think they did. They did in novels, for sure. Maybe Josephine had been trying to lure Kenny into her snare, had been foiled by Armando, had gotten mad at Kenny for some reason, and poisoned him!

I don't know. That theory seemed kind of shaky.

Anyhow, as I'd already surmised, it might just as easily have been Sarah Molina who'd become fed up with her beau's straying ways and done him in. Besides, it had been Sarah looking at the book of poisons. At least, I think it had been. Or maybe that cowboy Kenny'd had the fight with had decided enough was enough and slipped some arsenic into his barbecue—although I'd never offer that suggestion to Jack, who idolized cowboys and would taunt me—not that he ever needed a reason to do that.

Or maybe it had been one of Miss Strickland's keepers, Charles or Edward. Or both of them. Maybe they did away with anyone who paid too much attention to Miss Strickland. I wrinkled my nose when that thought crossed my mind.

Heavenly days, could it have been my very own brother-in-law, Richard MacDougall, who'd become jealous because his mistress Josephine Contreras had been flirting with Kenny? I couldn't bear the notion of that one, so I made my brain scoot back to the fighting-cowboy scenario.

Or, what the heck, maybe Hazel had decided not to wait for gossip to happen but to do something to stir some up on her own. That last thought was so silly, I decided I'd best stop muddying my brain with wild surmises, put my choir robe on and get ready to sing. So I did.

Every Sunday after church, we all gathered in what we call the Fellowship Hall, for cookies and punch and, once a month, a potluck supper. This was one of the punch-and-cookie Sundays. Lots of folks around Rosedale only saw other folks around town on Sundays, since they lived on ranches and farms quite a ways out from the town. Rodeo week was an exception, but we Rosedale folks still considered Sundays our primary social days.

Naturally, on that particular Sunday, the topic of conversation was Kenny's death. Myrtle and I sat at a table by ourselves, but that happy state of affairs didn't last long. Mae Shenkel, the high-school principal's daughter, soon joined us, as did Hazel Fish and Ruby Bond, her bosom buddy. I wasn't awfully fond of Mae, who had a brain the size of an English pea, but she was easier to take than Hazel. Ruby was okay. Quiet. I guess if you were used to hanging out with Hazel, you were also used to not talking much.

"Do you think Kenny was murdered?" Mae leaned over the table and whispered her question.

"Don't know how else he could have taken in enough poison to kill him," I said, considering my response only practical.

"Well, but, can't you get poisoned by accident sometimes?"

Not more than once or twice, probably, I thought but didn't say. "I don't see how. Under the circumstances and all."

Mae looked blank. She did that a lot. She was very pretty, with blonde hair and blue eyes and nice clothes, but, as I said before, there wasn't anything in her head except fluff, in spite of her being the high-school principal's daughter. "The circumstances? What circumstances?"

"The rodeo and barbeque and all," I explained patiently. "We all ate the same food and drank the same lemonade and cider and cocoa and stuff. If anything in the barbeque had been poisoned, we'd all have got sick. The way I figure it, somebody must have put poison in Kenny's cocoa or his coffee or in his food or something. Or his s'more." Which thought gave me pause. How did arsenic taste? Was it bitter? Did it have any flavor at all? Hmm. Maybe I should look at that poison book in the library myself.

"Oh," said Mae, blinking her big blue eyes and reminding me

of one of Zilpha's old china-headed dolls. "I guess that makes sense."

"But who could have done it?" Myrtle asked, punctuating her question by biting sharply into a sugar cookie.

"I don't know."

"I do." This, of course, came from Hazel.

"Yeah?" I was pretty darned doubtful myself, and I think my skepticism showed in my face. "Who do you think did it?"

Hazel tilted her head to one side and adopted an expression that was normal for her and that always made me want to slap her upside the head. It was her I-know-something-you-don't-know expression. "I don't know if I should say."

"If you know who murdered Kenny, you'd better say," I told her in plain, unadulterated English. "If you don't, you'll be obstructing justice, and that's a crime in itself." I didn't know this for a fact, but I'd read about obstruction of justice in a detective novel. I think that novel was set in New York City, but surely New Mexico had similar laws. Maybe.

Hazel didn't like having her little games batted about with the truth. She looked at me with annoyance. "Well, I didn't say I actually *know*," said she.

"Yes, you did," said Myrtle, my best friend. You can see why.

"Well, I didn't mean that I *know*. But I saw Armando Contreras and Kenny having a big fight right before the campfire last night."

"I saw them fighting, too, earlier," I admitted.

Hazel nodded in smug satisfaction. "This was later, though. Right before the campfire. So that makes it *two* fights."

Hmm. "Was it a fistfight or merely a fight with words?" I wondered if Kenny had gone out of his way to irritate so many people, or if it had been an inborn talent of his. If so, it seemed a mighty unprofitable one and one that might even have led to his death.

"Well, they didn't come to blows or anything. But they were sure yelling at each other. Armando called Kenny a—" Hazel paused and looked around to see if anybody else was close. "He called him a lousy son of a bitch." She said the last word so softly, we almost didn't hear it.

"Hmm," I said. A lousy son of a bitch was probably worse than a snake, which was what Armando had called Kenny in the fight I'd witnessed.

"I don't know what to think," said Myrtle. "What about you, Annabelle?"

"Me? I don't have a clue."

"Nuts. You're always solving mysteries."

"I am?" I was truly surprised by these words.

"Well, sure, you are. Remember last summer?"

How could I forget? A stranger had managed to get himself killed next to my aunt Minnie's chicken coop, and I'd fingered approximately six people in town, alternately, and had been totally taken by surprise when the real villains presented themselves and almost succeeded in killing Phil and me. In other words, I hadn't exactly comported myself with detectival brilliance last summer.

However, having been wrong before didn't stop me from mulling over, there in Fellowship Hall, the matter of Kenny's death. I decided Hazel's theory was silly. "I think you're wrong about Mando, Hazel. Sure, he has a hot temper, but I don't think he'd poison anybody." Not that I hadn't thought of him as a suspect myself. "He's more apt to pop someone in the jaw, I should think. And if he did that to Kenny, he'd probably be the one who got hurt."

"That's a good point, Annabelle!" Myrtle sounded as if she was proud of me. Turning to Hazel, she said, "What do you say to *that*, Hazel Fish?"

Hazel didn't get to say anything, because my mother and

father showed up at that point. "Let's get going, Annabelle," said Pa. "Your mother says the roast will burn if we don't get home soon."

With a sigh—of relief, actually, since except for Myrtle, I wasn't enjoying the company—I said, "Okay. Where's Jack?"

"I've got him," said Pa.

And, by gum, he did. By the collar of his shirt. Jack didn't look happy, so I guess Pa had found him out in some kind of mischief. How typical of him. He didn't even give it a rest in church. I told you Jack was obnoxious.

Myrtle spoke up then. "Are you going to go to the revival this evening, Mrs. Blue? I've been trying to get Annabelle to go with me, but she keeps not going."

Ma eyed me critically. "I think that would be a very good idea, Myrtle. I think Annabelle and Jack should both go. It will do them good."

Oh, brother. Every now and then my best friend could be a real snake in the grass—which wasn't as bad as a lousy son of a bitch, but hit mighty close. With a soul-deep sigh, I said, "All right. I'll go."

"I'll be there, too, Annabelle," said Hazel, as if she thought I'd be delighted to know it. "We can sit together."

Oh, goody. What an inducement.

"I've gone to two meetings, Annabelle. They're quite uplifting," said Mae.

Ruby, as usual, said nothing. But she smiled, as if adding her endorsement to the Stricklands' brand of ministry (I almost wrote "misery").

"You'll be glad you did," Myrtle told me, sounding so sincere, I wanted to smack her one. "Reverend Strickland is truly a wonderful preacher. And Miss Strickland has such a pretty voice." She clasped her hands to her bosom.

A voice wasn't all Esther Strickland had that was pretty. Since

I didn't dare say so, I just said, "Right," and went home with my family.

Phil, curse him, didn't show himself all morning long, at church or anywhere else where I was. I couldn't help but envision him dallying with Miss Esther Strickland and made myself miserable thinking about the two of them together, which made me hate myself, naturally.

At least Sunday dinner (which we took at noon, after church) was good. Other than that, my Sunday was pretty darned stupid. Except for *The Case of Jennie Brice*, which was very good.

Kenny's funeral was held that afternoon, at a graveside service. I know it sounds like they were rushing things, but you have to remember that back then bodies didn't keep very well, even in the autumn, which this was. Even though Kenny worked at the Texico Ranch, he was originally from Rosedale, so the South Park Cemetery got the privilege of accommodating him for all eternity.

I felt truly sorry for his mother, who was a well-off widow lady, and his sisters, who were in their twenties. While it's true they'd probably spoiled him rotten when he was a kid and were, therefore, primarily responsible for Kenny's swollen head, I'm sure they'd only pampered him because they loved him, he being the only boy in the family. And I suspect Kenny had been their rock and mainstay after his father died. In actual fact, I also suspected Kenny had taken work at the Texico Ranch, which was a long way away from Rosedale, in order to get away from his mother's smothering influence.

Whatever the circumstances of Kenny's life, his death was considered a tragedy by all, including me. His funeral turned out to be a truly dismal affair. The weather was blustery and cold, and fall leaves swirled everywhere. Mrs. Sawyer and Sarah, both wearing dull black dresses that had obviously been dyed especially for the funeral, sat together in folding chairs provided by Mr. Ballard, the undertaker. Kenny's two sisters were similarly garbed in black. They flanked the two chief mourners. The group of women together reminded me of a murder of crows, and I wish I'd never read the article about what-to-call-collective-nouns.

Most of the citizens of Rosedale were at the graveyard, as were most of the cowboys who'd worked with or competed against Kenny in the rodeo. The cowpokes all wore expressions of surprise and uneasiness, as if they couldn't understand how something like this could have happened to one of their own— even one who was generally regarded as an arrogant so-and-so. The rest of us probably appeared similarly befuddled. People just didn't poison each other in Rosedale, New Mexico. The fact that Kenny Sawyer had been a young, healthy, robust man in his prime also, I imagine, had something to do with the long faces of the funeral attendees. I mean, you aren't really surprised when, say, a ninety-year-old passes on, but a twenty-one-year-old? Such a passing seemed wrong, even when murder *wasn't* suspected.

Reverend Stone, the minister at the Bethel Baptist Church spoke the funereal words over the gaping hole where Kenny's coffin would soon be placed. I noticed that Ma and Pa were holding hands, which they didn't often do in public. But I imagine the notion of a child dying had made them think about their own family, and about how lucky they were that all of their five children had grown up to adulthood—except for Jack, who might yet be the exception, given his proclivities.

I spotted Myrtle in the crowd. She nodded soberly at me, and I nodded gravely back. Everybody was solemn that day. We were not only burying one of our own, but also one who had been foully dispatched by an unknown villain.

Phil wasn't there, and nobody else in his family showed up, either. I didn't consider this an unusual circumstance or one that displayed any kind of disrespect, given the fact that the Gundersons were probably preparing for the last day of the rodeo on Monday. The last day was mainly just for fun, with demonstrations of different events and lots of food and singing and so forth. I thought it was pretty mean of the murderer to cast such a dismal mood over this year's event, and not merely because everybody looked forward to the rodeo, but because I was especially fond of the Gundersons—and not just Phil, either.

The Stricklands showed up at the graveside service, too, and both of them appeared as gloomy as the weather. However (and I really hate to admit this) Esther looked perfectly lovely in her black suit and black hat, with her black stockings and black shoes. I'd never seen so fashionable a funeral costume. Because I didn't want to become so totally immersed in Esther-envy that I lost sight of the realities of life, I reminded myself that, in her capacity as sister to a minister, she probably had to attend lots of funerals, so it might pay to have an outfit specifically designated as one to wear to funerals.

Unfortunately, my attempt at kindliness didn't alter my perspective regarding Esther Strickland. I still couldn't stand the woman. This was especially true when she sang "Softly and Tenderly, Jesus is Calling" in her clear, perfect soprano voice, thereby reducing to tears everybody who was standing around that hole in the ground—including me. I wondered what Sarah thought of this addition to the service, but she had a veil on her hat, so I couldn't see her face. I sure could tell that both she and Mrs. Sawyer were in tears, though, because they were embracing each other and their shoulders heaved with their sobs.

Whoever had done Kenny in had a lot to answer for. And I hoped to goodness he—or she, since I couldn't get rid of the notion that poison was a woman's weapon—would be caught soon. The notion of a mad murderer running around Rosedale didn't appeal one teensy bit.

Usually after a funeral, people gathered at the home of the deceased for refreshments. Things had happened so fast after Kenny's demise that this custom wasn't honored. Mrs. Sawyer told people she'd have what she called a "wake" later in her son's honor, but that today wasn't the day. Nobody blamed her. I think we were all too stunned by the event itself even to think much about the lack of a get-together.

Poison. In Rosedale, New Mexico. Granted, this part of New Mexico has never been exactly what you'd call peaceful, having been home to innumerable Indian raids, cattle wars, outlaw incursions (remember Billy the Kid and Pat Garrett?) and so forth. But poison? Whatever next?

Unfortunately, I didn't have long to wait for the answer to that question.

CHAPTER SIX

Myrtle stopped by the house a little after five that evening, and we walked together to the revival tent, which was set up a few hundred yards west of the last house on Second Street. Rosedale wasn't much of an urban metropolis, being small and dull. Not that our size had anything to do with the revivalists, except that I always got the feeling folks like the Stricklands preferred hanging out in smaller towns rather than larger, more sophisticated ones. Not that we were inherently more gullible or stupid than any other population group, but, as demonstrated by Miss Strickland's comments about Blue's Dry Goods, folks *thought* we were. I resented their attitude.

Anyhow, you can probably tell that I wasn't looking forward to the revival meeting one little bit, and not only because I wasn't fond of Esther Strickland and her brother, the velvet-voiced Milo Strickland. I still felt sick about Kenny Sawyer.

That funeral had been truly awful. The deep and honest grief of Mrs. Sawyer and Sarah Molina had affected me strangely, making me feel as if the least little thing would set me off on a crying jag. That would be very embarrassing, mainly because people would probably think I was crying over Phil. And part of any crying jag in which I might wallow would have been that, but most of it would have been because thinking about life and its inevitable consequence—death—was really uncomfortable. Heck, I was only nineteen years old. I should live for years and years.

Yet Kenny had been in his early twenties, and he was as dead as the proverbial doornail. The notion made my tummy hurt. Or maybe it was my heart. Whatever it was, I wished it would stop.

"I love going to these meetings," Myrtle said, as we watched my obnoxious brother Jack and a couple of his friends from school racing on ahead of us toward the big tent. He was swinging his stupid baseball bat, and I wondered what in the name of Glory he aimed to do with a baseball bat at a tent revival meeting. I'd bet money that Ma and Pa didn't know he'd brought his bat along.

"Hmm," I said, thinking maybe Jack would be saved and behave like a human being for a couple of weeks. That would be nice, even if I wasn't anticipating much along those lines, Jack thus far in his life having proved himself impervious to most forms of discipline and spiritual enlightenment.

Besides, I had a sneaking suspicion that Jack and his pals had devious plans for the evening and that this plan didn't include religion. It wouldn't have surprised me any if they aimed to duck out of the revival, have a little game of baseball outside the tent, and let the rest of the town get themselves saved while they played ball—if they could see to play. It was pretty dark by then, and nobody had strung electrical wires around the tent as they had around the Gundersons' pasture.

Anyhow, as I've mentioned before, I didn't care for revivalists in general because they always seemed to get carried away and condemn people out of hand. I for one—and I wouldn't want the minister of my church to hear this—don't believe that everyone in the world who doesn't believe exactly as I do is going to hell. What about all those Buddhists out there? Or Moslems? Just because they haven't heard of God as I know Him doesn't mean they don't believe in God, does it? Didn't Saint John say something about that in the Book of Revelation?

Since I couldn't remember the exact passage, I probably ought to have asked Myrtle, who seemed to have been boning up on her Bible lately, but I didn't.

I was pretty sure Reverend Strickland didn't share my sentiments, and I didn't much like him because of it, although I acknowledged as we walked to the tent that I might have been jumping the gun. I hadn't heard him preach yet. For all I knew at that point, he was a very fair-minded, openhearted individual who would swing wide the gates of his notion of heaven to good people of all faiths.

As I'd feared, though, it turned out that he was every bit as narrow-minded as I'd expected, although you couldn't prove it by Myrtle, who was absolutely smitten with the man. The more fool she, in my humble opinion.

He sure was a powerful speaker, though. I appreciated the resonance of his voice and his delivery, even if I didn't much care for his message.

By the way, I was right about Jack. I didn't see hide or hair of my rotten brother during the entire time I spent in that stupid tent, which was, by the way, lit with kerosene lamps and smelled accordingly. I knew Jack was outdoors playing ball, the wretched fiend, and wondered what he was using for light so that the little sinners could see the game they were playing.

"Sinners!" Reverend Strickland cried, meaning us, I guess. "Come to Jesus! Jesus is the only way to eternal life! *Come* to the Lord! *Come* to the Lord!"

And more along those lines. I was immune, probably because I had so many hard feelings about the man's sister. Nevertheless, I had to give him credit for believing in what he spoke. I don't think I've ever heard a more impassioned sermon, especially when he begged the congregation to "come forth and be saved into eternal life."

A whole bunch of my fellow citizens took him at his word

and surged to the front of the tent, where he blessed them and embraced them. There was a lot of hugging and crying and a few wailed amens and stuff like that. I don't appreciate such displays. Maybe that's a sign of a sinful nature, but I think it's only my natural dignity—Jack would laugh at that, and maybe my mother and father would, too, but I think it's true—coming to the fore.

There were lots of songs, too, and several people who belonged to the Stricklands' entourage (including Edward and Charles, which surprised me) sang "Do Lord" and "Swing Low, Sweet Chariot" better than I'd heard them sung before or since. Fancy that: Edward and Charles (or Charles and Edward; I still couldn't figure out who was which) singing. Amazing. Then there was Esther, who sang a couple of solos and made me wish I'd been born with a soprano voice. In truth, everything about her made me feel puny and small and not worth much.

Therefore, since watching Esther made me miserable, I amused myself by watching the rest of the people who'd decided to attend the revival that evening. I didn't stay amused for very long. When one of the quartets was singing "All Hail the Power of Jesus' Name," I glanced at a clump of folks who were standing beside the riser where the preaching and singing went on, and I saw Phil and Esther, looking quite comfortable together and chatting. Phil had that lazy grin of his on his face, and Esther was simpering. Doggone it, Phil hadn't been to town all day long, not even for Kenny's funeral—and he certainly hadn't bothered to see *me*—but he'd come to town for the revival meeting.

I was about to look at something else, that particular sight making me feel sick to my stomach, when I noticed something interesting. Reverend Strickland came up behind Esther, took her arm, and said something into her ear. He had a frown on his face. She turned around, looked as if she wanted to tell him a thing or two, but didn't, and walked away with him, leaving Phil with a smile and a wave.

Hmm. Interesting, although not so interesting that I aimed to watch Phil anymore, mainly because I didn't want to see Esther come back and fawn over him again. Nuts.

So I allowed my gaze to wander elsewhere. That didn't make me feel a whole lot better, since the first couple it landed on was Josephine Contreras and my brother-in-law Richard huddled together at the back of the tent. They looked as if they were making plans, and I couldn't think of a single plan they might come up with that would be good for my family. In a tent revival, too! I couldn't decide if I was more shocked than worried or the other way around, but I sure hoped I was wrong about those two. The little bit of conversation I'd overheard in the library came crawling back into my head, as insidious as ants at a picnic, and I swatted it away. Any conjectures I could come up with were too ugly to be borne. Yet I couldn't figure out what benign purpose would have Josephine and Richard chatting together like a couple of base conspirators. Over and over again, too, what's more.

My mood wasn't enhanced when Hazel Fish spotted Myrtle and me in the congregation and scuttled over to sit with us. I darned near let out a groan. "Oh, Annabelle, I'm so glad you came this evening."

"Thanks, Hazel," I said without much enthusiasm.

Myrtle was more generous than I. "Isn't Reverend Strickland a wonderful speaker?"

Her eyes sparkled and she looked as if she fancied herself in love with Strickland. I wondered what had happened to her enchantment with Sonny Clyde, who was ever so much better looking—not to mention a whole lot more entertaining—than the preacher, but I didn't ask. Anyhow, she was talking to Hazel.

"He sure is. And Miss Strickland has the voice of an angel."

An angel? Maybe, but it was increasingly my opinion that she didn't act like one. I didn't share *that* sentiment with my companions, either.

After one more long, loud, impassioned sermon, we all got to sing for a while. Since I like to sing, that part of the meeting was enjoyable, if you discounted the fact that my heart was broken and the fellow I'd assumed I'd marry one day was ignoring me and devoting himself to a woman whom I *knew* was unworthy of him even though I had no proof of that and she'd only ever been nice to me, the vile seductress. She was a villain. Actually, both of them—Phil Gunderson and Esther Strickland—were villains. Not literally, of course.

I tried not to think about it.

"I'll be back in a minute," said Hazel, rising from her seat next to me.

Please don't bother, is what I wanted to tell her, but I didn't. I only said, "Okay."

Lots of other people besides Hazel started moving around during the singing, probably because their sitters were sore from having endured being verbally whipped by the preacher for forty-five minutes while sitting on hard wooden benches. As we sang "Amazing Grace," one of my favorite hymns, I saw Hazel, whom I had assumed had got up to get a glass of water from the back of the tent, fawning over Reverend Strickland.

Boy, I didn't understand what she and Myrtle saw in that man. True, he had a wonderful speaking voice, but he used his voice to ill purpose, if you asked me. Not that anybody did. Also, his looks were against him. While his voice was a powerful instrument, his physical person was reedy and small, and he looked trifling and insignificant to me. Or like a malnourished rat. I allowed as how I might have an itsy-bitsy hint of a prejudice against him because of his sister and his calling, but I still couldn't see why the rest of the girls in town swooned so darned much. Perhaps they were mistaking him for his message or something, if you know what I mean. Since I didn't much care for his message, either, I was still stumped. The man didn't appeal to me one little bit.

Anyhow, Hazel was gushing all over Reverend Strickland, who was smiling and nodding and seemed more than a little pleased with himself, and the rest of us were singing, when I saw Esther Strickland join her brother and Hazel. She said a few words, her face wreathed in smiles. It was interesting to watch the expression of rapture on Hazel's face fade. It was as if she were a watercolor painting somebody had left out in a storm. All her animation ran down her face like colors running in the rain. Then she said something, probably "Excuse me," or the equivalent, turned around and walked toward the back of the tent. She got a couple of paces away from the preacher and his sister, then ran for the opening. I thought she might be crying and felt a little sorry for her, although not quite sorry enough to go after her and find out what was wrong and try to comfort her. I know, I'm not a nice person.

I'd forgotten all about Hazel, and Myrtle and I and the rest of the congregation were clapping and singing a rousing version of "When the Roll Is Called Up Yonder," when Hazel came back. Even though I was supposed to be under the influence of Jesus by that time, I found myself not pleased to see her. She seemed to have recovered her composure. In actual fact, she was grinning like the Cheshire cat in *Alice In Wonderland.* Although I didn't much care to know why she'd endured this transformation, I was trying to be nice, so as soon as "When the Roll Is Called" was over, I asked her, "What's got you so excited all of a sudden?"

"I can't tell you now," she said. She would. Always trying to drum up drama, Hazel was. "But I *can* tell you that your little brother is a brat."

"I already knew that."

"Do you know that he and the Wilson boys are out there playing baseball when they're supposed to be in here at the revival meeting?"

"I suspected as much."

"They ought to be in here."

"I'm sure they should."

"I told Jack so, too."

Oh, boy. I bet that went over really well with my brainless brother. "Oh? And did he drop his ball and bat and rush to the tent to be saved?"

Hazel snorted. "I should say not. He chased me with that stupid bat of his."

That caught my attention. This conduct was more outrageous than usual, even for Jack. "Oh, dear. I'm really sorry, Hazel." I meant it sincerely, too, and wished I could tell Ma and Pa about my brother's horrid behavior without being considered a tattletale. "Jack's a real brute these days."

Hazel pruned up her lips. I guess she was trying to look like a long-suffering Christian martyr or something. "That's all right, Annabelle. Boys will be boys."

Oh, brother. I'd heard *that* one before—and always in reference to Jack, who didn't deserve to be let off the hook so easily in my opinion. *Boys will be boys,* my foot. "I guess. But I wish Jack would snap out of it. He's been a real monster lately, and I don't think people ought to excuse his outrageous behavior. They *ought* to tell our parents." If Hazel told on Jack, at least *I* wouldn't be blamed for tattling.

"That's not the *only* thing I saw out there, either." I guess Hazel found Jack too piddly a subject for her dramatic tendencies.

Not that I blamed her for not wanting to talk about my brother, since I didn't either, but I also didn't especially want to hear her other tale, either, since her tone of voice reeked with impending gossip. That being the case, I said merely, "Oh."

With much titillation, she said, "I'll tell you all about it later. And it's going to knock the socks off of everyone in Rosedale, too. Just you wait."

Guess I'd have to, which was all right with me. I was annoyed by Hazel's coyness. Here I was, trying to be a good Christian girl and behaving nicely to her—which was honestly and truly a hard thing to do sometimes, this being one of the times—and she played this silly game and made me want to wallop her. Maybe Hazel Fish was a test sent by God to see what I was made of. Well, I knew what I was made of: a whole bunch of petty human failings. I'm pretty sure I sighed again.

After we sang the last note of "When the Roll Is Called," the pianist struck up the opening chords of "The Battle Hymn of the Republic," and Hazel leaned over and whispered in my ear, "Just wait, Annabelle. You won't believe it! Nobody will!"

Since she apparently wasn't going to tell me what I wasn't going to believe, I became even more annoyed with her. "Yeah?" said I, and attempted to drown out with song any further efforts of communication that Hazel might make. Myrtle winked at me, and I felt a little better about things, although I devoutly wished Myrtle would return to earth from her heavenly plane and stop worshiping at the altar of Milo Strickland.

Hazel never did get to sling her latest dirty tidbit at us, presuming she had any intention of doing so, because, lo and behold, who should show up at that precise moment but Phil! I pretended not to notice when he came over to us. But when he said, "Hey, Annabelle, can I sit with you?" what could I do?

I said, "Sure," and scooted over. I'd just cleared my throat and begun singing the chorus to "The Battle Hymn" when my happiness in Phil's company suffered a severe setback. All of a sudden, as if she'd materialized out of thin air, Esther Strickland appeared before us. She leaned over and whispered something in Phil's ear.

Rising, Phil said, "I'm sorry, Annabelle, I have to help Esther out for a little bit." He rose from the space I'd just made for him.

Esther gave me one of her angelically innocent smiles. "I'm so sorry to intrude, Miss Blue, but my brother needs Mr. Gunderson for a minute." And she took Phil's arm and waltzed off with him.

Well! You can bet I saw red for a second, but then I calmed down. At least Phil had sought me out. If Esther had decided she didn't want him to have done so, I don't suppose it was Phil's fault. Well . . . all right, so it was Phil's fault in that he evidently hadn't repelled her advances. Heck, maybe he didn't even realize they *were* advances. He was a pretty naïve guy in many respects, and some men have absolutely nothing between their ears except blocks of wood when it comes to women.

Not only that, but the bitter truth was that even I wasn't sure Esther's motives were impure. Maybe she wasn't trying to lure Phil from my side. Maybe she'd told the truth, and it had been Milo Strickland who'd asked her to fetch him. She exuded an air of innocence that was almost too perfect for me to believe, but my judgment about people isn't always the best. I'd learned that the hard way during the summer, during which I'd mentally accused all sorts of people of murder, when the real murderers were a couple of folks I wouldn't have suspected in a million years.

Oh, pooh. I told myself that life just stank at the moment, and that it would get better eventually. Presuming I lived long enough, maybe I'd even be happy again one day. That thought made me think of Kenny and how he'd never get to see another day, much less go through the ups and downs of life, and I got all melancholy again.

Naturally both Hazel and Myrtle had seen Esther spirit Phil away. Myrtle, still singing, looked at me with an expression of such sympathetic understanding on her face that it galled me. Hazel went so far as to pat my hand. Then she leaned over and whispered, "Don't worry, Annabelle. By this time tomorrow, Phil will have seen the error of his ways. Believe me. In fact, everybody in Rosedale will know the truth."

I had no idea what *that* was supposed to mean, and I didn't appreciate the sentiment, being too peeved by Phil's defection and Myrtle's sympathy to appreciate anything at all at that moment. I just nodded at her to show her that I'd heard what she'd said, even if I didn't have a notion on earth what she meant by it, and continued singing. To heck with Phil Gunderson and Esther Strickland and Milo Strickland and Hazel Fish and Myrtle Howell and everybody else. I only wanted them all to go away and leave me alone. And, since I knew they weren't going to do that, I wanted to go away and leave *them* alone. Instead, I had to sit there, singing, and then endure another bout of fervent prayers from Reverend Strickland.

All in all, Sunday was a really lousy day.

It didn't get any better when, much later, after we'd all gone to bed, my entire family was awakened out of a sound sleep by the shrill ringing of the telephone. I was the first one to stumble out of bed, grab a robe, and stagger to the kitchen to answer it. When I bent over to retrieve the clock I'd knocked off my bedside table, I saw that it was twelve-fifteen. On Monday morning! I don't think I'd ever been awake at that hour of the morning before in my entire life, the nightlife in and around Rosedale being somewhat limited.

"Hello?" I said groggily, sounding sort of like one of the bullfrogs that inhabit the banks of the Spring River during the summertime.

"Is this the Blue residence?" a familiar female voice on the other end of the wire asked. I couldn't place it at first. I thought it sounded worried.

"Yes, this is Annabelle Blue."

"Oh, Annabelle!"

It was then I recognized the voice of Mrs. Fish, Hazel's mother. I got a sickish sensation in my stomach in anticipation of something awful to come. Nobody ever called other people at that hour of the morning unless they carried bad news. More awake now, I said, "What's the matter, Mrs. Fish?"

"It's Hazel! Have you seen her?"

Had I seen her? For a second I didn't understand the question. Of course, I'd seen her. Then it dawned on me what Mrs. Fish's question was meant to imply. "You mean recently? I mean, in the last few minutes or something?"

"Yes!" The poor woman sounded hysterical now.

"No, I'm sorry, Mrs. Fish, but I haven't. I saw her at the revival meeting this evening. Last evening, I mean, but I haven't seen her since then."

"Did you see her leave the tent with anyone?"

"Well . . . she left with Myrtle and me, actually, but then Myrtle and I walked home and I'm not sure where Hazel went. Why? You mean she hasn't come home yet?" I was becoming more alert, not to mention more alarmed, by the second.

"Yes!" wailed Mrs. Fish. "Oh, Annabelle, I'm just sure something awful has happened to her!"

"I . . . I can't imagine what." It was a stupid thing to say. "But let me get Pa. Maybe he and I can go out looking for her or something."

"Thank you." Poor Mrs. Fish started sobbing.

"Have you called the police station? I think they've got someone on duty all night."

"I'll do that now. Maybe Chief Vickers can organize a search party." Willard Vickers was the chief of police in Rosedale.

Technically, I suppose Mrs. Fish should have called Tom Greene, who was the Chaves County Sheriff, since the revival tent had been set up outside the city limits, but usually folks called the police station first and then the sheriff if it became necessary.

"Good idea. You call, and I'll run by the police station as soon as I'm dressed. Maybe I can show Chief Vickers where I last saw Hazel." The station was only a block away from our place.

"Oh, Annabelle, you're such a good friend to my Hazel."

If she only knew. Nevertheless, I muttered something meant to be consoling, said good-bye, hung the receiver on the hook and turned to see Ma and Pa and Jack all standing there, staring at me with bleary eyes. "Hazel Fish didn't go home after the revival meeting."

Ma clutched her wrapper to her throat. "Why, Annabelle, whatever do you mean?"

I thought I'd expressed myself pretty plainly, but maybe Ma was as groggy as I'd been. "I mean the person on the telephone was Mrs. Fish asking if I'd seen Hazel. I told her I'd seen her at the revival meeting, but not since. Then she said Hazel never made it home from the tent meeting."

Ma and Pa exchanged a glance. Jack said, "Let's go look for her!" He sounded bright and chipper and not the least as if he'd just been awakened from a sound sleep and then heard distressing news. Didn't I tell you he was a fiend?

He'd turned, presumably to rush to his room and get dressed, when Ma grabbed him by the tail of his pajama top. "Not you, young man. You're not going anywhere."

"Ma!" Jack cried piteously.

"No," said Pa in a voice I recognized. "You've got to go to school tomorrow, young man."

"But, Pa!"

"Jack," said Ma in that voice of hers.

Jack heaved a gigantic sigh. "Aw, shucks." But he shuffled on back to his room. I regret to say that I experienced a moment of grim satisfaction that my horrid brother's bad behavior was being curtailed. Ma followed him down the hall, I expect to make sure he did as he'd been told to do. You couldn't trust Jack to behave himself unless he was closely supervised.

I started off to my own room to change clothes when Pa asked, "Are they going to look for the girl?"

"Yeah. Mrs. Fish is going to call Chief Vickers and get a search party organized. I thought I'd stop by the police station after I get dressed and tell them the little I know about where I saw Hazel last."

"I'll go, too. The more people who look, the sooner we'll find her, I reckon."

"I guess."

"What can have happened to the girl?" Pa asked. I assume it was a rhetorical question, since I sure didn't have a notion.

"I don't know, but I told Mrs. Fish I'd help look."

"Annabelle," said Ma, who'd hesitated in the hall. "Why don't you leave any searching to the men."

Puzzled, I asked, "Why?"

"Well . . . in case they find anything . . . anything unpleasant."

"Unpleasant?" Then it dawned on me. "You mean in case they find her *dead?*"

"Annabelle." She frowned. "Really, you're such a tomboy. I wish you'd behave in a more ladylike manner. This behavior is most unbecoming."

Oh, boy. Here we were, living at the end of the earth, in Rosedale, New Mexico, home of cowboys and Indians and assorted outlaws, for Pete's sake—well, okay, so there weren't any Indians around any longer—but still. "Ma, something might have happened to Hazel. Maybe she fell down and sprained her ankle and couldn't get up again or something. I'm sure nothing worse could have happened to her. For heaven's sake, we don't live in . . . in Chicago!" That was the worst place I could think of at that time of night. The newspaper headlines were always screaming about gang warfare in Chicago and people shooting each other with Tommy guns and stuff like that.

Ma sighed. "Very well. Change your clothes and go out with your father. But stay with the men. Don't go wandering off on your own."

"I promise I won't go off by myself, Ma." I wasn't so fond of running around in the pitch dark that I'd do anything so stupid. Even if there weren't any Tommy-gun-toting bootleggers hiding out in the brush to shoot innocent citizens, there were plenty of gopher holes and rattlesnakes and scorpions and cacti and stuff like that lurking on the desert. No sensible person would tackle such a search alone, even in the daytime, much less at night.

It took all of five minutes for me to rebraid my hair and put on some dungarees and a shirt and grab a sweater. Then, while Pa was still struggling into his clothes, I ran to the police station, my flashlight bobbing wildly. I'd remembered to stuff a couple of extra batteries in my pocket, which, considering the lateness of the hour and the fact that I'd been sound asleep not ten minutes earlier, bespeaks a sensible nature. At least I think it does.

I was wrong about nothing worse happening to Hazel Fish than a sprained ankle. I was out near the revival tent with Earl Wilcox, a deputy sheriff (I guess Chief Vickers called the sheriff's department), holding my flashlight and bellowing Hazel's name when Chief Vickers, who had brought along his bloodhound Harley, set up a holler. "Over here!"

You might think it's easy to figure out where sounds are coming from on a normal night, but that's probably because you've never been searching for someone out on the southeastern New Mexico desert on a dark, cloudy night, with no illumination anywhere except what's coming from your flashlight. Earl called back, "Where are you?"

"Over here!" That helped a little, but not much.

However, we found them eventually by following the cries and mutters coming to us from the dark: a little clump of people standing around with Harley the bloodhound, who was merrily snuffling the ground at the chief's feet and wagging his tail. I adored Harley, but that isn't the point. As soon as Chief Vickers saw me, he said, "Don't come any closer, Miss Annabelle. I don't want you to see this."

Oh, dear. This sounded ominous. Earl and I looked at each other, then Earl left me with the flashlight and went over to the group of men. They were all gazing down at something on the ground. I had a horrible suspicion I knew what it was, and darn it, I wanted to see. If it was Hazel at whom they peered—and I presumed it was, because why else would they all be standing there looking as if they weren't sure what to do with themselves?—I wanted to know what had happened to her.

So I inched forward, trying to be inconspicuous. That wasn't too difficult, given the circumstances—meaning, of course, the lack of daylight and the interest the men were taking in something other than me. When I got to the ring of men, I stood on my tiptoes and peered over Earl's shoulder, since he was the shortest man there.

What I saw, thanks to several flashlights aimed at the ground, made me feel sick. I presume it was Hazel—or, I should say, Hazel's body. You couldn't really tell who it was because the poor thing's face had been battered, literally, to a bloody pulp. I swallowed hard and almost wished I hadn't been so nosy. On the other hand, I'd helped look for her, hadn't I? I deserved to see the results of our search, even if they were ugly. They were very, *very* ugly.

And, since I was there, I decided to butt in. What the heck. "Is . . . is it Hazel?" Squinting into the darkness, I couldn't make out what color the body's clothing was, or even if it was clad in a dress or trousers. Even under the light of several flashlights, it was much too dark, and there were too many shadows to see much except the horrible mess that had been made of the body's head and all the blackness that was, I presumed, blood. The scene reminded me of something out of a particularly grim motion picture—the kind I don't like to see.

Sheriff Greene frowned at me. "I thought we told you to stay back."

"Yeah, well, I didn't," said I. I'm not generally sassy with law-enforcement officers, but I was curious. And feeling guilty and sick.

"It looks like it's Hazel," Pa said, understanding why I'd come over to look. Good old Pa. He shined his flashlight away from the battered face to the clothes on the body. "Do you remember what Hazel was wearing this evening, Annabelle?"

Yeah, I remembered. Hazel had been wearing a brown-and-white-striped skirt and a white blouse and a brown sweater. I recognized the skirt and gulped. "Um . . . yes. That's her, I guess. I remember that skirt."

Sheriff Greene shook his head and appeared even grimmer than before. His jaw bunched like he was grinding his teeth. He muttered, "Damn," which was most unusual, as the sheriff generally watched his language.

I cleared my throat. "Um . . . how did it happen?"

"We don't know," said the sheriff.

"I mean, how did she get so . . . battered?"

"Blunt force trauma."

"With what?" We lived in the middle of nowhere, and there

132

weren't a whole bunch of trees around from which someone might grab a heavy branch if he were inclined to batter someone to death.

I got the feeling the sheriff didn't appreciate my questions. He frowned at me. "We don't know yet."

They might not know, but as I recalled the events of the past evening, I had a sinking feeling I might, although I didn't relish the notion. I allowed my flashlight to play around the field surrounding the men. Yup. There it was. "I think you'll find the instrument that did the deed right there," I said, focusing the light from my flashlight on the thing lying between a couple of scrub creosote bushes. Jack's baseball bat. I remembered only then that, while I'd seen him carrying the bat to the tent, I hadn't seen him bring the bat home from the revival meeting. Darn that little monster, anyhow!

I heard a gasp and was pretty sure it came from Pa. I nodded. "Yes, Pa. I'm afraid it's Jack's bat."

"Are you sure?" I *knew* Pa had asked that question.

I took a deep breath. "Yes. See? It's got blue tape wrapped around the grip. Jack put that tape on a week or so ago." I didn't think it necessary to point out that the wide part of the bat was matted with a substance that looked black, but which was probably blood. I also didn't mention that Jack had taken the blue tape from our dry-goods store without asking, since, even though I don't like my younger brother much, I'm not a snitch.

"Good God." Like the sheriff, Pa seldom took the Lord's name in vain. Maybe he didn't that time, either. I'm not sure where *Good God* falls in the overall scheme of English-language blasphemies. "What's his bat doing out here?"

I hesitated, wondering if I should tell on Jack. Then I glanced at Hazel's body, and the sight of her made up my mind for me. "He took it with him when we went to the revival tent."

Pa looked at me as if I'd smacked *him* with a baseball bat. "What did he take the bat for?"

I shook my head, feeling guilty about revealing Jack's dirty secret. "Um . . . I'm not sure. Hazel—" Suddenly my throat closed up and I had to swallow again. "Um . . . I don't know." It was a lie. And I really thought my brother was a louse. But I just couldn't make myself reveal the extent of his villainy.

Pa said, "Damn that boy," a sentiment with which I concurred even if it was improper, I suppose.

He moved toward the bat, but Chief Vickers took his arm. "Hold on there, Will. Don't touch it. Don't want to mess up any finger marks."

Finger marks. That's right. They might be able to tell who'd wielded the bat by checking for fingerprints. Except . . . "I expect all the kids in town will have left their prints on that bat, Chief Vickers. They were most of them out in this field playing ball this evening during the meeting."

Pa's head whipped around. "What do you mean, Annabelle? You went to the revival, didn't you?"

Oh, boy. One more look at what was left of Hazel prodded me onward. Besides, Jack didn't deserve any protection from me. I said firmly, "*I* did. Jack didn't. He and some of his friends played baseball instead."

"I'm going to skin that boy one of these days," Pa muttered.

It couldn't happen soon enough to suit me. "I guess he left the bat in the field," I said, thinking that, as idiotic as my brother was on an everyday basis, he didn't generally do things like leave his property lying about. Unless it had been. . . .

No. I couldn't make myself think about that. Jack couldn't have done . . . that—I looked down at the body that used to be kind of a friend of mine—could he? I shuddered.

"Where's your boy now, Will?" asked the sheriff.

"Where is he?" Pa looked confused for a second. "Why, he's

home, I reckon." He turned to me. "Isn't he home, Annabelle?"

I nodded, although with Jack, you could never be quite sure. "He has school tomorrow, so you and Ma wouldn't let him come out here and search for Hazel."

"Yeah. I didn't want him running around and getting in the way, either," said my father, for once voicing an opinion I agreed with.

"Maybe I ought to go to your house and talk to him," said Sheriff Greene. "You know, just to ask him if he remembers seeing Hazel earlier this evening."

My stomach pitched and for a second I wasn't sure what to do. Should I tell the sheriff that Jack and Hazel had an altercation? That, according to Hazel, Jack had chased her with the baseball bat? If I did, and if Jack lied about it, it might go hard on Jack. Then again, Jack probably deserved a little suspicion landing on him. Naturally, as rotten as he was, I didn't believe for a minute that he'd—

Oh, Lord.

CHAPTER SEVEN

Earl Wilcox waited beside the body for the coroner, Dr. Bassett, to arrive. (Dr. Bassett was our local dentist; I'm not sure why the dentist—and not one of Rosedale's many medical doctors—was chosen to be coroner, but he was.) The rest of us headed back to our house. Sheriff Greene carried the baseball bat, wrapped in a piece of oilskin he'd had in the back of his sheriff's car.

Ma met us at the door. I guess she hadn't been able to get back to sleep. Or maybe she'd had a premonition of what we were going to find—not that she could possibly have anticipated the terrible end poor Hazel had met. I'd never taken much to Hazel, for reasons already expressed probably too often, but I sure never wanted her to be beaten to death with a baseball bat. The mere notion made me shudder. Poor Hazel. Anyhow, Ma was dressed and had a pot of coffee on the stove when Sheriff Greene, Chief Vickers, Pa and I entered through the back door of our place, which led into the kitchen.

"Did you find her?" Ma was wiping her hands on her apron. I noticed the oven in the stove had been lit—Pa had ordered a self-regulating stove from the Sears and Roebuck catalog a year or so before—and I hoped Ma had a coffee cake or some other kind of delicious goody baking in there. I was hungry.

I guess we were all feeling pretty glum, because a general exchange of glances took place, although nobody spoke to answer Ma's question. Then Pa nodded at me and I realized I'd been elected spokesperson. Lucky me. "We found her body. Or Harley did, I reckon." I looked at Chief Vickers, who nodded. "Yeah. Harley found her body."

"Her *body?*" Ma's eyes grew huge.

I nodded. "I'm afraid so."

"Sweet heaven have mercy!" Ma cried, horrified. Her hands flew to her mouth. "What in the name of heaven happened to the child?"

Again nobody spoke for several seconds. This time it was Sheriff Greene who nodded at me. I heaved a sigh. Why me, Lord? "Somebody bashed her head in with Jack's baseball bat."

I don't think I've ever seen Ma's eyes open so wide. She sank into a chair. "What . . . what . . . *Jack's* baseball bat? I—I don't understand."

She understood, all right. She just didn't want to. I pulled out a chair, sat in it, and sighed again. "Jack and the Wilson boys and a few other kids didn't go to the revival this evening, Ma. They played ball out in the field instead. God knows how they managed to see anything in the dark," I muttered, then regretted my choice of words. Hurrying on before Ma or Pa could take me to task, I said, "I guess the tent spilled some light onto the field or something. Anyway, they played ball out there while the meeting was going on."

"I'm going to skin that boy," Pa said again, sounding more forceful about his intentions this time. Maybe I'd help him do it.

"Oh, but Will, I'm sure. . . ." Ma didn't reveal what she was sure of.

"He's been getting real wild lately, Susanna," said Pa. "And I aim to see that he starts behaving like a child of ours before another day passes."

Ma commenced chewing her lip, but she didn't argue anymore.

"I suppose he's asleep?" This, from the sheriff.

"Yes, but he won't be for long." Pa rose from his chair with an air of grim determination.

Ma grabbed his hand. "Oh, Will, don't wake him up. He has to go to school tomorrow. Today."

I looked at my folded hands, which were resting in my lap, my heart aching and a lump in my throat. But I had to tell what I knew. To do otherwise would have been withholding evidence that might be useful, although I hoped like anything it turned out not to be. Sucking in a big breath for courage, I said, "He chased Hazel with that baseball bat last night, Ma. Hazel told me he did it when she told him he ought to be in the revival tent instead of playing baseball."

Ma gasped and let go of Pa's hand. Looking more forbidding than I'd ever seen him, Pa continued on into the hall leading to the bedrooms.

After a moment of silence as everyone digested this latest revelation of my brother's wretched behavior, Sheriff Greene said, "He did, eh? He chased her with the bat?"

I nodded, feeling about as lousy as I'd ever felt. Then I said hurriedly, "But I'm sure he was only teasing her. Jack would never do anything like . . . that." I flapped a hand uselessly in the air, praying I was right.

"Well. . . ." Again Ma's voice petered out before she got a whole sentence spoken. She made up for it when she opened her mouth once more. "But please sit down, fellows. I don't know where my manners are. I've got something baking in the oven for you." She rose from her chair and went to the stove. Picking up a folded-over dish towel, she reached into the oven and removed a pan.

The lawmen did as she'd requested, pulling out chairs and sitting down. Sheriff Greene said, "That's right nice of you, Mrs. Blue." Very carefully, he put under his chair the tarpedwrapped baseball bat he'd been carrying. I eyed the thing with loathing, glad when it was out of sight. I didn't like the notion that it was in our house. It was as if the instrument of murder defiled the place or something.

"Sure is nice, ma'am," agreed Chief Vickers. "This is the first good thing to happen tonight."

I'd been right about Ma. She'd fixed a coffee cake to go with the coffee, God bless her. My mother has the instincts of a saint. Jack's stupid behavior is no reflection on our parents, who are both good people and who had always tried to teach him better—and their teachings worked on the rest of their children. Jack's just always been different. Or maybe difficult is the word I mean. I couldn't wait to see what disciplinary measures Pa aimed to impose on him. Jack certainly needed them.

"I'll help, Ma," I said, getting up and fetching a platter for the cake.

So she cut the coffee cake and I got a spatula, scooped the pieces out onto the platter, and carried them to the table, piping hot and steaming and smelling of cinnamon. Ma had already set out cups and milk and sugar for the coffee, and plates for the cake. I fetched several teaspoons and forks and said, "Here you go, gentlemen."

"Thank you kindly, Mrs. Blue, Miss Annabelle," said Chief Vickers, who dearly liked his food. His tummy pooched out over his belt a little more every day, or so it seemed.

Pa came back a minute later, leading Jack by the arm. Jack looked a little woolly and bewildered, and he was rubbing his eyes as if he'd just been awakened from a deep sleep, which he had. "You sit right there, young man," Pa said, shoving Jack into a chair and not being gentle about it. "Sheriff Greene and Chief Vickers have some questions to ask you, and I want you to answer them. Do you hear me?"

Jack, beginning to look a little worried, eyed Pa and said,

"Sure, Pa. I'll answer anything they want to ask." He glanced around the kitchen and reached for a piece of coffee cake, but Pa smacked his hand away.

"You can wait to stuff your face until you've answered those questions, young man."

Pa *never* called anyone "young man." He was more upset than I'd seen him since we got the telegram telling us my older brother George, an aeroplane pilot, had been shot down over France in the Great War. George survived so it turned out all right, but we all had a few rough days as we waited for word about his fate.

Frowning, Jack said, "Shoot. Okay, okay."

"And mind that mouth of yours," Pa commanded gruffly.

"All right." Clearly, Jack felt abused and mistreated. He turned to the sheriff. "Did you find that girl?"

"We did, son. That's what we want to ask you about."

"Me? What do you want to ask me anything for?"

The sheriff reached under his chair and withdrew the cylindrical package that had been resting there. "Well, son, I understand you might know something about this." He didn't put the bloody thing on the table, but carefully held it out and lifted the tarp so that Jack could see the baseball bat.

Jack stared. "What's that?"

"It's your baseball bat," I told him. My voice was hard, too.

"But . . . but what's that stuff all over it?" He reached out, but Sheriff Greene pulled the bat out of his grasp.

"Don't touch it, son."

"Is that my bat?" Jack looked up at me, as if he hoped I'd bail him out. After the way he'd been acting lately, he should have known better.

"It's yours," I said. "Don't you recognize the blue tape you stole from the store?"

"Annabelle!" Ma looked shocked.

"I didn't steal it!" cried Jack. "Hell—"

He didn't get to finish whatever statement he'd been going to make, because Pa smacked him, hard, on the back of his head, almost knocking him out of his chair. I really must be a horrible person, because I was glad of it. Jack had been acting far too badly lately, and I thought it was past time he was called to account for his behavior.

"Don't you ever use that word in this house again, Jack Blue," said Pa in the deadly voice he very seldom used, but which everyone—even Jack—obeyed.

Rubbing the back of his head, Jack said, "Yes, sir." He was sullen now.

"Answer the sheriff's questions, boy," Pa said.

"Yes, sir. But—"

"No buts." Pa said, using *that* voice again.

Jack looked daggers up at him. "I only wanted to know what that stuff on the bat is."

I decided the little beast could use another hard lesson, so I spoke up next. "That *stuff* is blood, Jack Blue. Hazel Fish's blood. Your baseball bat was used to murder Hazel Fish tonight. Someone used it to bash her head in."

He stared at me.

The sheriff glanced at me, too, and I got the feeling he'd just as soon I butt out, so I sat back in my chair, took a piece of coffee cake, and bit into it so as not to say anything else to my bratty brother. I wanted to shriek at him. Maybe use the bat on *him* and see how he liked it.

"So," Sheriff Greene continued. "This is your bat?"

Shooting his sulky glance my way, Jack muttered, "So Annabelle says."

Pa smacked his head again, harder. "Do you want to go outside and get a switch on your backside, boy? You're not too

141

big for me to whup, and if you think you are, I'll show you different."

"For heaven's sake, Jack, just answer the sheriff's questions," said Ma. She was exasperated with him, too, by this time.

"All right, all right. Yes. That's my baseball bat." There were tears in Jack's eyes, but I'm sure they were an automatic reaction to being whacked so hard. I was also sure he'd rather have died like Hazel than cry in front of that group—and probably any other. He was too stupid—or, more likely, too obnoxious, being twelve and all—to leave it at that, but added resentfully, "But I didn't have anything to do with killing that stupid girl."

He must have known he'd said the wrong thing, because he lifted both hands to cover his head. That didn't help much, because Pa lifted him out of the chair by his two arms and shook him as if were a rag doll. I hadn't realized how strong Pa was, but I guess he kept his muscles in tone by lifting supplies off wagons and chopping wood and stuff like that. "One more snotty remark, and you'll regret it for a long time, Jack Blue. I'm ashamed to call you my son."

That was probably the bitterest thing Pa could have said to any of his children. I know that Jack felt it more deeply than he'd felt the various smacks and shakes he'd received thus far that morning. He seemed honestly cowed. Pa slammed him back in his chair and knelt in front of him, not letting go of his arms.

"Now I'm going to tell this you one more time. Answer the sheriff's questions. Don't add any of your sassy remarks, and don't ask why. Just answer the questions. A girl was brutally murdered last night, by means of your baseball bat, which you carelessly left behind after you'd disobeyed your mother and me and played ball instead of attending the revival meeting. And if there's one person in this family who could use a good dose of

Jesus and the Good Book, it's you. Do you understand me, Jack Blue?"

Jack didn't seem to be sullen any longer. His eyes were huge when he said, "Y-yes, sir."

"Do you have anything else you want to say to the sheriff?" Pa punctuated this question with another shake.

Jack looked puzzled for only a moment. Then he licked his lips, looked up at Sheriff Greene, and said, "Sorry, sir."

The sheriff wisely didn't say, "That's all right," or anything of that nature. He only nodded and said, "Now, son, you confirm that this is your baseball bat?"

"Yes, sir."

"And you took it with you tonight when you and some other fellers went out to the revival tent?"

"Yes, sir."

"You didn't go to the meeting?"

Jack didn't hang his head, but he looked mighty uncomfortable. "No, sir."

"You and some of your friends played baseball instead?"

"Yes, sir."

"And during the time you played ball, did Miss Fish see you playing ball in the field, Jack?"

Jack took a deep breath and nodded. "Yes, sir."

"Did she speak to you?"

After licking his lips, Jack said, "Yes, sir."

"What did she say?"

"She said we ought to be in the tent and not playing baseball."

Pa muttered something under his breath, but I didn't hear what it was. Probably just as well.

The sheriff went on, "And did you chase Miss Fish at that time, and threaten her with your baseball bat?"

After a brief hesitation, Jack said, "But it was only a joke. I never—"

I guess Jack saw Pa make a movement as if to do something else to him, because he shut his mouth and when he opened it again, he only said, "Yes, sir."

"And did Miss Fish leave you alone after that?"

"Yes, sir."

"And when the revival meeting was over, did you go home with your friends?"

"Well, yes. You see, we'd stopped playing ball after the lights in the tent went so low we couldn't see anymore. Then we just loafed around and talked. I-I guess I forgot my bat after that. I sure never hit anybody with it." He shot a glance at Pa to see if this interjection would earn him another smack. It didn't, although Pa looked as if he'd just as soon flush Jack down the drain as acknowledge his presence in his house.

"All right. Now, can you give me the names of the other boys who were playing ball with you last night?"

"None of them—" Another movement on Pa's part brought this editorial comment to a halt. Jack cleared his throat. "Um . . . there was Jesse Lee Wilson. Adolph Wilson. Bill Wilson. Um . . . Clarence Small and Joe Piney. I guess that was all."

Ma shook her head sadly. "Poor Mrs. Wilson. As if she didn't have enough worries without you leading her sons astray, Jack Blue. I'm ashamed of you. I'll call her up and apologize to her in the morning."

Boy, that must have been a blow, hearing both of his parents tell him how ashamed they were of him in one evening. Morning. Whatever it was by that time.

I had to agree with Ma, though. Mrs. Wilson had a hard life, even when her children didn't misbehave. Her husband, a Methodist preacher who used to ride the circuit between Rosedale and East Grant Plains, had died only a couple of days after their fifth child was born, leaving Mrs. Wilson with five of her own children to rear without a father, as well as six children from his previous marriage to Mrs. Wilson's best friend, who had died years earlier. What's more, she had to rear all those kids in a three-room house, working as a seamstress. It seemed to me, as it must have seemed to my parents, that Jack could have thought of something better to do with his time than get the Wilson kids to play hooky from a meeting that even I could see might have done them more good than a sneaked-in baseball game. Even if the message was delivered by the Reverend Strickland and his seductress of a sister.

Looking stricken, Jack started to say, "I wasn't—" But he didn't get any farther than that, because he glanced at Pa and thought better of it. A wise decision on his part. It was undoubtedly the first wise decision he'd made in a very long time.

Ma just sat there shaking her head and gazing at Jack as if the son she'd born twelve years earlier had turned into a hydra-headed monster before her very eyes. My secret glee was undoubtedly evil of me, but I've already said more than once that I'm not very nice.

The sheriff went on as if he was used to family dramas like this and they didn't faze him. "Do you recall where you left the bat when you boys stopped playing, Jack?"

Jack thought for a minute or two. "We were sitting on the fence a little way from the tent. I guess I put it down there. When the tent emptied, I guess I forgot it was there."

"When people started leaving the tent, what did you boys do?"

"We joined the crowd and headed home."

I was surprised when the sheriff directed his next question at me. "Did you see Jack as you left the tent, Annabelle?"

"No, I don't remember seeing him at all after we left home to go to the revival meeting."

"Well, I was there!" cried Jack, as if I'd told the sheriff he was a liar.

"I didn't say you weren't," I pointed out. "I only said I didn't see you. There were a lot of people there."

"Who were you with, Jack?" asked the sheriff.

"Davy and the Wilson kids," Jack said, as sullenly as he thought he could get away with. I know that because he shot Pa another glance to make sure he wasn't going to get whomped again.

"Good," said Sheriff Greene, making a note. "I'll check with them in the morning."

Jack said, "Huh," and gave yet another glance at Pa, who was standing right next to his chair by that time, towering over him, with his arms folded across his chest. Pa looked as if he was just waiting for the next opportunity so he could knock Jack out of his chair and kick him out into the dark, cruel world. Not that Pa would ever do anything like that. In fact, when he'd mentioned a switch, it had surprised me, since he'd never laid a hand on any of us that I could recall until that night when he'd whupped Jack, who'd more than deserved it.

"And Miss Annabelle," the sheriff went on, "did you say that Hazel was walking with you when you left the tent?"

"Yes. For a minute or so, then she veered off."

"Do you remember which direction she went?"

I thought about it. "Um . . . not really. She walked a few steps with Myrtle and me, and then she wasn't there any longer. At least. . . ." I shook my head. "I'm sorry, but can't remember."

"Do you recall if she said anything to you when she left you?"

I wracked my brain to think of anything Hazel might have said that registered with me. I regretted then that I had become so accustomed to ignoring her. "I don't think so."

"Who else was walking with you at that time?"

"Myrtle Howell and I went to the tent together, and we

walked home together. Hazel walked with us for only a few yards, then she. . . ." Then I remembered something. "Oh, yes! She said she wanted to thank Reverend Strickland again for preaching such a moving sermon. I think she went back to the tent to talk to him."

"I see. All right, then. If you remember anything else that you think might be helpful—anything at all—let me know. All right?"

"Yes, sir," I said, vowing to try to remember every single little tiny thing that had happened the evening before. It just seemed incredible to me that a girl I'd known all my life, had gone to school with, for heaven's sake, had been so brutally murdered. Things like that didn't happen in Rosedale, New Mexico. Kind of like poisoning. Mercy sakes.

"And, Jack, you too. If you can think of anything else, let me know. All right? Anything at all."

Jack said, "Yes, sir." He had finally got his comeuppance, by gum, and I silently rejoiced in the fact, although I felt kind of guilty at the same time. Not about Jack, but about feeling glad of anything at all under the circumstances.

The lawmen rose, and Sheriff Greene chucked the wrapped baseball bat under his arm. I wondered what they were going to do with it. Hold it for evidence, I reckoned. I then wondered if they had equipment to identify fingerprints here in Rosedale, or if they'd have to send the bat to Albuquerque or Santa Fe or someplace like that to have the fingerprinting done. I'd have asked, but such a question didn't seem appropriate under the bleak circumstances.

"Thank you kindly for the coffee cake, Mrs. Blue. Thank you for helping us look for that poor girl, Mr. Blue and Miss Anna-belle."

Pa and I nodded, and I heard Pa say something, but I couldn't make out the words.

"And Jack," said the sheriff. He was standing in front of Jack and looking down at him in what I could only regard as a calculated manner, and I grinned inside. Sheriff Greene might look like a hick, but he knew a thing or two about getting people to pay attention to him. "I think it's about time you remembered where you live and who your parents are. There aren't two finer people living on this earth than William and Susanna Blue, and I should think a feller like you would do everything you can do to make them proud of you." He didn't wait for Jack to say anything, which was just as well—if Jack had been totally humiliated instead of just a little bit humiliated, he might have rebelled even harder—but shook Pa's hand and headed for the back door.

Jack hung his head.

I said, "We'll let you know if we hear anything, Sheriff and Chief Vickers."

"Thank you kindly, ma'am," Chief Vickers said to Ma, giving a last, longing glance at the coffee cake.

Ma and I cleaned up the kitchen after the men left, while Pa and Jack went back to bed, Jack without saying another word to anyone. I was curious to discover if the events of that night would affect his behavior from then on. I was hoping for the best, but not anticipating much, if you know what I mean. The obnoxiousness of twelve-year-old boys is a tenacious disease. Besides, after being called to task that evening, he might even be more inclined to misbehave. Pa might have something to say about that if he tried it.

With a sigh, Ma said, "I don't know what the world is coming to."

I'd collected the plates, forks, cups, and spoons and deposited them on the sink. As Ma began washing the dishes, I wiped down the table. "I sure never expected to find Hazel like. . . ." I couldn't repress another shudder. "Like that. It was really awful, Ma."

"I'm sure it was. I'm sorry you had to see her that way, Annabelle."

"I just hope they catch whoever did it. And soon. It's kind of creepy, thinking there's a vicious murderer in town. And right after Kenny was poisoned, too."

"Mercy sakes, that's right. That's two murders in as many days. In *Rosedale*. I just can't take it in."

"It's pretty astonishing," I agreed. "I wonder if the same person committed both murders."

"I guess whoever it is must have. It's difficult to imagine there being two murderers in a town this small."

"Well. . . ." I didn't want to disagree with my mother, but I'd read lots of murder mysteries. "The thing is that the two murders were so different. Don't murderers generally stick to one method?"

"I have absolutely no idea, Annabelle Blue, and I don't want to." Ma's tone was acerbic as she rinsed the last dish and put it in the drainer.

"Well, I guess I'd rather think there's one person in town murdering people than two of them." I started wiping the dishes dry and putting them away.

Ma had picked up the wash bucket and headed for the door to pour the used water on the vegetable garden out back. She paused at the door and looked at me. "Do you really think it's somebody from town, Annabelle? I can't imagine it."

"Well, I can't either, really. But don't forget that there are lots of people in town these days who aren't *from* here. There are all the rodeo people and all the revivalists. And there are always drummers and salesmen and cattlemen and so forth coming through town, too. We live in a small place, but lots of folks pass through."

She looked thoughtful. "True. That's true."

"It's probably one of them. I can't imagine anybody we

know. . . ." Again, Hazel's bloodied head loomed in my mind's eye, and I tried to shove it out.

Ma shook her head and turned the doorknob. "I just can't believe it."

"It's hard." I tried to keep the image of Hazel's battered head from recurring to my mind's eye, but didn't have much luck. Deciding it would be better not to mention this problem—after all, I had volunteered to search for her and then disobeyed the sheriff when he'd told me not to look at her body—I considered suspects.

There really *were* lots of people to consider. Including Jack. Who slept in the room right next to mine.

Shoot, I wished I hadn't thought about that.

As I was hanging up the dish towel, I remembered how Hazel had acted when she'd come back to our bench after talking to Reverend Strickland, being run off by Esther Strickland, and going outside and being run off by Jack. What was it she'd said to me? Something about having seen something that would knock the socks off the entire town of Rosedale? She never had told me what it was she'd seen, but I decided I'd best tell the sheriff what she'd said to me anyway. I couldn't imagine how it could help him, but you never knew.

When Ma came back indoors, we both went to bed. I didn't think I'd be able to sleep, but I did. Soundly. In fact, Ma had to shake me awake at seven-thirty that morning. She didn't generally let me sleep so late, but I guess she figured I'd had a rough night and needed my rest.

She was right.

CHAPTER EIGHT

For the first time since I could remember, Jack didn't whine about having to do his chores in the store that afternoon after he got home from school, which, following tradition, let out at noon during rodeo days. He swept the whole place out without saying a word. That was fine by me, since I generally had to listen to him gripe and grouse, and it was always difficult for me to keep my temper with him. And, naturally, when I lost my temper, he reacted by being even more of a brute than usual.

That afternoon, however, there were no arguments. In actual fact, there was no noise at all, except for the broom scratching across the scarred wooden floor and then the clunk of tin on tin as Jack restocked the canned-goods section. I peacefully read *The Case of Jennie Brice* when I could tear my thoughts away from Hazel's murder. The occasional customer was certain to come in and interrupt me, but I didn't mind that.

Pa was out back mending the fence, and Ma was in the garden, probably harvesting the seven billion pounds of squash and pumpkins the vines always produced at this time of the year. Even though we Blues owned a dry-goods and grocery store, Ma always preserved as much food as she could in order to save money feeding the family. I loved the results, although I wasn't too keen on helping her can pumpkins and squash. I'd much rather clerk in the store, which was lucky since that's what I generally got to do.

The first person to show up in the store after lunch was the sheriff. Tom Greene was a tall, rangy fellow, a little on the thin side, and with an air of authority Pa claims he got when he was a Texas Ranger. I wouldn't know about that, but I liked him all right. He also had a nice daughter, who was a little bit older than I.

"Hey, Sheriff." Out of the corner of my eye, I saw Jack duck behind a table filled with bolts of fabric. He clearly didn't want another confrontation with the law. Well, we'd see about that.

"How-do, Miss Annabelle?"

"I'm fine, thanks. And you?"

"Tell the truth, I'm a little low, Miss Annabelle. Two murders, and one a young woman." He shook his head.

"I know. The whole town's upset." I shook my head to show how much sympathy I felt for everyone.

"For good reason."

I nodded. "I couldn't agree more." Because I was curious, I asked, "Have you discovered anything? Anything you can tell me about, I mean."

"Not really." Sheriff Greene looked glum. "But that's why I'm here."

My heart scrunched painfully, even though I knew I hadn't killed anyone and there was no reason for it to be acting oddly. "Oh?"

"Yeah. We know all about the weapon that killed Miss Fish, but we haven't traced the poison that killed Kenny Sawyer. Do you recollect anybody buying rat poison recently?"

I blinked a couple of times. "Rat poison?" The notion of anybody feeding anybody else rat poison made my insides curl up in revulsion. "You think it was rat poison that killed Kenny?"

The sheriff removed his hat, scratched his head, and sighed. "Seems most likely. According to Doc Bassett, the kind of poison in Kenny's stomach was the kind that's most often found in rat poison."

Ew. That was totally disgusting. However, I did want to help; therefore, I tried to recall whether I'd sold any rat poison recently. "Well . . . people are always buying rat poison, you know." Especially out here, where farmers and ranchers lived, rat poison was nearly a staple when it came to keeping vermin out of barns and so forth. Shoot, we Blues even used rat poison behind the shelves. We didn't want to sprinkle it out in the open, just in case a kid or a dog or cat might stumble on it.

He heaved a bigger sigh. "Yeah, I know." He sounded tired and discouraged, poor guy.

Wanting to help out if I could, I thought hard. "Let me see. Miss Libby bought some a couple of months ago." Aunt Minnie and Miss Libby lived more in the middle of nowhere than most of us, in a house way out on the desert that used to be the hub of my uncle Joe's ranching operation. Since Joe died, Millie didn't ranch anymore, but there were still acres of land near her house that were home to any number of voles, field mice, ground squirrels, and other pests.

I thought some more. "Phil bought some for his brother's hardware store. He said there were mice in the storeroom. And Miss Whitesmith got some to keep in the break room at the library. I guess somebody saw mouse droppings." I felt my brow wrinkle as I tried to remember anybody else who'd bought rat poison. I didn't think the list I'd offered so far tendered much scope for the sheriff in finding Kenny's murderer, since I couldn't feature any of the folks I'd mentioned having anything to do with so ghastly a crime. Except. . . .

"I suppose anybody might have gone into the Gundersons' barn and found the rat poison they keep there and used it. After all, the whole town was at the Gundersons' for the rodeo."

"Yeah." Another huge sigh issued from the sheriff. "You're right. Well, it was a thought. Let me know if you remember anybody else buying the stuff."

"I sure will. Oh, and Sheriff, last night at the meeting, Hazel told me she'd discovered something that would surprise everyone in Rosedale. Her exact words were that her knowledge, whatever it was, would 'knock the socks off' the whole town."

"Oh?" He perked up slightly. "Did she tell you what this momentous discovery was?"

"Sorry. No, she didn't. She was kind of annoying about it, actually."

His perk popped, and his shoulders drooped. "Yeah. That is real annoying." He plopped his hat back onto his head. "Well, thanks, Miss Annabelle."

"Sure thing, Sheriff. And I'll be sure to let you know if I remember anything useful."

"Or even anything you don't think is useful. You never know about these things."

I imagine he was right about that. "Will do."

The sheriff left, and Jack came out from hiding.

The first customer to show up at the store after that was Myrtle, and she wasn't really a customer any more than the sheriff was. I think she'd just dropped by to chat during her afternoon break from her job at Joyce Pruitt's drugstore next door to Blue's, where she mainly stood behind the cosmetics counter and sold face powder to the old ladies in town. She looked as if she'd been crying.

I didn't feel so hot myself, but I was glad to see her. I smiled when I saw her heading toward the counter and shoved my library copy of *The Case of Jennie Brice* aside. "Hey, Myrtle."

"Oh, Annabelle, did you hear the terrible news? Hazel is dead!"

"I heard," said I. "Heck, I was out searching for her along with some other people last night. This morning, I mean. Mrs. Fish telephoned our house a little after midnight, asking if I'd seen Hazel."

"You were *there?*" Myrtle yanked a hankie from her skirt pocket and blew her nose, which was shiny and red and might profit from discreet use of some of the cosmetics Myrtle sold at Pruitt's.

I nodded. "Mrs. Fish called to ask if we'd seen Hazel because she hadn't come home after the revival meeting. Pa and I went out with the sheriff and Chief Vickers to look for her." Remembering that telephone conversation and the results thereof, I sighed. "I thought maybe she'd fallen and hurt herself or something. Sprained her ankle, maybe. Or been bitten by a rattler. I had no idea. . . ." For some reason, I was reluctant to bring Jack's baseball bat into the conversation.

It turned out I needn't have had any qualms about sullying my rotten brother's reputation, since word had spread already. "Annabelle, I feel so sorry for your poor parents! To think that your brother's baseball bat was the weapon that was used to . . . to *kill* her."

"So that information is out, is it?" Oh, joy. Oh, rapture. Oh, how I wished I could thump Jack on his stupid head! Right where Pa had thumped him. When I glanced around to see if he was there and had heard, I saw him straightening bolts of fabric, head down, shoulders hunched. I reckon he'd heard, all right. Served him right.

Myrtle nodded and stuffed her hankie away. "I just can't believe it. First Kenny and now Hazel. What's the world coming to?"

"What's Rosedale coming to, is more like it," I said, thinking Hazel's demise probably couldn't be laid at the feet of Esther Strickland. Whoever heard of a woman bashing somebody over the head with a baseball bat? Poison, I could believe. This bat thing, I couldn't. A woman bashing another woman was never to be found in any of the mystery novels I read.

"Do you think the same person killed both of them?"

Shaking my head, I said, "I don't know. It's hard to imagine two brutal murderers in a town this size."

"It's hard for me to imagine one of them."

I heaved a sigh. I'd been doing that a lot lately. "Yeah. That's true."

"Pa said he's going to put a lock on the front door. Can you imagine it? Locked doors in Rosedale." She shook her head and sighed, too, the notion that her family might not be safe in the tiny town of Rosedale, New Mexico, where nothing ever happened, being almost too much for her to comprehend, I reckon.

Not that I blamed her. The only reason we Blues locked the doors to our house was because of the store, and the fact that our house was an extension thereof. There are people everywhere who steal—especially when they're poor and hungry. I'm sorry to say that there are poor people everywhere, too, including Rosedale. At least the hardware store owned by Phil's brother would probably be getting a boost in business since he stocked locks. "It's really creepy, isn't it, knowing there's a murderer loose in town. Or maybe even more than one murderer."

"It certainly is." Myrtle glanced around the store, acting kind of surreptitious about it. Leaning over the counter, she whispered, "You don't think that Jack. . . ." Her words trailed off, but I knew what she was thinking. I'd wondered the same thing.

After heaving yet another big sigh and thinking I'd better brace myself for more questions of a like nature, I said softly, "I doubt it. Jack's a pain in the neck and a brat, but I think that's only because he's twelve. I don't think he'd do anything like . . . like that."

Myrtle nodded. "You're probably right. My cousin Dennis was absolutely awful when he was that age, but he got over it."

"I'm beginning to think Jack never will, although he seems to have taken Hazel's murder with his own bat pretty hard.

Especially after the talking-to he got from Pa last night. This morning. Whenever it was." Even though I'd slept late, I was still tired and had to keep smothering yawns.

"Serves him right, if you ask me," said Myrtle. Have I mentioned that she's the best and truest friend a person could have? Even in spite of her new religious streak.

"My sentiments exactly."

More people began trickling into the store. Mae Shenkel came in with Ruby Bond, who had, as I've already mentioned, been a very good friend of Hazel's. Ruby seemed kind of shaky, and I felt sorry for her. I hadn't cared a lot for Hazel, but she'd been a good friend to Ruby, who was shy and plain and could use all the friends she could get. I smiled at the two of them even though I didn't much like Mae, either. Boy, I really needed to drink of the milk of human kindness and work some on my Christian charity, didn't I?

"Hey, Mae. Hey, Ruby."

"Hey, Annabelle," said Mae. Ruby only gave me a crooked smile. I got the feeling she was trying not to cry.

Because I couldn't think of anything better to do, I said, "I'm awfully sorry about Hazel, Ruby. I know you two were close."

Ruby yanked a handkerchief out of her pocket and burst into tears, thereby ruining her best effort to hold her emotions in check. "Oh, Annabelle!"

As you can imagine, I felt like two cents. Maybe less. Ducking under the counter, I hurried over to her. Mae was hugging her on one side, so I took the other side. Myrtle stood in the background making comforting noises. "I'm so sorry, Ruby," I said. "I didn't mean to make you feel worse than you already did."

"No, no," she said, her words thick with tears. "You didn't make me feel bad. You were being kind."

Well, that was a first. "Would you like some water, Ruby? A

cup of tea?"

She shook her head. "I'm sorry. I didn't mean to cry like this."

"Here," I said, hauling up one of the chairs that we keep near the stove, so that people can thaw out on cold days. "Sit down. I'll get you some water."

Ruby sat, and I rushed in back to the house and fetched a glass of water. Ma was there, sweating over a huge kettle filled with canning jars into which she was going to stuff squash, I reckon, and she looked at me oddly. I didn't stick around to explain myself, but filled a glass with water and dashed back to the store. Ruby looked as if she were about done crying, thank God, and was mopping her face.

"Here, Ruby." I thrust the glass at her.

She looked up, gave me a watery smile and said, "Thanks, Annabelle. I don't know why I broke down like that."

Both Mae and Myrtle were kneeling beside her, offering her solace, and I wondered how I'd feel if anything happened to Myrtle. At least as bad as Ruby, I'm sure. That being the case, I said, "It's really hard to lose someone you love, Ruby. Please don't apologize."

Then Mae said, "I hear it was your brother who did it, Annabelle. I'm surprised you opened the store today," and I almost collapsed myself. "Your poor parents must be beside themselves."

"*What?*" I shrieked.

I think the noise shocked Ruby right out of any tendency that might have remained in her to cry. She, Myrtle, and Mae all jumped.

"For heaven's sake, Annabelle—" Mae started, but she didn't get any further because I interrupted.

"Jack did *not* kill Hazel Fish, Mae Shenkel, and I'd really appreciate it if you don't start spreading that rumor around town!"

I almost said something about Mae taking over rumor-mongering duties from Hazel, but, for Ruby's sake, I stopped myself. "My idiot brother left his baseball bat out in the field next to the revival tent, which was stupid of him—especially since he was supposed to be at the revival meeting and not playing baseball—but it was somebody else who used the bat to kill Hazel."

Mae looked doubtful, although Ruby nodded. "I was sure he didn't do it, Mae," she said, bless her. "Nobody from Annabelle's family could do anything so horrid."

"Well—"

Again I interrupted Mae. I'd always kind of resented her big blue eyes and pretty blonde curls, and I knew she was about as bright as your average boulder, in spite of being the high-school principal's daughter, but I'd never known her to be gossipy before. "My brother is a brat and about as loathsome as a boy can be, but our parents didn't rear any murderers, Mae."

A big crash from the west side of the store made us all jump again. We turned to see Jack, his face flaming, scrambling around, picking up tins of Clabber Girl Double-Acting Baking Powder.

Mae grimaced. "Oh, dear, I didn't see him there."

"Would it have made a difference?" I asked.

She looked at me blankly. "Well, of course, it would. I'd never have said that if I knew he could hear."

"Ah," I said—and my voice was like ice. "You only talk about people behind their backs? Is that it?"

Mae hung her head, reminding me of Jack. "I'm sorry, Annabelle. I'm sure that you're right and that Jack didn't do it."

"If he'd done it, don't you think the sheriff would have locked him up?"

I know, I know. I'd suspected the little monster myself. But it's one thing to have doubts about your own detestable brother.

It's quite another thing when people outside the family start shoveling dirt about him at you.

"You're right." Mae brightened. "Of course, he would! Oh, Annabelle, I'm sorry I even mentioned it."

"It's all right, Mae. And it's true that his bat was the weapon used and that he's been behaving like a beast lately, but Jack didn't do it."

"Of course not."

"And I'd really appreciate it if you wouldn't say such things to anyone else."

"Oh, no, I won't," Mae assured me.

As I returned to my position behind the counter, I got the impression that she wasn't entirely convinced of Jack's innocence, but that I'd made inroads. I believed her when she said she wouldn't spread any further rumors. It wasn't so much because I could acquit her of malicious behavior, but because she was thick as a plank and would probably forget all about Jack as soon as she and Ruby left the store. At least I hoped so.

Anyhow, at that moment, the entire Gunderson family—Mr. and Mrs. Gunderson, Phil, and Davy (Phil's three older brothers had married and moved away from the family ranch already)—came into the store, effectively shutting off the gossip tap. And thank God for it, I might add. Mae and Ruby drifted out of the store. Myrtle said, "I'd better go back to work," and after greeting the Gundersons, she left, too.

"Hey, Annabelle," said Phil. He was looking very sober that morning. Well, heck, everybody I'd seen so far that day was looking sober. A couple of murders in town will do that to a community.

"Hey, Phil. Good morning, Mrs. Gunderson, Mr. Gunderson. Davy."

"Hey, Annabelle," said Davy. He, too, looked as if he'd had a bucket of cold water poured over his head. "Is Jack here?"

I pointed to the corner, where Jack had managed to get the baking powder situation under control once more. Davy rushed over to him. "Jack! You all right? I heard about the bat. Can you come to the ranch with me when we go back home today?"

Looking sheepish, Jack swept the store with his gaze. He spoke to Davy under his breath, but I heard him when he said, "I've got to ask my mother and father, Davy. Um . . . and finish my chores first."

"I can help you," Davy offered. I'd often noticed before that people who don't *have* to do things are more eager to do them than the people to whom such tasks are a duty. I guess it's the Tom-Sawyer syndrome or something. Davy turned to his father. "Is that okay, Pa?"

"Sure, go ahead and help Jack." He winked at me, as if he too were amused that his son was so happy to do somebody else's chores. I'll bet Davy's eagerness never occurred at home.

"Is it all right if Jack goes back with you?" I asked Mrs. Gunderson. "I think he'd like to get out of town for a while today." I gave her a significant look, which she seemed to understand.

"I'm sure that's so," said Mrs. Gunderson with a knowing glance at her son and Jack, who had begun talking in very earnest undertones as they straightened shelves.

"Although," I said, after thinking it over for a minute, "maybe it would be good for him to stay here and face the music. So to speak."

Mr. Gunderson chuckled. "You may be right, but we'll see what your folks have to say. According to Davy, school was quite a trial for Jack today."

"Oh, dear." I hadn't even thought about Jack at school. Kids could be really cruel to each other, though, and I suspect his fellow students had teased Jack unmercifully. I wish I could have been there to see it. "Were the kids mean to him?"

"According to Davy, they were," said Phil, who didn't sound

awfully cut up about it.

Mr. Gunderson's smile vanished. "We're not going on with the rodeo. After talking it over and consulting with the sheriff and Chief Vickers, we decided it wouldn't be respectful to continue with what is supposed to be a celebration. Two deaths, and murders, at that . . . well, a celebration simply doesn't seem appropriate."

"I'm sorry to hear that, but I sure do understand. It's a terrible shame that these dreadful things had happened this year, when you folks were hosting the rodeo."

Mrs. Gunderson said, "Well, you know how it is on the last day of the rodeo. We were going to have some demonstration events this afternoon—calf roping and that sort of thing—and have one last potluck supper, and end it all with a big friendly fire and some songs. But after what happened . . . well, we just think it will be better to cut the rodeo short this year."

I sighed. "Yeah, I'm sure you're right. It's such a shame."

Phil said, "The only good thing to come of it is that Pete's business is booming." He called this afternoon to see if I could come to town and help him out." And Phil shook *his* head. "Seems everybody's buying locks and needing wood for bolts to put on their doors."

"I'd heard that Myrtle's parents are putting a lock on their door. I suppose other people will be doing the same thing."

"Are your folks home, Annabelle?" asked Mrs. Gunderson. "George and I want to tell them about the plans for the day."

Mr. Gunderson added, "We thought that, even though we won't have the demonstration events or promote a party atmosphere, we might could have a campfire and some songs and have some sort of . . . what do you call it?" He glanced at his wife, silently asking for clarification.

Mrs. Gunderson helped him out. "A memorial service for the two young people whose lives were so tragically cut short. Not anything formal, or anything, but just a remembrance." She shook her head, too. There'd been a whole lot of head-shaking going on in Rosedale during the past couple of days. "A prayer or two. Some songs. A potluck supper with the whole town contributing a dish or two in honor of the bereaved families. That sort of thing."

I was touched. "That would be very nice. I think everybody would appreciate it, and especially Mr. and Mrs. Fish and Mrs. Sawyer. Ma's in the kitchen boiling jars, and Pa's out back fixing the fence."

I lifted the counter, since I didn't think a couple of old folks like the Gundersons would want to duck under it. Come to think of it, maybe they weren't all that old. I was just used to thinking of my friends' parents as old, I guess.

"Say, Annabelle," Phil said, giving me a shy smile. "Why don't we go back to the ranch together after work?"

"Well . . . I don't know, Phil. I'm probably going to have to drive the family out there this evening."

He appeared disappointed, which was moderately encouraging.

"Or you could go with us," I said, hoping I didn't sound too eager.

"Naw," he said after a few seconds of contemplation. "I guess it was a dumb idea, come to think of it. I reckon I'll be going out to the ranch with Pete and his family."

"Ah. Yes, I suppose so." If anyone had come into the store and seen us, they'd probably have deduced we'd each lost our favorite aunt or something, we both looked so gloomy. Which was almost the case. Although neither of the deceased was a particular favorite of either of us, the circumstances were ghastly enough to give anyone the galloping glooms.

We were both quiet for a moment or two. Then I said, "What a stupid rodeo *this* one's been, huh?"

Phil nodded and looked discouraged. "It sure has been."

"Usually the rodeo is the highlight of the year."

"Yeah. Not this time." Phil jammed his hands into his back pockets.

"But what's going to happen now?"

Leaning against the counter and still looking as if he'd just lost his favorite hound dog, Phil said, "What do you mean?"

"Well. . . ." I shrugged, feeling helpless. "I mean, are the police and the sheriff going to let everyone just leave and go home? All the cowboys and ranchers and people who came to see and participate in the rodeo? Don't they have to talk to them or something? Question them? In order to find the killer, I mean."

"Oh. Yeah, I see. No, Sheriff Greene said nobody's supposed to leave town until his office has finished talking to anybody who might have seen anything."

"But that's probably everybody in the whole town."

He shrugged. "I imagine so."

"Oh, boy, that's not going to make people very happy."

"No, but it has to be done. I guess some of the cowboys were drinking and whooping it up at the wagon yard near our place last night. For all anyone knows, one of them might have done poor Hazel in."

Involuntarily, I grimaced, recalling the ghastly sight of Hazel's bashed-in face. If I hadn't recognized the clothes she'd been wearing, I'd not have known it was her. She. Whatever it's supposed to be.

"I guess that's not impossible. Some guy gets drunk and sees Hazel and tries to . . . uh . . . you know." Dang, I could get myself in more trouble just by opening my mouth than anyone else I knew.

Phil blushed, an endearing trait of his when anything indelicate cropped up in a conversation. "Yeah."

"It's terrible. First Kenny, now Hazel." Those words were a recurring theme that day. For several days, in fact.

Phil heaved himself away from the counter, took his hands out of his back pockets, and sighed. "Well, I'd better get going to Pete's store. He's got a lot of stuff to do, and he wants me there to sell people locks." He shook his head. "It's a crying shame our town has come to this. Locked doors in Rosedale. Wonder what's next." The theme of locked doors in Rosedale was also popular that day.

Phil left to go to Pete's store, and I picked up my book once more. I didn't get much reading done, though. It seemed as if the entire town of Rosedale paid the store a visit that afternoon. Sometimes people bought stuff, but most often they only came in to chat about the murders—and my stupid brother's baseball bat.

It was discouraging to know how many people believed my brother could have done Hazel in. Even people who'd known our family forever had their suspicions. I wished I could hide behind the potbellied stove when I saw Aunt Minnie and Miss Libby storming across the street toward the store.

Jack was washing the west windows with Davy helping him and didn't see Minnie and Libby advancing. It occurred to me to warn him there was trouble headed his way, but I held my tongue. Maybe such reticence on my part was unkind, but in my opinion, it was way past time he understood that his reckless behavior in recent months had given people an impression that he was capable of committing horrible crimes. And if there was anybody on earth who wouldn't hesitate to tell him all about it, it was Miss Libby. That was one of the few times I'd considered Miss Libby to be of use to anyone. Normally, I could think of only one thing that made worthwhile the space Miss Libby took up on the world, and that was her cooking, which was superb.

"Annabelle Blue, whatever is your family is coming to?"

Miss Libby had a very loud voice. Everyone who was in the store at the time started and turned to look. Jack dropped his rag, and I distinctly heard him say, "Aw, shit."

It was definitely the wrong thing to say. Miss Libby bellowed, "Watch your filthy tongue, young man!"

"My family?" My spine stiffened like cement setting, and I glared at the old bat. "I beg your pardon? What do you mean? My family isn't *coming* to anything."

"You heard me, and it is so. What is your family coming to? How did your parents manage to rear such a despicable boy?"

I couldn't argue with her adjective, but her attitude was insufferable. I muttered, "Ask them yourself," and turned to Minnie. While Libby muttered about how rude the younger generation was, I said, "How are you doing today, Minnie?"

"Not so chipper. These terrible murders. Those poor young people. Oh, Annabelle, your uncle Joe is beside himself."

Now that would be something to see, considering Uncle Joe had been dead for almost fifteen years. "I'm sorry to hear that."

Miss Libby, paying no attention to Minnie, which was probably the best thing to do with her, roared, "You! Jack Blue. What the devil do you mean by bringing evil on your family?"

Poor Jack. If I hadn't been so angry with him myself, I might have felt sorry for him. He tried to stand up straight and look Libby in the eye, but she was a mountain of a woman, and I could tell he was scared. "I didn't do anything," he muttered.

"You *did* do something, you insufferable boy! Your wickedness and carelessness led to that poor child's murder! I hope you're ashamed of yourself, because the family is ashamed of you!"

I hoped like thunder Jack wouldn't point out that Miss Libby wasn't technically a member of the family because such a comment, while true, would only escalate the unpleasantness.

He didn't. I breathed a silent sigh of relief when he only repeated sullenly, "I didn't do anything."

"You call disobeying your parents nothing?" Miss Libby screeched. "And then leaving your cursed bat lying about for someone to use as a murder weapon? That's nothing?"

"I didn't kill anyone." Jack sounded a trifle desperate.

"You'd best talk to your Maker, Jack Blue, and ask Him to guide you onto a clean path, because the one you've been traveling lately will lead you only to wickedness and hell." She shook her finger at him. "Your poor parents. I expect they both rue the day you were born. I've never known another member of your family to bring such shame to the name Blue, young man. Your father ought to take you out to the wood pile and teach you the meaning of respect."

Personally, I didn't think walloping a child taught him much about respect, although the threat of it might discourage lousy behavior. I guess a smack or two might be worthwhile for the same reason.

Davy patted Jack on the back. I could tell that Jack was holding something back, but I couldn't tell if it was rage or tears.

"I'm sure Jack already feels bad about the whole thing, Miss Libby," I said, aiming for conciliation. I should have known better. Miss Libby doesn't cotton to being pacified when she's on a rampage.

"Don't you talk back to *me*, young lady! Anyhow, you're a fine one to talk, after the trouble you brought down on your aunt last summer!"

Now that comment shocked me. I hadn't brought a darned thing down on Aunt Minnie last summer. In point of fact, it had been Aunt Minnie who had made me come stay in her house out in the wilds of the southeastern desert, and I'd had nothing at all to do with the ensuing troubles, all of which centered around a bootlegging operation. Because I knew firsthand the futility of arguing with Libby, I sniffed to show her I thought she was a beastly old woman and again turned to Aunt Minnie. "What does Joe have to say about everything that's gone on lately, Minnie?"

As Libby stomped over to Jack and Davy, both of whom held up pretty well as she approached—I'm reminded of the mountain and Muhammad here—Minnie said, "Oh, he's just so upset, Annabelle. You know, the Gundersons' ranch is just down the Pine Lodge Road from us."

"I know." How could I not?

"And you know how violent death always upsets those on the Other Side."

Well, no, I actually hadn't known that. I said, "Mmm."

"And to think that a poor young woman was so cruelly murdered. Joe could almost understand somebody killing Kenny Sawyer. Joe said Kenny was too full of himself—but that girl! Why, I don't know what the world's coming to." And, naturally, Minnie shook her head.

Libby had made her way to Jack by this time and was loudly haranguing him. I was kind of surprised that Jack just stood there and took it. I guess he'd been more intimidated by recent events than I'd thought.

It didn't surprise me when Ma showed up, wiping her hands on her apron. I expect she'd heard Libby and had come into the store to rescue her son—although she'd waited a good long while to do it. I got the feeling she, too, wasn't awfully sorry that Jack had become the brunt of so much ill feeling. She smiled at Minnie, ducked under the counter, and gave her a hug. "It's good to see you, Minnie. Do you need anything special from the store?"

"I can use another sack of flour and one of sugar," said Minnie. She glanced at the corner into which Libby had driven Jack and Davy. "Oh, dear, I hope Libby isn't being *too* forceful with poor Jack."

Ma looked, too, and sighed. "I'm sure she's only telling him what he needs to hear from people other than his parents. He's been so wild lately. I don't know what the world is coming to." Which was yet another common sentiment expressed that day.

And so it went. When Libby and Minnie left, others came to take their place. Sometimes someone would offer sympathy that our family, however remotely, had been involved in the demise of Hazel Fish, but most of the time, they only wondered: (1) what the world was coming to; (2) what Rosedale was coming to; and (3) who had killed first Kenny and now Hazel.

I was very glad when we locked up early that afternoon. I was considerably less glad when Myrtle came to get me to go to another stupid revival meeting shortly after work.

"It's sort of a memorial service for Kenny and Hazel," she explained eagerly. "Reverend Strickland says he felt called by God to put on a special service under the circumstances."

Oh, brother.

However, my mother said, "What a wonderful thing to do. Go on, Annabelle. I'll fix a covered dish to take to the Gundersons' while you and Myrtle go to the revival." She eyed my brother with disfavor. "Jack, you go, too. And *this* time, attend the meeting. You need it."

Looking sulky but chastened, Jack muttered, "Yes'm." Miss Libby, not to mention everyone else, had evidently put the fear of God into him, so maybe the revival meeting actually *would* get through his thick skull, although I doubted it. Anyhow, Jack was bad enough the way he was. If he got religion and started trying to save everybody, I didn't think I could stand it.

In spite of Jack's presence, which always casts a dark cloud over any event at which I was present, the revival meeting wasn't too dreadfully bad. Reverend Strickland seemed honestly appalled by the two murders that had taken place in Rosedale.

Charles and Edward sat in the row of chairs behind the pulpit and didn't look any more glum than usual. They always looked as if they were either headed for or coming home from a funeral. Esther seemed pale and drawn, but she sang like an angel in heaven. Huh. Some angel.

Then I told myself not to be such a cat. Just because Esther Strickland was beautiful and made it a practice to bat her eyes at other women's gentlemen friends didn't make her a bad person. Heck, for all I knew, she hadn't even known Phil was supposed to be my beau. Or Kenny, Sarah's beau. Then I told myself I wouldn't put anything underhanded past her. And *then* I told myself to shut up and listen to the sermon, because I needed it almost as much as Jack did.

My charitable mood didn't last long. Mind you, I agreed with everybody in town that Milo Strickland was a powerful speaker. But I still couldn't force myself to believe that all the human beings in the world except for the people in that tent at that time were going to hell, which seemed to be the message he was trying to get across.

Therefore, I squinted around the tent, looking at people and wondering if any of them could have committed two heartless murders in as many days. There were Armando and Josephine Contreras, who were holding hands. Did that mean that Armando had forgiven Kenny for flirting with his wife? Or Josephine for flirting with Kenny? Did it mean that Josephine and my brother-in-law Richard MacDougall weren't having an illicit affair?

Of course, it didn't mean any of those things. On the other hand it didn't prove that Josephine and Richard *were* involved with each other, either. I sure couldn't think of any other reason she and Richard should be so often, and so secretly, in each other's company. I tried to convince myself that my suspicions only meant that I was a small-minded individual with a limited outlook on life, but I didn't care much for that line of thinking, for obvious reasons.

Giving up on Josephine and Richard for the nonce, I concentrated my attention on Armando. I could feature him knocking somebody's block off, but I couldn't imagine him poisoning an enemy. Nor, for that matter, could I see him battering a young woman to death with a baseball bat. Well, maybe in the heat of passion, he might, but he'd have to have a darned good reason, and I doubted that Hazel's usual brand of gossip would qualify. For all I knew, Hazel and Mando never said two words to each other.

Then I recalled Hazel's excitement Saturday night, and her statement about knocking the socks off the city of Rosedale, and pondered. Could she have seen Armando doing something really bad? Worse than fighting with Kenny? What could it have been? Unless she'd seen him burying a bottle labeled "Arsenic—Poison," and deduced that he'd killed Kenny Sawyer, I couldn't think of a single other thing.

But wait. What exactly *had* Hazel said to me? Since we were supposed to be praying by that time, I shut my eyes and tried to filter out Reverend Strickland's voice—not an easy task, since he apparently wanted God to hear him loud and clear—and concentrate.

Hadn't Hazel said something about Phil seeing the error of his ways? And hadn't she said something about everybody in Rosedale knowing the truth? I think she had. But what truth had she been talking about? And why would any kind of truth make Phil see the error of his ways?

It all beat me. And, that being the case, I decided to heck with thinking. After Reverend Strickland said his powerful "Amen," I went back to surveying the congregation.

Sarah Molina hadn't come to the meeting today, which didn't surprise me in the least. After all, the man she loved had been poisoned not four days since, and a woman who had done her best to take that man away from her was a big part of this revivalist business. I expected Sarah would prefer to see as little as possible of Esther Strickland.

What about Sarah, anyhow? I guess I could feature her poisoning Kenny, although it was a stretch. But battering Hazel with a baseball bat? Sarah cried all the time. To the best of my knowledge, she'd break down in tears before she'd strike out in rage. I'd noticed before that people with open emotions either got sad or mad, but didn't generally switch reactions.

Still, there was that poison book at the library. But I wasn't even sure the person who'd been looking at the book had been Sarah. Actually, I hadn't really seen *anyone* looking at the poison book, which had been open on a table when I saw it. Nuts. That line of thinking was only serving to confuse me, so I moved on.

One also had to consider the cowboys Kenny had fought with, over the course of the rodeo. I could see one of those guys bashing *Kenny* with the baseball bat, especially if he had a snootful of prohibition gin in him, but I could not fathom a cowboy killing Hazel. And I knew good and well that Phil wouldn't poison *or* bash anybody. He was too darned nice. Heck, he seldom got mad at me, even when I was being stupid.

That line of thinking made *me* want to cry, so I stopped it and concentrated on a subject guaranteed to make any hint of tears evaporate: my brother Jack.

Okay. So Jack had been particularly beastly lately. I tried to envision him poisoning someone and couldn't do it. Oh, I suppose he might have been doing some sort of idiotic experiment that went awry, but would he have experimented with arsenic? Where the heck would he have got hold of any arsenic? Sure, *I'd* read about people soaking flypapers in water and feeding people the liquid thereafter, and I knew that most of the rat poison we sold in the store contained arsenic, but Jack and I didn't read the same books, and I couldn't feature him reading the labels on cans, either. Jack didn't like to bother with stuff that didn't concern him directly.

Could he, in a childish rage, have struck someone with a baseball bat? Possibly, but I doubt that he'd have kept on battering that person until her head was mush. Also, I couldn't imagine him hurting a female. I know he'd chased Hazel with his dumb bat, but our mother and father's teachings were pretty darned strong and definitely hard to ignore, even when you wanted to. As much as Jack had been flaunting them recently, I doubted that deep down in his soul he could forget them so utterly that he'd actually murder a person.

It occurred to me that families of most murderers probably felt the same way about their lethal kin as I did about Jack. Normal, everyday people just didn't *expect* their relatives to be vicious murderers.

I brightened slightly when I considered the possibility that Charles and Edward were the culprits. The good Lord knew they both looked the part, being sour and dour and grim. I don't think I'd ever seen either one of them smile, even though they did sing well together. Maybe they believed it was their duty, as Esther Strickland's guardians, to protect her from lecherous cowboys and unmitigated gossips. Perhaps they took their duties a little too seriously. Perhaps they'd taken the Reverend Strickland's preaching too much to heart and had decided they'd been put on earth to carry out Strickland's interpretation of God's word.

Cut it out, Annabelle Blue, I commanded myself. Then I told myself to reign in my vivid imagination. Just because Charles and Edward were both stuffed shirts didn't necessarily make them killers, although I wouldn't have minded in particular if the law fingered either one of them. Or both of them, for that matter.

Nuts. Other than being annoyed at the sight of Phil and Esther sitting together—Phil holding a stack of pamphlets and Esther looking particularly innocent and virginal—surveying the congregation didn't offer any hint of enlightenment.

Chapter Nine

Right after the revival meeting, my mother, father, slightly-less-bratty-than-usual brother Jack and I climbed into the Model T, and I drove us out to the Gundersons' ranch. Ma had prepared a potluck favorite of mine: a salad made with peas and mayonnaise and little bits of chopped onion and cheese. It was safe to use mayonnaise that day, since the weather, which had turned chilly on Sunday, was still chilly that Monday.

It wasn't unheard of for us to get snow in October. On that dismal Monday afternoon the sky was full of lowering black clouds that hung over Rosedale as if the weather was mourning right along with us. It wouldn't have surprised me if snow fell before the night was over. I only hoped it would hold off until after we'd all eaten our fill and said our final good-byes to Kenny and Hazel—and to the rodeo. For some reason, it seemed important to me that we bid the two deceased young people a proper good-bye.

Rodeo days were supposed to be jolly and carefree. This year's rodeo days had been neither of those things, thanks to some very evil person, whom we all prayed would be caught and brought to justice soon. It may sound silly, but I resented the evildoer not only for killing two people I knew, but for doing so when the Gundersons, some of my favorite people, were acting as hosts for what was supposed to be a big party for the entire town.

Although the purpose of this evening's gathering was to offer comfort to the families of the deceased, I have to admit to being kind of surprised when I drove up to the field where everybody was parking their cars and wagons and saw Mr. and Mrs. Fish and Hazel's two sisters and her brother walking toward the ranch house. I felt awfully sorry for them all. Hazel might have been a pain in the neck, but she'd been *their* pain in the neck. Anyhow, she might have improved with age. Sometimes people did. Maybe even Jack would, although I often harbored doubts about that particular hoped-for transformation. But neither Hazel nor Kenny Sawyer would have the chance to evolve into better people. Some awful person had seen to that. It wasn't fair.

I was less surprised when we took our pea salad to the table reserved for salads and saw Kenny's mother and two sisters standing with Sarah Molina, almost as if they had formed a reception line—which might have been the case, come to think of it. Sarah saw us coming, and hurried over to me.

"Oh, Annabelle, I'm so glad to see you. This was awfully kind of the Gundersons, but it sure is hard on all of us." Naturally, her eyes were dripping. Poor Sarah. If I found life so miserable that I had to cry about it all the time, I might just jump off a cliff and get the whole thing over with. Except that there aren't any cliffs around Rosedale. If you jumped off Mescalero Ridge, chances are good you'd only break your leg or something.

Nevertheless, I gave her a quick hug. "This is going to be a special occasion, Sarah. We'll be celebrating Kenny's life. And Hazel's." I'd heard such sentiments (celebrating deceased people's lives, that is) before, and was kind of proud of myself for thinking of the idea then. If Sarah could think of this as a party for a couple of dear folks who weren't there, maybe she'd feel better about it all. Fat chance. But I did try.

As far as feeling better about how things went, my own personal capacity for doing so suffered a severe check when I saw Phil Gunderson, Esther Strickland on his arm, walking slowly toward the food tables. Doing my best to act as though the sight didn't make me want to hurl pea salad at the both of them and then stomp them both flat, I smiled. "Hi, there." I peered over Phil's shoulder and, sure enough, Miss Strickland's keepers, Charles and Edward—or Edward and Charles (I never did figure out which was which)—were tagging along right behind them.

Oh, brother. I'd hate to be followed everywhere I went. On the other hand, maybe Miss Strickland needed them to keep her out of mischief. For a second or two I tried to think of what kind of mischief Miss Strickland might be tempted to get into, but I couldn't do it. She was so . . . I don't know. Sweet. Innocent. Pure. Good. Perfect, curse it.

That day Esther Strickland appeared particularly gorgeous. She had on a gorgeous black dress with black embroidery around the neckline and hem. Her black stockings looked as if they were silk, and her shoes seemed plain, but weren't really. I'd seen shoes like that in a catalog, and they'd cost a fortune. Cynically, I thought that the revivalist business must be good. Esther looked pale and beautiful, and her blue eyes stood out like jewels against her white cheeks. The little black hat she wore on top of her pretty blonde curls was a creation of charm and elegance. I hated her. Which says a lot more about me than it does about her.

"Hey, Annabelle," said Phil, giving me a sheepish smile. As well he might, the rotten traitor. He was in his Sunday best, too: dark gray sack suit and vest, white shirt, fresh white collar, silk four-in-hand with a muted red pattern on dark blue, and polished black shoes. His hair was brushed, and he carried a black derby hat, not his usual rancher's Stetson. He looked, in short, quite the handsome gentleman—for *her* sake, no doubt. Oh, sure, I know we were ostensibly there to pay tribute to

Kenny and Hazel, but I couldn't shake the notion that Phil wouldn't have dressed so grandly for Kenny Sawyer's sake. Or Hazel Fish's, either, even though he was invariably polite to women.

"How do you do, Miss Blue? My, isn't that a charming frock."

Before I could catch myself, I glanced down at my gray shirtwaist with a lowered waistline and black trim, made for me by my mother's very own hands with love and care. I'd worn it today out of respect for the dead, because we wouldn't be climbing any fences, because it was pretty, and because I felt good when I wore it. Or I had. Until Esther Strickland spun her evil magic around me and made me feel like an ill-clad backwater hick. Darn it, I just hated that I fell into her traps every time I spoke the woman!

Of course, the true crux of the problem lay in the fact that Esther had merely complimented me on my dress. I'd added those interpretations to her comment all by myself, without any help from her. Talk about making mountains out of your basic old molehills. I was clearly a mistress of the art.

I only said, "Thank you," and hoped I didn't sound as furious and frustrated as I felt.

Phil's brother Davy rushed up to the salad table and skidded to a halt before me. "Hey, Annabelle. Do you know where Jack is?"

It was the first time in several years I'd been happy to see Davy Gunderson. But on that day he provided a useful diversion from my seething emotions. "I imagine he went over to the campfire, Davy. I'm not sure."

"Okay, thanks." Davy paused, looked at his brother and Esther, then back at me. I got the feeling he wanted to say something.

"What is it, Davy?" I asked, aiming for a gentle tone in order to let Phil know he was losing a peach of a girl if he threw me over for Esther Strickland.

"I . . . I. . . ." He glanced again at his big brother, then dug the toe of his shoe into the dust at our feet. "I just wanted to say that I'm sorry about playing baseball and getting Jack into trouble. About the bat, you know."

"I know. Thank you, Davy. I appreciate your apology and hope you and Jack will behave more responsibly from now on."

Boy, I hadn't realized I could sound so much like my mother. The knowledge was kind of daunting. Fortunately Myrtle and her family showed up at that moment, so I didn't have time to dwell on it. Was I ever relieved to see her! "Hey, Myrtle!"

One of Esther's goons, the tall one, said, "Reverend Strickland needs you, Miss Strickland. He asked us to fetch you."

Esther let out an aggrieved sigh, caught herself doing so, and smiled seraphically at the two fellows. "Thank you, Charles."

I looked quickly at the men, but couldn't tell which one she'd addressed. So I still didn't know which was which.

Smiling sublimely at Phil, Esther said, "I'll see you later, Phil, dear."

Phil, dear? Good Lord, what next? Without looking at Phil, I spoke to Myrtle. "Come on, Myrtle. Let's get a good seat around the fire. I guess this is supposed to be a kind of a memorial service for Kenny and Hazel. I brought a blanket to sit on, 'cause I don't want to get my skirt dirty." Even if it was homemade and I was wearing plain old cotton stockings.

"Good. I brought one too," Myrtle said. "Remember what Reverend Strickland said at this afternoon's service?"

No, actually, I didn't, having done my best to ignore the good reverend's entire sermon. I felt a little bad about that now, since it wasn't his fault his sister was a conniving harpy. If she was. Maybe she really was as sweet and innocent as she acted, although I'd yet to meet anyone *that* pure. Nevertheless, I said, "Yes. It was a good sermon, wasn't it?"

Myrtle looked at me as if she was surprised I'd said anything positive about one of the Stricklands. I'd have been surprised, too, in her place. And I felt a teeny bit guilty because the only reason I had for saying a nice thing was because I didn't want Phil to think I cared in any way whatsoever that he'd fallen for the preacher's sister. The preacher's *beautiful* sister, who looked like an angel and sang like one, too, curse them both.

I didn't mean that.

Oh, who am I trying to kid? I did mean it, but wished I didn't.

So Myrtle and I strolled off in one direction, and Esther Strickland strolled off in another direction, between her two keepers. I didn't know what Phil did and told myself I didn't care, either, which was a big fat lie. Therefore, I jumped when I felt somebody grab my arm rather roughly. Wheeling about, I was surprised to find it had been Phil who'd done so. I lifted an eyebrow at him.

"Annabelle, I have to talk to you."

I eyed him, deliberately forcing myself to appear indifferent. My innards were far from indifferent. They were screaming that they didn't want to hear anything he had to say, since they didn't want all my suspicions about him and Esther Strickland to be confirmed. Not only that, they couldn't think of another reason he'd want to talk to me. "Oh?"

"Yeah." Phil shuffled his feet and looked uncomfortable. As well he might, the beast.

"Well. . . ." I debated with myself. Did I want to hear Phil tell me he was madly in love with another woman? Stupid question. Of course I didn't. However, among my many character traits, some of which really stink, I am practical and commonsensical. I figured it was better to know the truth than to keep guessing. After all, the sooner I heard the hateful words from Phil's own mouth, the sooner I could get over it. "Okay. When and where?"

"Um. . . ." I guess he hadn't thought that far ahead.

Myrtle tapped me gently on my arm. "I'll save you a seat at the fire circle, Annabelle."

"Thanks, Myrtle. Here. Please take my blanket with you."

"Sure."

"Save two seats, please," said Phil.

Hmm. Was that a promising statement, or was it not? Darned if I knew. As Myrtle walked away, I said, "Okay, Phil, what's this about?"

"Let's go find somewhere where we aren't in the middle of things."

Humph. If, as I suspected, he aimed to throw me down for another woman, I'd just as soon the whole town knew what kind of a cad he was.

Or did I?

No, I did not. I absolutely hated people feeling sorry for me.

Also, since I expected it would be difficult for me to keep from crying and I didn't want *anyone* to witness my total humiliation, I went along with this plan. When he dumped me, I aimed to pretend to the world that it didn't hurt, and that would be exceptionally difficult to do if I was bawling my eyes out. "How about behind the barn?"

"Good idea." He took my hand and fairly towed me behind him.

Since I was wearing my Sunday shoes, pretty black pumps that I'd adorned this day with modest black bows, I protested. "Slow down, Phil. I can't walk that fast."

He stopped instantly, and turned, looking contrite. "I'm sorry, Annabelle. I guess I've been wanting to say this for a long time."

Uh-oh. This didn't bode well. My insides gave an enormous spasm. Wow, I hadn't realized how much I cared for Phil. Or was it merely my pride aching? Honestly, I didn't know.

I'd loved Phil from the time I was a little girl, but I'd always told myself that it was the kind of love you have for a dear, wonderful friend. I'd always told myself that I wanted adventure before I got married and settled down. That I wanted to meet more men—dashing men. Allan Quartermain–type men. Or men like Rudolf Rassendyll from *The Prisoner of Zenda.* Sydney Carton. Men who'd sacrifice for me. Honorable men who'd go to the guillotine to protect me from an evil fate. Who'd rescue me from the clutches of a wicked knight who'd fallen madly in love with me and kidnapped me because his clan and mine were mortal enemies and who'd taken me to his castle and locked me in a tower.

I know, I know. Romantic nonsense. But *you* try being nineteen years old and having lived nowhere but in Rosedale, New Mexico, and see how practical *your* heart is. I mean, I wouldn't mind marrying Phil—eventually. But I'd like to get at least one African safari under my belt first. Or a trip to Europe. Something exciting. *Anything* exciting.

That evening, I wasn't so sure anymore. Not that it mattered. If Phil had become tired of me and decided he'd rather go after the preacher's spectacular sister, there wasn't much I could do about it. Heck, for all I knew, Phil harbored a couple of romantic fancies of his own and had been longing to run into a deathless beauty for years now.

Demoralizing thought, as I sure wasn't deathlessly beautiful and never would be. I also couldn't picture myself as a romantic heroine, except maybe by accident, in which case Allan or Rudolf or Sydney would, of course, come to my rescue.

Nuts.

"That's all right," I said. And we proceeded toward the barn more slowly. I felt as though I were marching to my execution. Anne Boleyn: that's me all over.

We approached the barn with me feeling as if my life were about to be shattered. I didn't have a clue as to what Phil was thinking, but I hated him for it all the same. When we turned the corner and went behind the barn, I wanted to hightail it out of there and never come back. I didn't *want* to hear Phil tell me he no longer cared for me. However, what I wanted and what was about to happen had no correlation with each other.

As soon as we stopped walking, I sucked in a deep breath and tried to brace myself mentally for the blow that was about to fall. I wished then that I'd practiced this scene so that I'd be better prepared to handle it. I was flipping through possible re-actions in my mind, trying to select an appropriate one and knowing it was too late, when Phil spoke.

"Annabelle, I've got a confession to make."

Here it came. I braced myself some more. "Oh?"

"Yes. I . . . I haven't been entirely honest with you lately."

If I braced myself any further, my spine would snap. Instead, I allowed my temper to snap instead. "Oh, for Pete's sake, Phil, just spit it out." Then I could have kicked myself, mainly because I didn't want to hear it. Even though I knew I had to, and the sooner the better. Can you tell I was a quivering bundle of conflicting emotions just then? Well, I was.

"Darn it, Annabelle, how come you're always picking on me?"

I stared at him, my quivering bundle forgotten for the nonce. "I beg your pardon?"

He looked as if he were losing his temper now, which was very unusual. Phil epitomized the easygoing, honest-to-the-bone cowboy the novelists are always writing about, and he seldom got angry—except with me. "Darn it, do you have any idea what it feels like to have somebody you . . . uh . . . care about ignore you? Act as if you don't matter to them? Treat you like dirt? Make you feel like two cents?"

I think my mouth fell open. He'd just described my whole entire life during the past few days. Should I confess it?

And rip my pride to shreds?

Good Lord, no!

Well . . . maybe.

"Um . . . well, yes, I do, actually."

He blinked at me. "You do?"

I hesitated and then decided *what the heck.* If Phil knew how much his hanging around with Esther Strickland had hurt me, he was too much of an innate gentleman to tell anybody else and compound my misery. Heck, the rest of my friends had been doing that with their understanding sympathy and consoling looks and words for days now; he didn't have to. "Yes, Phil, I do."

He stared at me for a moment or two as he pondered my answer. Then he said tentatively, "Are . . . I mean . . . is that because you thought Miss Strickland and I were, um, interested in each other?"

He turned a brilliant beet red. Phil was ever a modest person; it must have embarrassed him to say those words because it implied that both Esther Strickland and I cared for him, and he would consider that boasting, which is something Phil never did. Silly boy. Phil was tall, handsome, well built, and about the nicest guy in the universe. What female in her right mind *wouldn't* care for him?

I stood my ground, wondering if my own face was flaming. I was surely embarrassed enough for it to be. Trying to sound practical and down to earth, I said as sarcastically as I could, "Yes, Phil. My feelings were hurt when you seemed to throw me over for Esther Strickland. Wouldn't your feelings be hurt if I threw you over for Kenny Sawyer?" Not that Kenny had ever paid the least bit of attention to me. I guess I wasn't pretty enough for him.

"You mean . . . you mean you were *jealous?*"

He sounded so utterly incredulous, I stamped my foot. Childish gesture, I know, but Phil had looked and acted so astounded, I couldn't believe this was an honest reaction on his part. He couldn't possibly be that naïve, could he?

Shoot, maybe he could. "Well, of course, I was jealous, you idiot!"

"But . . . but you never acted jealous," he said wonderingly.

"That's because I have my pride, darn it. But how would you feel if I'd waltzed off with another man? You've been ignoring me ever since the Stricklands came to town. You've been all over Esther Strickland, and she's been all over you!"

"I never!" he cried indignantly.

"You were, too!" I was having none of his fatuous protests. "Do you have any idea how humiliating it's been for me to watch you hovering over her? Do you know how many of my friends have offered me sympathy because they thought you'd fallen madly in love with that woman and forgotten about me? How many times have you bought *me* Whitman's Samplers? Never! That's how many times, Phil Gunderson! And you did it right in front of my friends!" My throat started to close up and I was on the verge of tears. By that time I was so mad at him, I *really* didn't want him to see me cry. I'd already confessed too much, blast my always-overeager tongue.

"Whitman's Samplers?" Phil stared at me. "But that was from her brother because she was sick. He gave me the money and asked me to get something at the store. Did you think *I* was giving her candy?"

I stared back at him. "The candy was from her *brother?* You didn't tell me that! You didn't tell anybody that! You waltzed right into my own parents' store and asked for candy to give to another woman, Phil Gunderson, right in front of my friends, me, and God almighty Himself! How do you think that made me feel?"

He threw his hands in the air in a gesture of frustration. "But

Annabelle, it didn't mean anything." His mouth pressed into a tight line for a second, and then he burst out, "Doggone it, Annabelle Blue . . . all right, I'll admit it. I *was* trying to make you jealous, but you never acted jealous, so I didn't think you were! You never showed by so much as a sidelong glance that you gave a rap one way or another whether I courted Esther Strickland. Or Hazel Fish, for that matter!"

"Well, of course, I didn't!"

"Why *not?*"

"I already told you! I have my pride!"

"How the devil was I supposed to know that? How can I tell what you're thinking? I'm not a mind reader. Why didn't you *say* something?"

"Because I didn't want to look like a fool, for heaven's sake!"

"Well, *damn* it!" Phil whapped his leg with his black derby hat. He must have been really aggravated, because he never swore in front of ladies—not even me, whose status as a lady had been called into question more than once.

We stood there, eyeing each other, for several seconds. I don't know about Phil, but I didn't have a clue what to say next. I was, however, beginning to lose that my-heart-is-broken-in-half-and-the-only-reason-I'm-still-upright-is-because-my-brain-doesn't-have-sense-enough-to-stop-working feeling. Had he really been hanging around with Esther in an attempt to make me jealous? Really? How . . . how gratifying. Or something.

I licked my lips. "Um, Phil, did you mean what you said just now?"

He glared at me, his eyebrows forming a splendid V over his nose. He looked quite the rakish gent for a second or two. Almost like one of my romantic heroes. "Are you accusing me of lying, Annabelle?"

"Well, no, not really. But, well, I just wondered."

"I don't lie."

"Of course not. But . . . well, um. . . ." I wanted him to repeat what he'd said. Just in case I'd misunderstood him the first time.

Thank God, he did. "For your information, I was trying to make you jealous. I know it was a stupid thing to do, since you clearly don't give a hang about me, but—"

"*What?*" I couldn't believe my ears. "What do you mean I don't give a hang about you? That's not true! You know that's not true!"

"Oh, yeah? You couldn't prove it by me. You've never treated me like anything but a pal. A buddy. A *brother,* for Pete's sake. Damn it, Annabelle, I want to marry you someday! I love you! I don't want to be your damned brother!"

I *know* my mouth fell open that time. And my brain went blank. And my heart stumbled. After I don't know how long, I whispered, "You love me?"

He rolled his eyes. "Geez Louise, Annabelle Blue, I know you're not stupid, but that's about the dumbest question anybody's ever asked anybody else."

"No it's not. You've never told me before that . . . that you love me." My voice had suddenly gone very small and squeaky.

"Well, why should I? You've never given me any indication that you'd care to hear the words, have you? And you sure as hell have never mentioned that you return the sentiment."

"Um . . . I. . . ." Shoot, he was right. And he was right because, as much as I cared about him, I was still totally ambivalent about marriage. Marriage was so . . . permanent. Sort of like a life sentence, if you know what I mean.

"See?" Phil demanded. "That's what I mean. You *don't* want to hear it. Yet you think I ought to pay attention to you and ignore other girls. But you never let me know if it's worth the effort. Whether I'm succeeding. Whether you even want me to hang around you. Well, darn it, Annabelle, that's not fair."

I hung my head. He was right.

"So I started paying attention to Esther, hoping that might jar you off your damned high horse."

"It did." I said it humbly.

"Yeah, well, you still don't seem to be very happy to know I love you. How do you think that makes *me* feel?" He turned around, making a complete circle, and threw his arms in the air again. I'd never seen Phil so upset. He was still glaring.

Something in me snapped. Risking everything—or so it seemed at the time—I rushed over and threw my arms around him. He dropped his hat as he embraced me. "But I *do* love you, Phil! I do! I just don't want to get married right now."

He nuzzled the hair around my hat. "You do? Love me?"

I'd started crying. For some reason, it didn't seem humiliating, perhaps because we seemed to have broken through some sort of barrier. "You stupid man! Of course, I love you. But I'm only nineteen years old. I want to see the world—a little bit of it, anyhow—before I settle down on a ranch in the middle of nowhere and hide away from the world forever."

"Well, hell, so do I," he said. I think he was laughing, although I wasn't sure because I didn't lift my head.

"Really?"

"Really. I'm only twenty-one myself, Annabelle. We have lots of time before we settle down. I've got to save up some so I can support a wife and family. And I'd like to see something of the world, too. You're not the only one who's interested in seeing something outside Rosedale, New Mexico."

"Oh, Phil, I'm sorry I've been so silly."

"And I'm sorry I've been so stupid."

And that was that. I felt *so* much better about life. After I mopped my cheeks and asked Phil several times if he thought anybody would know I'd been crying, and having been assured almost as many times that they wouldn't, although I'm pretty sure he was lying because men never pay attention to stuff like that, we strolled back to the campfire hand in hand. My heart was singing.

The afternoon seemed brighter, too. The chilly weather seemed pleasant to me now, instead of oppressive and ugly. The clouds, which had before appeared menacing, had taken on an aspect of benevolence, reminding me that autumn had arrived, and that pretty soon we'd be celebrating Halloween and Thanksgiving and then Christmas, my very favorite holidays of the year. I remembered that I loved fall and winter in New Mexico, and that we had the most beautiful sky in the world. Okay, so the rest of the landscape wasn't exactly the stuff of dreams, but it was vast and open and impressive, and a magnificent example of God's blessings to those of us who were privileged to live here—give or take a scorpion or two and the occasional rattlesnake and skunk.

Possibilities opened before me. I hadn't known that Phil, too, desired adventure and romance. Maybe we could pursue those two goals together.

Or maybe not. After all, I couldn't shake the notion that I'd really like to meet a few more men before Phil and I got hitched.

Okay, so Phil could have his own adventures, and I could have mine. Naturally, he wouldn't meet anyone whom he'd rather be with than me. As for me . . . well, I wouldn't do anything wrong with any of the men who courted me and swore their undying devotion before I came home and married him.

It's probably clear that reality and I didn't have much more than a nodding acquaintance in those days. Still and all, my heart was pure. And I was so very young.

I'm ashamed to say that when I noticed Esther Strickland looking at us as if she wished we were both being roasted alive over a spit, I felt a totally unworthy surge of satisfaction.

CHAPTER TEN

Was it my imagination, or was everyone sitting around the campfire looking at Phil and me and smiling—well, except for Charles and Edward, who never smiled? I know for a fact that Myrtle smiled when she turned and saw us coming to take the seats she'd saved. Of course, her happy mood might have been due to the fact that Sonny Clyde was sitting on her other side.

I saw Mayberry and Zilpha on the other side of the fire circle and waved. They waved back. So did Hannah and Richard, who were together—and sitting right next to Josephine and Armando Contreras. My joy slipped a trifle when I took in that particular combination of humanity. If Josephine and Richard *were* carrying on a clandestine love affair, they were being mighty subtle about it at the moment.

Oh, well. There wasn't anything I could do about anybody else's romantic affairs. Heck, I couldn't even handle my own.

Phil and I had just sat, and I'd just adjusted the skirt of my lovely gray dress, when Mr. Gunderson stepped up on the platform. He looked as solemn as I'd ever seen him.

Holding up his hand, he addressed the audience through a megaphone. "Ladies and gents, we're gathered here today on what was supposed to be the last day of a festive occasion. Somebody destroyed it for all of us when he took the lives of our friends, Ken Sawyer and Hazel Fish."

A subdued murmur went around the fire circle, Sarah sobbed once, loudly, and my mood wavered a little more. Two murders.

In Rosedale. It didn't seem possible. And during the rodeo, which was supposed to be the lighthearted conclusion of a hard year of ranching. Good Lord.

Mr. Gunderson continued, "I've asked Reverend Milo Strickland, who will be leaving our fair city tomorrow—"

I sat up straighter, my mood improving dramatically. Then I leaned over and whispered to Myrtle, "Did you know he was leaving tomorrow?"

"—to lead us in prayer."

"Yes. He told me he was cutting his revival short because of the tragedy. Tragedies."

Myrtle had spoken quickly and quietly, as if she wanted to hear every word Mr. Gunderson said, so I didn't ask her any more questions, but listened, too.

"It's a sad day when religion has to take a backseat to crime," said Mr. Gunderson. "And I hope the Stricklands and their friends understand that we here in Rosedale are, for the most part, law-abiding, Christian citizens. I'm not casting aspersions on anybody, but I *know* that no one from Rosedale committed these two terrible crimes."

The crowd's reaction to that declaration was another murmur, this one of agreement. I wasn't so sure myself, but I sure wanted to believe him. It's pretty awful to think that the guy who lives next door, figuratively speaking, might be a homicidal maniac. Phil took my hand again, and my heart beat a little tippity-tap in my chest. I shot him a quick smile, but he wasn't looking at me. With a sigh, I turned my attention back to Mr. Gunderson.

"So, I'm going to shut up now," he said. "And let Mr. Strickland take over. After the prayer, the Baptists and the Methodists will lead us in a few hymns to honor the fallen."

It sounded as if he were referring to people killed in a war. We used to hold services for the fallen at the Methodist Church during the Great War. I was too young to understand exactly what was going on, but I remember feeling very sad for all the people in the congregation who were crying. As out-of-the-way a place as Rosedale was, we lost a whole lot of boys in that awful conflict. Our present-day killings seemed to me to be even more senseless than the war killings, and my newly happified mood suffered a rather severe setback.

"Then, after we sing a few hymns, we'll have a little supper. Then we'll all gather round the fire again to conclude our evening." Mr. Gunderson stepped from the platform. He offered the megaphone to Reverend Strickland, but the latter, with a small smile, shook his head. I guess he already knew he could be heard for miles around without help.

Reverend Strickland delivered a moving prayer. I couldn't fault the man for lack of sincerity. He seemed truly impassioned as he begged God to forgive the sinner who'd killed two innocents. I'm not sure how innocent Kenny was, and I didn't think God was any too fond of gossips, but I appreciated the preacher's point. He didn't mention any special wish that the sinner who'd murdered the two young people be caught and punished, but I figured maybe ministers hesitated to voice such entreaties to a loving God. Then again, what did I know? Obviously, not much.

Our Methodist preacher led us in "Amazing Grace," and the Baptist preacher had us sing "Gather at the River," and then we all solemnly trooped over to the food tables. Before we dug in, we expressed our condolences to Mr. and Mrs. Fish and Mrs. Sawyer and Sarah Molina. Reverend Strickland had arranged that little lineup, I guess. I also guess it was appropriate, but it sure cast a damper over the meal. Which was appropriate, too, I suppose, this being in the nature of a solemn occasion. All I know for sure is that my mood, which had initially soared into the skies after Phil and I had made up with each other, was now hovering down around my pretty black pumps.

The weather didn't help. By that time of the evening, it was pitch black outside and freezing cold—almost literally. I kept pulling my sweater more tightly around my shoulders, but it didn't help much. I should have brought my heavy winter coat, but hadn't because it's brown wool and wouldn't have gone well with my gray dress, and I'd wanted to look my best for Phil in case he still cared. Now that I knew he *did* still care, I berated myself as a fool. *What price vanity, Annabelle Blue?* Probably pneumonia. Besides that, I knew as well as I knew my own name that Phil didn't give a rap what people wore. He didn't pay attention to stuff like that.

"You look chilly, Annabelle," he murmured as he followed me in the chow line. We served ourselves that evening.

Feeling silly, I murmured back, "I should have brought my coat."

"I can run fetch you one."

I turned a grateful glance upon him. "Would you really? That would be very nice of you, Phil."

"Sure. As long as you don't mind it being kind of big on you." He gave me one of his heart-stopping smiles, and I decided then and there that I wouldn't mind anything at all, ever, as long as I knew Phil was there with me.

Ergo, I smiled back. "Thanks." I almost added *you're a pal,* but stopped myself in time. After our mutual confessions behind the barn, I figured that statement would be in the nature of a reminder to him that he'd accused me of treating him like a brother.

He made as if to go right that minute, but I forestalled him. "Wait until you've filled your plate, Phil. You don't have to go right this minute."

"Nuts. You're cold now. I can see you've got goose bumps." And off he went.

It was then I realized Esther Strickland and her brother had been right behind us in the line. I, feeling magnanimous, smiled at the both of them. Milo Strickland returned my smile with one of generous benevolence, as befitted a man of God. Esther already had a smile pasted on her face. It didn't alter a single iota, but I couldn't help but wonder if Phil's attentions to me were making her a teensy bit jealous. I hoped so. Petty of me, I know, but there you go. I never claimed to be a saint.

Since I didn't want to eat alone, I stepped out of the line, saying as I did so, "I'd better wait for Phil."

The preacher nodded and moved forward a pace. Esther either didn't hear me or pretended not to. With that same vacant smile on her face and a plate in her hand, she followed her brother.

I don't care what anybody says, *I* thought the woman was strange.

It didn't take Phil long to run to his house, grab a jacket, and head on back out to the food line. When I saw which jacket he'd deemed appropriate for his pending fiancée to wear at a potluck supper, I grinned to myself.

"I got you the warmest one I could find," he said, panting to a stop before me.

"Thanks, Phil." And I stuffed my arms into a sheepskin-lined corduroy jacket, the sleeves of which reached way past my fingertips. Phil rolled them up to my wrists for me. The jacket itself came down to my knees. No doubt about it: I'd be warm for the rest of the evening. And so what if the jacket didn't match my dress? I felt like a newly crowned princess.

So Phil and I got back into line, at the end of it this time. It didn't matter. People in Rosedale don't believe in skimping, and there was plenty of food left, including a last couple of spoonfuls of my mother's pea salad. I shared them with Phil, which goes to show my state of mind by that time. I was willing to concede undying love to Phil Gunderson and even share the last of my mother's pea salad, as long as we both got to see a little of the world before we recited the matrimonial vows.

Since clouds had rolled in, obliterating the stars, and it was dark as the inside of a cave, most of us took our plates back to the fire circle so we could see what we were eating. Phil and I sat beside Myrtle and Sonny again, and this time Zilpha and her husband Mayberry joined us, too. As Phil and Mayberry started talking about saddles, Zilpha said, "What did you get Hannah for her birthday, Annabelle?"

"I embroidered a scarf for her."

"That's nice."

I sensed an air of suppressed excitement in my sister that evening. Eyeing her critically as I munched a bite of Mrs. Gilchrest's smoked brisket (which wasn't as good as Miss Libby's, although I'd never tell her that, and it was pretty darned good), I swallowed, then said, "What is it, Zilpha? You look like the cat that's swallowed the canary."

"I do?" Zilpha made an attempt to appear sober and serious, but her eyes still danced.

"Yes," I said firmly, "you do. What's up?"

She put her fork down and laid a hand on my arm. "Annabelle," she whispered, "if I tell you, you have to promise that you won't tell another soul."

Oh, yeah? This was odd. It wasn't like Zilpha to keep secrets. "Okay. I guess I can promise. Unless you tell me you're the murderer." I'd meant it as a joke, but it was a bad one and inappropriate.

She shook her head. "Of course, I'm not, but that's the reason I don't want you blabbing. I don't want you to tell anyone else because this is supposed to be a solemn occasion, and I don't want to spoil it. And anyhow, if anybody should be celebrating in spite of the occasion, it's Hannah, because her birthday's tomorrow."

Hmm. How could one spoil a solemn occasion? By laughing uproariously, I guess, but I doubted Zilpha's secret involved comedy. "Okay. I promise I won't tell anybody."

"You can tell Ma and Pa after you get home."

This concession to the no-blabbing rule puzzled me. If she wanted Ma and Pa to know something, it wasn't like her to go through an intermediary. But I wasn't going to cavil. By that time I was wildly curious. I only said, "Okay."

She leaned over and whispered in my ear, "Mayberry and I are going to have a baby!"

"*What!*" I cried, so astonished I almost dropped my plate. Then I saw Zilpha's furious frown and clapped a hand over my mouth. Lowering my voice to a whisper, I said, "I'm sorry. But, Zilpha, this is wonderful news!" I could see now why she didn't want the whole world to know it. Not at this particular memorial service. It wouldn't be fair to the families of the bereaved to know that other people were still able to experience the joy and gladness of welcoming new life into the world.

"I think so, too, but don't tell anybody, for heaven's sake. Not for another week or so, anyhow. Because . . . well, you know."

"Yes, I know. I'm sorry your happy news has to be kept secret because of some rotten murdering villain." The more the world went on the way it normally did, the more I resented whoever it was who had cast a blight over my little community. I sure hoped the police or the sheriff would catch the scoundrel soon. Neither of Rosedale's law-enforcement groups had a whole lot of experience in nabbing murderers, but I guess they were competent. "How far along are you?"

Zilpha cast a furtive glance around the fire circle to see if anyone was watching us. I guess my initial reaction had been kind of loud. "Only about two months, I think. I'm going to see Dr. Hilliard next week."

I was surprised. "You have to see a doctor? Is everything all right?" I couldn't remember Ma going to the doctor when she was going to have Jack. Then again, I'd been awfully young at the time.

"According to the magazines, ladies who are expecting babies, especially their first, should be thoroughly examined by a doctor as soon as possible and keep seeing the doctor all during their pregnancy."

"Oh." There seemed to be a whole lot I still didn't know about being an adult. It was probably a good thing Phil and I had decided to wait until we were older to tie the knot.

"Anyway, I'm very excited about it, but I don't want to let on. At least not here and now. It wouldn't be fair."

"I understand." For a second, I imagined the impact Zilpha's news might have on Mrs. Fish or Mrs. Sawyer, both of whom had just lost children born of their own wombs. The very idea made me want to cry, so I suppressed it.

Zilpha heaved a happy sigh. "Mayberry is going to be such a wonderful father."

"You're going to be a wonderful mother, too," I said, meaning it sincerely. Of my two sisters, Zilpha was the more loving and caring. And she was right about Mayberry. He was a genuinely good man. I had a feeling any child of theirs would be a happy one.

Zilpha and I continued to chat with each other, and Phil continued to chat with Mayberry. Occasionally, Myrtle and Sonny would join in the conversation with Zilpha and me, but for the most part they seemed engrossed in each other. I thought that was sweet, and I was happy for Myrtle. Sonny Clyde was a nice fellow, although I hoped he didn't aim to cowboy for a career, since it was a fairly unstable one, and cowboys didn't make much money.

I know, I know. A girl's supposed to marry for love, and she's not supposed to be money-grubbing and materialistic. And I'm not advocating gold digging when it comes to selecting husbands. But, doggone it, I knew firsthand that love didn't put food on the table. Every time I doubted it, all I had to do was think about Mrs. Wilson and her eleven kids (more than half of whom weren't even her own) to make me recall that life wasn't fair. It was just as rough on the good as it was on the bad. I couldn't think of a nicer or better or more Christian woman than Mrs. Wilson—and look what life had thrown at her. I sure didn't want Myrtle to be the next generation's Mrs. Wilson. If you know what I mean.

Zilpha had just told me what she'd got for Hannah for her birthday ("A beaded evening handbag. I ordered it from the Sears and Roebuck catalog. You know, for when she has to attend important dinners with Richard.") when I felt a tap on my shoulder. When I swiveled to see who'd tapped, my heart crunched when I espied Mr. Gunderson. His presence brought too forcefully to my mind what had happened the last time he'd tapped me on the shoulder at a campfire.

My initial reaction lessened when I realized he was smiling. Thank God! He wouldn't be smiling if somebody else had been poisoned or battered to death with a baseball bat. So I smiled back.

"Can you come and help Mrs. Gunderson for a minute, Miss Annabelle? We've got the makings for s'mores, and Mrs. G. needs help carrying stuff out to the campfire."

"Sure," said I. "I'll be happy to help Mrs. Gunderson." I rose from my place, gathered my empty plate and silverware and tapped Phil on the shoulder.

He turned his head and smiled up at me. "Hey, Annabelle."

"I'm going to help your mother with dessert, Phil. Be right back."

"Need help?"

I shook my head. "Naw. I think we can handle it. But thanks."

So I took my plate and silverware back to the picnic tables and left it on the table designated for the collection of dirty dishes, and went to the Gundersons' house. Knocking lightly on the kitchen door, I didn't wait for a reply, but pushed it open and went right on in. That's the way we did things in Rosedale. We weren't formal.

Mrs. Gunderson was pleased to see me, and we gathered together a couple of boxes of graham crackers, several chocolate bars, and two bags of marshmallows. People were expected to cut their own sticks on which to roast the marshmallows. Or mushpillows, as Jack used to call them when he was a baby. I think that was the only cute or endearing thing Jack ever did. Perhaps his recent bad behavior had driven all the other instances of demonstrated charm out of my mind.

Mr. Gunderson opened the door for us. I carried the tray with marshmallows and chocolate bars, Mrs. Gunderson carried the boxes of graham crackers, and we all three headed back to the campfire. Since I was in the middle, I said, "This was a very nice thing for you folks to do—you know, have this little memorial when you were expecting a happy occasion. I know Mr. and Mrs. Fish and Mrs. Sawyer appreciate it. We all do."

Shaking her head and looking sad, Mrs. Gunderson said, "It's the least we could do. I can't even bear to think of losing one of my children. Nothing can possibly be worse."

I'm sure every parent there that evening felt exactly the same. I thought of Zilpha carrying a new life in her body, and of somebody someday killing that new life, and my blood ran cold.

It ran even colder when I got close enough to the campfire to see that someone new had been added to the little group of which I'd formerly been a member. And, darn it to heck, it was Esther Strickland. She was smiling at Phil and batting those long eyelashes of hers, too. Shoot, I'd thought Phil and I had sorted through this nonsense and that he'd have brains and courage enough to repel any further advances from Miss Strickland.

But that had been silly thinking on my part. Phil would *never* be rude to a woman. Heck, he found it difficult to be rude to a man. He was too darned nice.

I frowned as I realized that Esther was holding out a cup to Phil. Must be cocoa, I decided, since there was a big pot of it bubbling over the fire.

When I glanced at Reverend Strickland, I saw him standing, staring at Esther, horror writ large upon his rather small features. Wondering why he should look as though he were witnessing a hanging, my gaze slid sideways and I saw Charles and Edward. They were both hurrying toward Esther and Phil, and both of them also sported expressions of alarm on their usually stoic faces. Now what in the world were they . . . ?

And then I understood everything. In the horror of understanding, I dropped my tray and bolted like a spooked hare toward the fire circle, waving my arms and screaming at the top of my lungs.

"No! Phil, don't touch that cup!"

Both Esther and Phil jumped a foot in the air and turned to see what the commotion was all about. I saw Phil take the cup from Esther's fingers. I saw the sweet, innocent smile creep over Esther's perfect features. I saw Phil lift the cup to his lips.

I shrieked, *"No!"* again.

And then, like a baseball player heading to score at home plate, I lunged at him and smacked the cup away from his hand before he'd had the chance to take a sip.

Then I lay there on the ground, covered my face with my

hands, and sobbed. *Thank God. Thank God. Thank God.*

Naturally, my histrionic display had caused absolute silence to descend upon the fire circle, kind of like I'd sloshed a bucket of ice water on the gathering. Everyone stood up and tried to see the idiot who'd screeched like a banshee and spoiled the get-together. Myrtle leaped to her feet and hurried to help me rise, as did Zilpha. Mayberry and Phil just sat there and goggled at me, both looking as if they'd been turned to stone.

With the help of my sister and Myrtle, I staggered to my feet. My pretty gray dress and Phil's jacket were both covered with dust, and my black stockings had holes in the knees—and my knees were bleeding. I was still crying, although I'm not sure why—a combination of leftover terror and relief, I guess.

Wiping my eyes with the back of my hand, I saw that Charles and Edward had taken Esther by the arms, one man on either side of her. One of them stooped—I still didn't know which was whom—and I realized he was reaching for the cup. I shouted, "Don't let him take that cup!"

Zilpha shook me slightly. "What in the name of Glory is the matter with you, Annabelle Blue?"

I pointed a shaking finger at Esther. "It's her," I said ungrammatically. "She's the one who killed Kenny and Hazel. She tried to poison Phil just now. I know she did."

If the gasp I heard from the collection of folks around that campfire had been exhaled instead of inhaled, the fire would have been blown out. Shooting a murderous look at me, one of Esther's keepers grabbed the cup. Phil, thinking fast, jumped up and grabbed it back. Then he turned and frowned at me. "What the devil are you talking about, Annabelle?" He must have been really rattled, or he'd never have said the word *devil* in company.

I nodded at the cup. "Test it. Have the pharmacist test it. Have Mr. Pruitt test it." In spite of Phil's jacket, I was cold. I started shivering.

Reverend Strickland rushed up and took his sister from Charles and Edward. "Really, Miss Blue, there's no need for this . . . this. . . ."

I turned on him like a termagant. "Isn't there? Why do you have those guys hovering over her all the time, then? Why is it that when a man she's set her eyes on goes back to his girlfriend, he ends up dead?" I turned on Esther herself. "What did Hazel see, Miss Strickland? Eh? She said it would knock the socks off everyone in Rosedale. What was it?"

Her blue eyes were as empty as a summer sky, and she still smiled. "She was such a silly creature."

The entire mob swiveled to stare at Esther.

"That's enough now, Esther," said her brother in a soothing tone. "You needn't say anything."

She turned upon him such a look of scorn, it almost withered me, and I wasn't even its recipient. "Don't be a fool, Milo. Why shouldn't I talk? It's not my fault God works through me to punish people who disobey His laws. I'm only doing His work."

I'm sure I wasn't the only one gaping at her by that time, but I was the only one who spoke. "You kill people for God?" The woman must be mad, I told myself.

"I am God's instrument," she replied calmly. She turned back to Reverend Strickland. "Tell her, Milo."

Turning on the so-called man of God in my own right, I demanded, "Yeah, preacher, tell us. You knew your sister was loony, didn't you? That's why you had Charles and Edward follow her around everywhere, isn't it? Because you didn't trust her not to kill people who got in her way. Your own sister!"

Milo Strickland buried his head in his hands and started sobbing. Wow, you don't often see men crying like that, at least not in Rosedale, New Mexico. "Not my sister," he said brokenly. "My wife."

Boy, if my initial accusation had caused a loud gasp in the

audience—and it had—Milo Strickland's statement precipitated an entire hurricane of incredulity.

Esther frowned at her . . . husband? Oh, boy. "Milo, you told me never to tell anyone, and now you've told. You're being very silly."

My temper spiked. Two people had died because these blasted revivalists and their entourage had kept Esther's . . . heck, I guess it was insanity . . . a secret. I'm not even sorry to confess that I hollered at Milo Strickland. "Do you mean to tell us that you *knew* this woman was a murderer, and yet you allowed her to roam free among the rest of the people in the world? When you *knew* what she was capable of? You *do* realize that she murdered two people here in Rosedale, don't you? And she damned near murdered *Phil?* How many other people has she killed?" I've very seldom had violent urges in my life, but I wanted to take Jack's baseball bat and batter both the Stricklands to death right then.

"I don't know why you're so upset, Miss Blue," said Esther serenely. "It's my duty to mete out justice. You're being quite ridiculous about this. I'm God's chosen one. Any man who prefers somebody like you to me"—you should have seen the look of disgust she aimed at me—"deserves punishment. As for that silly Hazel creature, why, she was going to tell people about Milo and me, and that's supposed to be a secret. Milo said so. People who can't keep secrets are wicked." She cast another scathing look at her husband. If she were allowed to go free, I wouldn't bet my socks that Milo Strickland might not have been her next victim.

I could scarcely believe my ears. I stood there, my fists clenched, my head spinning, unable to comprehend the total battiness of the woman. Phil came over and put his arm around me. I returned the favor. So there we were, our arms around each other's waists, staring at Esther Strickland, whose beautiful face was now marred by a frown.

"You see?" said she, nodding at Phil and me. "That's just wrong, you and Phil being together. It's wicked. I thought you knew better than to pay any more attention to that creature, Mr. Gunderson."

"That creature?" I said. "Meaning me, I suppose."

She gave me a pitying look. "Of course. It's unnatural for a man to prefer someone like you to someone like me. God made me beautiful. God made me perfect. Anyone who prefers someone less than perfect needs to be punished." She looked me up and down as if she were sizing up a freak at a sideshow.

"So you were going to poison me? Like you poisoned Kenny?" Phil's voice was soft, and he sounded gentle, as if he were talking to a little kid.

She looked sort of sad. "I didn't want to, Phil, dear. But I have to do God's will."

Oh, brother. I hadn't realized the sheriff had pushed his way through the crowd and come up behind me. When he spoke, he startled me.

"So you're the one who killed Kenny, Miss Strickland? And Miss Fish?"

With absolute, unfeigned, wide-eyed innocence, she said, "I did God's will. Mr. Sawyer was a bad man. And Miss Fish needed to be stopped."

"Using my brother's baseball bat?" I asked, pretty darned enraged by that time.

She eyed me sympathetically, as if she couldn't figure out how anyone could be so dense. "It was clearly God's will that your sinful brother leave his bat there, so that I could carry out God's commands."

Milo Strickland sobbed aloud. Charles and Edward, stoic as ever, remained at Esther's sides, each hanging on to her by an arm. She looked so slim and tiny and fragile, anyone might have taken her for a child.

By that time, I was willing to chalk up Esther's murderous actions to total insanity. She seemed to be living in some other atmosphere altogether, one she'd made up and believed in. But Milo Strickland didn't have the excuse of insanity to absolve him from the guilt. As far as I'm concerned, he was the more culpable of the two if he knew what she was capable of and hadn't had her locked up before this.

Releasing Phil, I took a step toward the minister until I was standing right smack in front of him. He wasn't much bigger than I was, and I wanted to get a few things straight, both for my own sake and for the sake of the citizens of Rosedale. "I think it's time you stopped blubbering and told us what's going on, Mr. Strickland. You knew it was Esther who'd killed Kenny and Hazel, didn't you? Your *wife*. Yet you did nothing to stop her. You didn't tell anyone what you know about her. You didn't do *anything!* Were you going to let her kill Phil tonight? And if she'd succeeded, what would you have done? Nothing, as usual?" I was so mad, I was shaking.

The sheriff laid a hand on my shoulder, and I stiffened. However, I guess he didn't intend to haul me away, but to back me up. His support was really pretty gratifying. "Yeah, Reverend Strickland," said Sheriff Greene. "Suppose you tell us what's going on here. And I suggest you do so quickly."

Strickland allowed his hands to drop from his face, which was red and splotchy and wet. "It's true. It's all my fault. I should have done something to keep Esther from hurting people. But I thought I had her under control when I hired Charles and Edward!" He had the nerve to look accusingly at his henchmen.

I said, "Ha! It's not *their* fault that you—"

The sheriff's hand tightened on my shoulder. It hurt, but I got the message and shut up.

"I hired Charles and Edward to watch out for her. To see that she was never by herself. If they'd kept an eye on her. . . ." His words petered out. I guess even *he* could tell his lame excuse wouldn't wash.

"I think you're worse than she is," I told him, my voice clearly conveying disgust at his criminal behavior.

"I think you'd all better come with me," said Sheriff Greene. "Reverend Milo Strickland, I guess I'm going to have to arrest you as accessory to murder."

You should have heard the gasp *that* time.

"You'd better arrest Charles and Edward, too," I said. The two men frowned at me, but I was relentless. "If they knew why they'd been hired, they're as culpable as Strickland."

The sheriff sighed heavily. "Right. And until we get this mess figured out, I reckon I'm going to have to arrest your sister—I mean, your wife, too. If she's as loony as it looks like she is, she'll probably end up in a hospital somewheres."

Humph. I wasn't sure I approved of that, but that's because I didn't like her.

Esther shook her head. She still appeared serene and unruffled. "I carry out God's will. I am His instrument." With a sweeping glance at the crowd, she said, "You people don't know what you're doing. That's what Jesus said on the cross. It's the same with me, you see."

Oh, boy. Now she was setting herself up as our savior? Talk about nuts.

"Yeah, maybe." Sheriff Greene didn't sound too interested in anything Esther had to say, probably because it was obvious by that time that she was totally removed from reality. He nodded to Charles and Edward. Unless it was Edward and Charles. "You fellers come along, too. We've got a lot of sorting out to do."

Because I was furious as well as curious, I spoke up one last time. "Before you go, Reverend Strickland, I'd really like to know how many people your wife has killed during your career as a revivalist."

Strickland's face scrunched up, he shook his head, and he didn't answer me. Earl Wilcox took his hands and slapped handcuffs on him.

Disgusted, I said, "Coward!"

Phil whispered in my ear, "Annabelle, let's step aside and let the law handle this."

Nuts. I wanted to yell at them all some more.

However, as the sheriff and his deputy led Milo and Esther Strickland and Charles and Edward away to their waiting automobiles, and even before the crowd could commence buzzing over the excitement, another distraction occurred in the form of two small bright lights aimed directly at the campfire. They came a little closer, and I could see that they were headlights. Most people parked their automobiles and wagons in the field on the other side of the Gundersons' ranch house, so this was kind of alarming at first. My initial thought was that the Stricklands had prepared for an emergency of this nature and had planned a disturbance that would discombobulate everybody and allow for their escape. I know that sounds melodramatic, but it's what I thought.

Turned out I was wrong, but the experience was still really eerie at first. The headlights kept coming, heading directly at the crowd, and people had begun to shuffle uncomfortably. The headlights had practically reached us when the driver of the automobile to which they were attached started squeezing his horn. Loud blasts of what sounded like *"Ooga! Ooga!"* ripped through the night, and everybody jumped a mile or so in the air and started screaming and scattering in all directions.

Then the most enormous car any of us had ever seen came to a halt right smack beside the fire circle, and who should emerge but Josephine and Armando Contreras and my brother-in-law Richard MacDougall! I wasn't the only one whose mouth dropped open. Phil, standing beside me still, tightened the arm he'd put around my waist in order to prevent me from slaughtering the preacher.

Hannah cried, "Richard!" Her voice sang out loud and clear above the throng, since all other noises had stilled. It was as if an angel had passed over and blessed the congregation with the gift of silence, and Hannah'd shattered it. "What in the world are you doing?"

His smile a mile wide, Richard hurried over to Hannah, his arms extended. Taking her hands in both of his, he cried, "Happy birthday, darling! This is your present!"

And by gum, if Richard hadn't bought my own very sister, Hannah Rachel Blue MacDougall, a brand-new, spiffy, bright-green, four-door Cadillac Touring Car, the fanciest automobile anyone in Rosedale—perhaps in the entire state of New Mexico—had ever seen in our collective lives.

"Oh, Richard!" Hannah threw her arms around her husband right there, in front of everybody in the town and God Himself, and kissed him on the lips.

After she let him go, Richard's sheepish glance slid around the accumulated people, including the sheriff and the Stricklands, whose forward progress had been halted because of the commotion. "Sorry, Sheriff. And I know it's kind of a bad time to be celebrating anything at all, but tomorrow is Hannah's birthday, and we—Armando and Josephine and I—had planned this surprise for a long time."

Sheriff Greene, shaking his head at the foolishness of men, I guess, said nothing, but recommenced his path toward the automobiles that were going to take the Stricklands and their cronies to jail.

"You see," Richard went on, "Armando came to me a few

weeks ago and proposed that the bank give him a loan so he could establish an automobile dealership here in Rosedale."

Murmurings erupted in the crowd. Until that time, Rosedale didn't have anybody in town who sold cars. If you wanted to buy an automobile, you had to go to Albuquerque, Santa Fe, or El Paso. So this news was really pretty darned exciting, if you discounted the circumstances, which, as Richard had said, were kind of bum.

"So, after looking the proposition over every way we could, we did it!" Richard concluded. "Contreras Auto Works will be coming to Rosedale in January of nineteen twenty-four! What do y'all think of that?"

And darned if everybody didn't start whooping and stomping their approval, thus proving that life goes on, in spite of people like Milo and Esther Strickland.

The party broke up shortly after that. My obnoxious brother Jack, in spite of his recent offensive behavior, got to ride in the Cadillac back to town with Hannah and Richard. I didn't really mind, since that meant he wouldn't be able to annoy me as I drove the Model T and my parents home.

"That was something, when those lights showed up, coming toward the fire circle," I said. "It was really scary at first."

"It was, indeed. Good old Richard," said Pa indulgently.

"I'm happy for Hannah," said Ma.

I was, too. And I was positively ecstatic to find out conclusively that Richard wasn't having an affair with Josephine Contreras.

CHAPTER ELEVEN

Thus ended rodeo season, 1923. It had been an exciting time, but I was glad it was over. What's more, I prayed that nothing quite that exciting would ever happen again in my little town. Rosedale might not be a garden spot, and it might sit in the middle of the desert in the middle of nowhere, but darn it, it was my home, and I didn't appreciate people like Milo and Esther Strickland coming in and gumming up its works.

I got to ride in Hannah's new car, too. She drove Zilpha and me out to the Bottomless Lakes for a spin the following Saturday, leaving Jack at home, and we took along a picnic lunch. We had a wonderful time, and the car was great. That was the last picnic anyone in Rosedale indulged in that year, because winter came in hard before October was over. The weather turned icy, the wind blew day and night, and by the time Christmas rolled around, I was ready for summer again.

The evil days of the Stricklands had left the good citizens in Rosedale more than a little shaken. It's not every day a homicidal lunatic visits our semi-peaceful little town. The fact that the lunatic in this case was a small and ethereally lovely woman was especially troubling, at least to me. We'd all had a firsthand gander at true insanity. The real problem was that insanity in this case looked so normal. And *that* meant that, try as one might, one couldn't ever be sure of anything or anybody. Frightening thought.

I could, however, be sure of Phil. He's such a sweetheart. I'm not sure to this day how he did it, but for my birthday, late in November, he gave me a Whitman's Sampler. I think he and Ma conspired, but she never did let on and neither did he.

Something else good came of the Stricklands' murderous intrusion into Rosedale. Jack, while still twelve years old and uncivilized because of it, never did regain his full measure of obnoxiousness. I guess having somebody use something of yours to commit a vicious, bloody crime—and all because you'd been an idiot—makes even people like my brother think better of their wicked ways. He was subdued for a month or two after the rodeo, he paid more attention to his teachers that was his usual wont, and, for a few weeks, he actually did his homework without whining.

As for the Stricklands themselves, Esther was found to be as crazy as she appeared to be, and was sent to the lunatic asylum in Las Vegas, New Mexico. As far as I know, she's still there. For some reason, my heart hurts when I think about her. God knows, I didn't like her. Heck, I didn't even much like the two people she'd murdered in Rosedale, and I'd been terribly jealous of her. But she truly was a beautiful woman on the outside. It seemed a terrible shame that she should be so absolutely devoid of conscience. We never did learn how many victims she'd left in her mad wake, but we were all sure there were more than just the two we knew about. Why else would Milo Strickland have hired watchdogs for her?

What makes people turn out like Esther Strickland, anyhow? I wanted to ask my old psychology teacher, but he'd retired and moved to Phoenix, so I couldn't. I looked up a couple of books in the library, but they didn't answer my question. Maybe nobody knows, which is almost as frightening as that sort of craziness itself.

I'm not sure what happened to Charles and Edward, but I hope they got their just desserts.

Milo Strickland was tried and convicted of being an accessory to murder and of obstructing justice, both of which verdicts were fair and just in my opinion. He was sentenced to several years in the state pen, and I do believe a couple of other states had at him after New Mexico was through with him. Stupid man.

I suppose he took up his ministry again in prison, which might be a good thing. I don't know. The whole Strickland episode left a nasty taste in my mouth.

It did the same to Myrtle. We talked about the Stricklands a lot in the weeks after the rodeo. It didn't seem possible that we'd never be annoyed by Hazel Fish again in our lifetimes. I felt terribly sorry for Mrs. Fish, even though I knew I wouldn't miss Hazel a whole lot.

And Kenny Sawyer. I'm not sure what to say about Kenny. He'd been boastful and full of himself, and he'd been a blowhard, and he fooled around on Sarah Molina, but darn it, those are pretty pathetic reasons to kill a man. Anyhow, Miss Esther didn't kill him for any of those reasons. She'd killed him because he'd not paid her the attention she felt she deserved. Is that conceit, or is it insanity? Maybe it's both.

Anyhow, she might well have done the same thing to Phil. That thought made me shudder every time I entertained it, so I tried not to. And that, as you can imagine, was sort of like trying not to think about an elephant when it's standing in front of you, snuffling in your pockets for peanuts with its big long trunk.

Nevertheless, life went on. Halloween came and went, and Thanksgiving, and my birthday, and Christmas, and then, lo and behold, springtime showed up, dry and windy and miserable. When the March cattle drives started, we were all ready for them—although I'm pretty sure everybody in town was a little anxious, after what had happened in October.

The following October, Phil took all the top prizes during the rodeo. Being Phil, he disparaged his accomplishment, telling anyone who congratulated him that he'd never have done so well if Kenny had been there. I don't think that's true—but his honest modesty made one more reason for me to love Phil.

The two of us haven't spoken of marriage since that day at the fall rodeo, and I hope he doesn't bring it up any time soon.

I still haven't had any adventures, darn it.

ABOUT THE AUTHOR

Award-winning author **Alice Duncan** lives with a herd of wild dachshunds (enriched from time to time with fosterees from New Mexico Dachshund Rescue) in Roswell, New Mexico. She's not a UFO enthusiast; she's in Roswell because her mother's family settled there fifty years before the aliens crashed. Alice would love to hear from you at alice@aliceduncan .net. And be sure to visit her Web site at http://www.aliceduncan .net.